THE BLOOD
OF THE VAMPIRE

BY

FLORENCE MARRYAT,

AUTHOR OF

"LOVE'S CONFLICT," "A PASSING MADNESS," ETC.

British Library Cataloguing-in-Publication Data
A catalogue record for this book is available from
the British Library

THE BLOOD
OF THE VAMPIRE

THE BLOOD OF THE VAMPIRE.

CHAPTER I.

It was the magic hour of dining. The long Digue of Heyst was almost deserted; so was the strip of loose, yellow sand which skirted its base, and all the *tables d'hôtes* were filling fast. Henri, the youngest waiter of the Hôtel Lion d'Or, was standing on the steps between the two great gilded lions, which stood rampant on either side the portals, vigorously ringing a loud and discordant bell to summons the stragglers, whilst the ladies, who were waiting the commencement of dinner in the little salon to the side, stopped their ears to dull its clamour. Philippe and Jules were busy, laying white cloths and glasses, etc., on the marble tables in the open balcony, outside the *salle à manger,* where strangers to the Hotel might dine *à la carte,* if they chose. Inside, the long, narrow tables, were decorated with dusty geraniums and fuchsias, whilst each cruet stand had a small bunch of dirty artificial flowers tied to its handle. But the visitors to the Lion d'Or, who were mostly English, were too eager for their evening meal, to cavil at their surroundings. The Baroness Gobelli, with her husband on one

side, and her son on the other, was the first to seat
herself at table. The Baroness always appeared with
the soup, for she had observed that the first comers received a more generous helping than those who came
in last. No such anxiety occupied the minds of Mrs.
Pullen and her friend Miss Leyton, who sat opposite to
the Baroness and her family. They did not care sufficiently for the *potage aux croutons,* which usually formed
the beginning of the *table d'hôte* dinner. The long
tables were soon filled with a motley crew of English,
Germans, and Belgians, all chattering, especially the
foreigners, as fast as their tongues could travel. Amongst
them was a sprinkling of children, mostly unruly and
ill-behaved, who had to be called to order every now
and then, which made Miss Leyton's lip curl with disgust. Just opposite to her, and next to Mr. Bobby
Bates, the Baroness's son by her first marriage, and
whom she always treated as if he had been a boy of
ten years old, was an unoccupied chair, turned up
against the table to signify that it was engaged.

"I wonder if that is for the German Princess of
whom Madame Lamont is so fond of talking," whispered
Elinor Leyton to Mrs. Pullen, "she said this morning
that she expected her this afternoon."

"O! surely not!" replied her friend, "I do not
know much about royalties, but I should think a Princess would hardly dine at a public *table d'hôte.*"

"O! a German Princess! what is that?" said Miss
Leyton, with a curled lip again, for she was a daughter
of Lord Walthamstowe, and thought very little of any
aristocracy, except that of her own country.

As she spoke, however, the chair opposite was

sharply pulled into place, and a young lady seated herself on it, and looked boldly (though not brazenly) up and down the tables, and at her neighbours on each side of her. She was a remarkable-looking girl—more remarkable, perhaps, than beautiful, for her beauty did not strike one at first sight. Her figure was tall but slight and lissom. It looked almost boneless as she swayed easily from side to side of her chair. Her skin was colourless but clear. Her eyes were long-shaped, dark, and narrow, with heavy lids and thick black lashes which lay upon her cheeks. Her brows were arched and delicately pencilled, and her nose was straight and small. Not so her mouth however, which was large, with lips of a deep blood colour, displaying small white teeth. To crown all, her head was covered with a mass of soft, dull, blue-black hair, which was twisted in careless masses about the nape of her neck, and looked as if it was unaccustomed to comb or hairpin. She was dressed very simply in a white cambric frock, but there was not a woman present, who had not discovered in five minutes, that the lace with which it was profusely trimmed, was costly Valenciennes, and that it was clasped at her throat with brilliants. The new-comer did not seem in the least abashed by the numbers of eyes which were turned upon her, but bore the scrutiny very calmly, smiling in a sort of furtive way at everybody, until the *entrées* were handed round, when she rivetted all her attention upon the contents of her plate. Miss Leyton thought she had never seen any young person devour her food with so much avidity and enjoyment. She could not help watching her. The Baroness Gobelli, who was a very coarse feeder, scattering her food over her plate and not infrequently over the table cloth as well, was nothing compared to the young stranger. It was not so much that she ate rapidly and with evident appetite, but that she kept her eyes fixed upon her food, as if she feared someone might deprive her of it. As soon as her plate was empty, she called sharply to the waiter in French, and ordered him to get her some more.

"That's right, my dear!" exclaimed the Baroness, nodding her huge head, and smiling broadly at the newcomer; "make 'em bring you more! It's an excellent dish, that! I'll 'ave some more myself!"

As Philippe deposited the last helping of the *entrée* on the young lady's plate, the Baroness thrust hers beneath his nose.

"'Ere!" she said, "bring three more 'elpings for the Baron and Bobby and me!"

The man shook his head to intimate that the dish was finished, but the Baroness was not to be put off with a flimsy excuse. She commenced to make a row. Few meals passed without a squabble of some sort, between the Hotel servants and this terrible woman.

"Now we are in for it again!" murmured Miss Leyton into Mrs. Pullen's ear. The waiter brought a different *entrée,* but the Baroness insisted upon having a second helping of *tête de veau aux champignons.*

"*Il n'y a plus, Madame!*" asseverated Philippe, with a gesture of deprecation.

"What does 'e say?" demanded the Baroness, who was not good at French.

"There is no more, mein tear!" replied her husband, with a strong German accent.

"Confound their impudence!" exclaimed his wife with a heated countenance, "'ere, send Monsieur 'ere at once! I'll soon see if we're not to 'ave enough to eat in 'is beastly Hotel!"

All the ladies who understood what she said, looked horrified at such language, but that was of no consequence to Madame Gobelli, who continued to call out at intervals for "Monsieur" until she found the dinner was coming to an end without her, and thought it would be more politic to attend to business and postpone her feud till a more convenient occasion. The Baroness Gobelli was a mystery to most people in the Hotel. She was an enormous woman of the elephant build, with a large, flat face and clumsy hands and feet. Her skin was coarse, so was her hair, so were her features. The only things which redeemed an otherwise repulsive face, were a pair of good-humoured, though cunning blue eyes and a set of firm, white teeth. Who the Baroness had originally been, no one could quite make out. It was evident that she must have sprung from some low origin from her lack of education and breeding, yet she spoke familiarly of aristocratic names, even of Royal ones, and appeared to be acquainted with their families and homes. There was a floating rumour that she had been old Mr. Bates's cook before he married her, and when he left her a widow with an only child and a considerable fortune, the little German Baron had thought that her money was a fair equivalent for her personality. She was exceedingly vulgar, and when roused, exceedingly vituperative, but she possessed a rough good humour when pleased, and a large amount of natural shrewdness, which stood her instead of cleverness. But she was an unscrupulous liar, and rather boasted of the fact than otherwise. Having plenty of money at her command, she was used to take violent fancies to people —taking them up suddenly, loading them with presents and favours for as long as it pleased her, and then dropping them as suddenly, without why or wherefore —even insulting them if she could not shake them off without doing so. The Baron was completely under her thumb; more than that; he was servile in' her presence, which astonished those people, who did not know that amongst her other arrogant insistences, the Baroness laid claim to holding intercourse with certain supernatural and invisible beings, who had the power to wreak vengeance on all those who offended her. This fear it was, combined with the fact that she had all the money and kept the strings of the bag pretty close where he was concerned, that made the Baron wait upon his wife's wishes as if he were her slave. Perhaps the softest spot in the Baroness's heart was kept for her sickly and uninteresting son, Bobby Bates, whom she treated, nevertheless, with the roughness of a tigress for her cub. She kept him still more under her surveillance than she did her husband, and Bobby, though he had attained his nineteenth year, dared not say Bo! to a goose, in presence of his Mamma. As the cheese was handed round, Elinor Leyton rose from her seat with an impatient gesture.

"Do let us get out of this atmosphere, Margaret!" she said in a low tone. "I really cannot stand it any longer!"

The two ladies left the table, and went out beyond the balcony, to where a number of painted iron chairs and tables were placed on the Digue, for the accommodation of passing wayfarers, who might wish to rest awhile and quench their thirst with *limonade* or lager beer.

"I wonder who that girl is!" remarked Mrs. Pullen as soon as they were out of hearing. "I don't know whether I like her or not, but there is something rather distinguished-looking about her!"

"Do you think so?" said Miss Leyton, "I thought she only distinguished herself by eating like a cormorant! I never saw anyone in society gobble her food in such a manner! She made me positively sick!"

"Was it as bad as that?" replied the more quiet Mrs. Pullen, in an indifferent manner. Her eyes were attracted just then by the perambulator which contained her baby, and she rose to meet it.

"How is she, Nurse?" she asked as anxiously as if she had not parted from the infant an hour before. "Has she been awake all the time?"

"Yes, Ma'am, and looking about her like anything! But she seems inclined to sleep now! I thought it was about time to take her in!"

"O! no! not on such a warm, lovely evening! If she does go to sleep in the open air, it will do her no harm. Leave her with me! I want you to go indoors, and find out the name of the young lady who sat opposite to me at dinner to-day, Philippe understands English. He will tell you!"

"Why on earth do you want to know?" demanded Miss Leyton, as the servant disappeared.

"O! I don't know! I feel a little curious, that is all! She seems so young to be by herself!"

Elinor Leyton answered nothing, but walked across the Digue and stood, looking out over the sea. She was

anticipating the arrival of her *fiancé*, Captain Ralph
Pullen of the Limerick Rangers, but he had delayed his
coming to join them, and she began to find Heyst
rather dull.

The visitors of the Lion d'Or had finished their meal
by this time, and were beginning to reassemble on the
Digue, preparatory to taking a stroll before they turned
into one of the many *cafés-chantants,* which were situated
at stated intervals in front of the sea. Amongst them
came the Baroness Gobelli, leaning heavily on a thick
stick with one hand, and her husband's shoulder with
the other. The couple presented an extraordinary appearance, as they perambulated slowly up and down the
Digue.

She—with her great height and bulk, towering a
head above her companion, whilst he—with a full-sized
torso, and short legs—a large hat crammed down upon
his forehead, and no neck to speak of, so that the brim
appeared to rest upon his shoulders—was a ludicrous
figure, as he walked beside his wife, bending under the
weight of her support. But yet, she was actually proud
of him. Notwithstanding his ill-shaped figure, the Baron
possessed one of those mild German faces, with pale
watery blue eyes, a long nose, and hair and beard of a
reddish-golden colour, which entitled him, in the estimation of some people, to be called a handsome man, and
the Baroness was never tired of informing the public
that his head and face had once been drawn for that of
some celebrated saint.

Her own appearance was really comical, for though
she had plenty of means, her want of taste, or indifference to dress, made everyone stare at her as she passed.

On the present occasion, she wore a silk gown which had cost seventeen shillings a yard, with a costly velvet cloak, a bonnet which might have been rescued from the dustbin, and cotton gloves with all her fingers out. She shook her thick walking-stick in Miss Leyton's face as she passed by her, and called out loud enough for everyone to hear: "And when is the handsome Captain coming to join you, Miss Leyton, eh? Take care he ain't running after some other gal! 'When pensive I thought on my L.O.V.E.' Ha! ha! ha!"

Elinor flushed a delicate pink but did not turn her head, nor take any notice of her tormentor. She detested the Baroness with a perfectly bitter hatred, and her proud cold nature revolted from her coarseness and familiarity.

"Tied to your brat again!" cried the Baroness, as she passed Margaret Pullen who was moving the perambulator gently to and fro by the handle, so as to keep her infant asleep; "why didn't you put it in the tub as soon as it was born? It would 'ave saved you a heap of trouble! I often wish I had done so by that devil Bobby! 'Ere, where are you, Bobby?"

"I'm close behind you, Mamma!" replied the simple looking youth.

"Well! don't you get running away from your father and me, and winking at the gals! There's time enough for that, ain't there, Gustave?" she concluded, addressing the Baron.

"Come along, Robert, and mind what your mother tells you!" said the Herr Baron with his guttural German accent, as the extraordinary trio pursued their way down.

the Digue, the Baroness making audible remarks on everybody she met, as they went.

Margaret Pullen sat where they had left her, moving about the perambulator, whilst her eyes, like Elinor's, were fixed upon the tranquil water. The August sun had now quite disappeared, and the indescribably faint and unpleasant odour, which is associated with the dunes of Heyst, had begun to make itself apparent. A still languor had crept over everything, and there were indications of a thunderstorm in the air. She was thinking of her husband, Colonel Arthur Pullen, the elder brother of Miss Leyton's *fiancé,* who was toiling out in India for baby and herself. It had been a terrible blow to Margaret, to let him go out alone after only one year of happy wedded life, but the expected advent of her little daughter at the time, had prohibited her undertaking so long a journey and she had been compelled to remain behind. And now baby was six months old, and Colonel Pullen hoped to be home by Christmas, so had advised her to wait for his return. But her thoughts were sad sometimes, notwithstanding.

Events happen so unexpectedly in this world—who could say for certain that she and her husband would ever meet again—that Arthur would ever see his little girl, or that she should live to place her in her father's arms? But such a state of feeling was morbid, she knew, and she generally made an effort to shake it off. The nurse, returning with the information she had sent her to acquire, roused her from her reverie.

"If you please, Ma'am, the young lady's name is Brandt, and Philippe says she came from London!"

"English! I should never have guessed it!" observed Mrs. Pullen, "She speaks French so well."

"Shall I take the baby now, Ma'am?"

"Yes! Wheel her along the Digue. I shall come and meet you by and by!"

As the servant obeyed her orders, she called to Miss Leyton.

"Elinor! come here!"

"What is it?" asked Miss Leyton, seating herself beside her.

"The new girl's name is Brandt and she comes from England! Would you have believed it?"

"I did not take sufficient interest in her to make any speculations on the subject. I only observed that she had a mouth from ear to ear, and ate like a pig! What does it concern us, where she comes from?"

At that moment, a Mrs. Montague, who, with her husband, was conveying a family of nine children over to Brussels, under the mistaken impression, that they would be able to live cheaper there than in England, came down the Hotel steps with half a dozen of them, clinging to her skirts, and went straight up to Margaret Pullen.

"O! Mrs. Pullen! What is that young lady's name, who sat opposite to you at dinner? Everybody is asking! I hear she is enormously rich, and travelling alone. Did you see the lace on her dress? Real Valenciennes, and the diamond rings she wore! Frederick says they must be worth a lot of money. She must be someone of consequence I should imagine!"

"On the contrary, my nurse tells me she is English and her name is Brandt. Has she no friends here?"

"Madame Lamont says she arrived in company with another girl, but they are located at different parts of the Hotel. It seems very strange, does it not?"

"And it sounds very improper!" interposed Elinor Leyton, "I should say the less we have to say to her, the better! You never know what acquaintances you may make in a place like this! When I look up and down the *table d'hôte* menagerie sometimes, it makes me quite ill!"

"Does it?" rejoined Mrs. Montague, "I think it's so amusing! That Baroness Gobelli, for instance——"

"Don't mention her before me!" cried Miss Leyton, in a tone of disgust, "the woman is not fit for civilised society!"

"She is rather common, certainly, and strange in her behaviour," said Mrs. Montague, "but she is very good-natured. She gave my little Edward a louis yesterday. I felt quite ashamed to let him take it!"

"That just proves her vulgarity," exclaimed Elinor Leyton, who had not a sixpence to give away, herself, "it shows that she thinks her money will atone for all her other shortcomings! She gave that Miss Taylor who left last week, a valuable brooch off her own throat. And poor payment too, for all the dirty things she made her do and the ridicule she poured upon her. I daresay this *nouveau riche* will try to curry favour with us by the same means."

At that moment, the girl under discussion, Miss Brandt, appeared on the balcony, which was only raised a few feet above where they sat. She wore the same dress she had at dinner, with the addition of a little fleecy shawl about her shoulders. She stood smiling, and looking at the ladies (who had naturally dropped all discussion about her) for a few moments, and then she ventured to descend the steps between the rampant gilded lions, and almost timidly, as it seemed, took up a position near them. Mrs. Pullen felt that she could not be so discourteous as to take no notice whatever of the new-comer, and so, greatly to Miss Leyton's disgust, she uttered quietly, Good evening!"

It was quite enough for Miss Brandt. She drew nearer with smiles mantling over her face.

"Good evening! Isn't it lovely here?—so soft and warm, something like the Island, but so much fresher!"

She looked up and down the Digue, now crowded with a multitude of visitors, and drew in her breath with a long sigh of content.

"How gay and happy they all seem, and how happy I am too! Do you know, if I had my will, what I should like to do?" she said, addressing Mrs. Pullen.

" No! indeed!"

"I should like to tear up and down this road as hard as ever I could, throwing my arms over my head and screaming aloud!"

The ladies exchanged glances of astonishment, but Margaret Pullen could not forbear smiling as she asked their new acquaintance the reason why.

"O! because I am free—free at last, after ten long years of imprisonment! I am telling you the truth, I am indeed, and you would feel just the same if you had been shut up in a horrid Convent ever since you were eleven years old!"

At the word "convent", the national Protestant horror immediately spread itself over the faces of the three other ladies; Mrs. Montague gathered her flock about her and took them out of the way of possible contamination, though she would have much preferred to hear the rest of Miss Brandt's story, and Elinor Leyton moved her chair further away. But Margaret Pullen was interested and encouraged the girl to proceed.

"In a convent! I suppose then you are a Roman Catholic!"

Harriet Brandt suddenly opened her slumbrous eyes.

"I don't think so! I'm not quite sure what I am! Of course I've had any amount of religion crammed down my throat in the Convent, and I had to follow their prayers, whilst there, but I don't believe my parents were Catholics! But it does not signify, I am my own mistress now. I can be what I like!"

"You have been so unfortunate then as to lose your parents!"

"O! yes! years ago, that is why my guardian, Mr. Trawler, placed me in the Convent for my education. And I've been there for ten years! Is it not a shame? I'm twenty-one now! That's why I'm free! You see," the girl went on confidentially, "my parents left me everything, and as soon as I came of age I entered into possession of it. My guardian, Mr. Trawler, who lives in Jamaica,—did I tell you that I've come from Jamaica?— thought I should live with him and his wife, when I left the Convent, and pay them for my keep, but I refused. They had kept me too tight! I wanted to see the world and life—it was what I had been looking forward to— so as soon as my affairs were settled, I left the West Indies and came over here!"

"They said you came from England in the Hotel!"

"So I did! The steamer came to London and I stayed there a week before I came on here!"

"But you are too young to travel about by yourself, Miss Brandt! English young ladies never do so!" said Mrs. Pullen.

"I'm not by myself, exactly! Olga Brimont, who was in the Convent with me, came too. But she is ill, so she's upstairs. She has come to her brother who is in Brussels, and we travelled together. We had the same cabin on board the steamer, and Olga was very ill. One night the doctor thought she was going to die! I stayed with her all the time. I used to sit up with her at night, but it did her no good. We stopped in London because we wanted to buy some dresses and things, but she was not able to go out, and I had to go alone. Her brother is away from Brussels at present so he wrote her to stay in Heyst till he could fetch her, and as I had nowhere particular to go, I came with her! And she is better already! She has been fast asleep all the afternoon!"

"And what will you do when your friend leaves you?" asked Mrs. Pullen.

"O! I don't know! Travel about, I suppose! I shall go wherever it may please me!"

"Are you not going to take a walk this evening?" demanded Elinor Leyton in a low voice of her friend, wishing to put a stop to the conversation.

"Certainly! I told nurse I would join her and baby by-and-by!"

"Shall I fetch your hat then?" enquired Miss Leyton, as she rose to go up to their apartments.

2 *

"Yes! if you will, dear, please, and my velvet cape, in case it should turn chilly!"

"I will fetch mine too!" cried Miss Brandt, jumping up with alacrity. "I may go with you, mayn't I? I'll just tell Olga that I'm going out and be down again in five minutes!" and without waiting for an answer, she was gone.

"See what you have brought upon us!" remarked Elinor in a vexed tone.

"Well! it was not my fault," replied Margaret, "and after all, what does it signify? It is only a little act of courtesy to an unprotected girl. I don't dislike her, Elinor! She is very familiar and communicative, but fancy what it must be like to find herself her own mistress, and with money at her command, after ten years' seclusion within the four walls of a convent! It is enough to turn the head of any girl. I think it would be very churlish to refuse to be friendly with her!"

"Well! I hope it may turn out all right! But you must remember how Ralph cautioned us against making any acquaintances in a foreign hotel."

"But I am not under Ralph's orders, though you may be, and I should not care to go entirely by the advice of so very fastidious and exclusive a gentleman as he is! My Arthur would never find fault with me, I am sure, for being friendly with a young unmarried girl."

"Anyway, Margaret, let me entreat you not to discuss my private affairs with this new *protégée* of yours. I don't want to see her saucer eyes goggling over the news of my engagement to your brother-in-law!"

"Certainly I will not, since you ask it! But you hardly

expect to keep it a secret when Ralph comes down here, do you?"

"Why not? Why need anyone know more than that he is your husband's brother?"

"I expect they know a good deal more now," said Margaret, laughing. "The news that you are the Honourable Elinor Leyton and that your father is Baron Walthamstowe, was known all over Heyst the second day we were here. And I have no doubt it has been succeeded by the interesting intelligence that you are engaged to marry Captain Pullen. You cannot keep servants' tongues from wagging, you know!"

"I suppose not!" replied Elinor, with a *moue* of contempt. "However, they will learn no more through me or Ralph. We are not "Arry and 'Arriet' to sit on the Digue with our arms round each other's waists."

"Still—there are signs and symptoms," said Margaret, laughing.

"There will be none with us!" rejoined Miss Leyton, indignantly, as Harriet Brandt, with a black lace hat on, trimmed with yellow roses, and a little fichu tied carelessly across her bosom, ran lightly down the steps to join them.

CHAPTER II.

THE Digue was crowded by that time. All Heyst had turned out to enjoy the evening air and to partake in the gaiety of the place. A band was playing on the movable orchestra, which was towed by three skinny little donkeys, day after day, from one end of the Digue to the other. To-night, it was its turn to be in the

middle, where a large company of people was sitting on
green painted chairs that cost ten centimes for hire each,
whilst children danced, or ran madly round and round
its base.   Everyone had changed his, or her, seaside
garb for more fashionable array—even the children were
robed in white frocks and gala hats—and the whole
scene was gay and festive.   Harriet Brandt ran from one
side to the other of the Digue, as though she also had
been a child.   Everything she saw seemed to astonish
and delight her.   First, she was gazing out over the
calm and placid water—and next, she was exclaiming
at the bits of rubbish in the shape of embroidered
baskets, or painted shells, exhibited in the shop windows,
which were side by side with the private houses and
hotels, forming a long line of buildings fronting the
water.

She kept on declaring that she wanted to buy that
or this, and lamenting she had not brought more money
with her.

"You will have plenty of opportunities to select and
purchase what you want to-morrow," said Mrs. Pullen,
"and you will be better able to judge what they are
like.   They look better under the gas than they do by
daylight, I can assure you, Miss Brandt!"

"O! but they are lovely—delightful!" replied the
girl, enthusiastically, "I never saw anything so pretty
before!   Do look at that little doll in a bathing costume,
with her cap in one hand, her sponge in the other!   She
is charming—unique!   *Tout ce qu'il y a de plus beau!*"

She spoke French perfectly, and when she spoke
English, it was with a slightly foreign accent, that greatly
enhanced its charm.   It made Mrs. Pullen observe:

"You are more used to speaking French than English, Miss Brandt!"

"Yes! We always spoke French in the Convent, and it is in general use in the Island. But I thought—I hoped—that I spoke English like an Englishwoman! I *am* an Englishwoman, you know!"

"Are you? I was not quite sure! Brandt sounds rather German!"

"No! my father was English, his name was Henry Brandt, and my mother was a Miss Carey—daughter of one of the Justices of Barbadoes!"

"O! indeed!" replied Mrs. Pullen. She did not know what else to say. The subject was of no interest to her! At that moment they encountered the nurse and perambulator, and she naturally stopped to speak to her baby.

The sight of the infant seemed to drive Miss Brandt wild.

"O! is that your baby, Mrs. Pullen, is that really your baby?" she exclaimed excitedly, "you never told me you had one. O! the darling! the sweet dear little angel! I love little white babies! I adore them. They are so sweet and fresh and clean—so different from the little niggers who smell so nasty, you can't touch them! We never saw a baby in the Convent, and so few English children live to grow up in Jamaica! O! let me hold her! let me carry her! I *must!*"

She was about to seize the infant in her arms, when the mother interposed.

"No, Miss Brandt, please, not this evening! She is but half awake, and has arrived at that age when she is frightened of strangers.   Another time perhaps, when she has become used to you, but not now!"

"But I will be so careful of her, pretty dear!" persisted the girl, "I will nurse her so gently, that she will fall to sleep again in my arms.   Come! my little love, come!" she continued to the baby, who pouted her lips and looked as if she were going to cry.

"Leave her alone!" exclaimed Elinor Leyton in a sharp voice.   "Do you not hear what Mrs. Pullen says —that you are not to touch her!"

She spoke so acridly, that gentle Margaret Pullen felt grieved for the look of dismay that darted into Harriet Brandt's face on hearing it.

"O! I am sorry—I didn't mean—" she stammered, with a side glance at Margaret.

"Of course you did not mean anything but what was kind," said Mrs. Pullen, "Miss Leyton perfectly understands that, and when baby is used to you, I daresay she will be very grateful for your attentions.   But to-night she is sleepy and tired, and, perhaps, a little cross. Take her home, Nurse," she went on, "and put her to bed!   Good-night, my sweet!" and the perambulator passed them and was gone.

An awkward silence ensued between the three women after this little incident.   Elinor Leyton walked somewhat apart from her companions, as if she wished to avoid all further controversy, whilst Margaret Pullen sought some way by which to atone for her friend's rudeness to the young stranger.   Presently they came across one of the *cafés chantants* which are attached to the seaside hotels, and which was brilliantly lighted up. A large awning was spread outside, to shelter some dozens of chairs and tables, most of which were already occupied. The windows of the hotel salon had been thrown wide open, to accommodate some singers and musicians, who advanced in turn and stood on the threshold to amuse the audience. As they approached the scene, a tenor in evening dress was singing a love song, whilst the musicians accompanied his voice from the salon, and the occupants of the chairs were listening with rapt attention.

"How charming! how delightful!" cried Harriet Brandt, as they reached the spot, "I never saw anything like this in the Island!"

"You appear never to have seen anything!" remarked Miss Leyton, with a sneer. Miss Brandt glanced apologetically at Mrs. Pullen.

"How could I see anything, when I was in the Convent?" she said, "I know there are places of entertainment in the Island, but I was never allowed to go to any. And in London, there was no one for me to go with! I should so much like to go in there," indicating the *café*. "Will you come with me, both of you I mean, and I will pay for everything! I have plenty of money, you know!"

"There is nothing to pay, my dear, unless you call for refreshment," was Margaret's reply. "Yes, I will go with you certainly, if you so much wish it! Elinor, you won't mind, will you?"

But Miss Leyton was engaged talking to a Monsieur and Mademoiselle Vieuxtemps — an old brother and sister, resident in the Lion d'Or—who had stopped to wish her Good-evening! They were dear, good old people, but rather monotonous and dull, and Elinor had more than once ridiculed their manner of talking and voted them the most terrible bores. Mrs. Pullen concluded therefore, that she would get rid of them as soon as courtesy permitted her to do so, and follow her. With a smile and a bow therefore, to the Vieuxtemps, she pushed her way through the crowd with Harriet Brandt, to where she perceived that three seats were vacant, and took possession of them. They were not good seats for hearing or seeing, being to one side of the salon, and quite in the shadow, but the place was so full that she saw no chance of getting any others. As soon as they were seated, the waiter came round for orders, and it was with difficulty that Mrs. Pullen prevented her companion purchasing sufficient liqueurs and cakes to serve double the number of their company.

"You must allow me to pay for myself, Miss Brandt," she said gravely, "or I will never accompany you anywhere again!"

"But I have lots of money," pleaded the girl, "much more than I know what to do with—it would be a pleasure to me, it would indeed!"

But Mrs. Pullen was resolute, and three *limonades* only were placed upon their table. Elinor Leyton had not yet made her appearance, and Mrs. Pullen kept craning her neck over the other seats to see where she might be, without success.

"She cannot have missed us!" she observed, "I wonder if she can have continued her walk with the Vieuxtemps!"

"O! what does it signify?" said Harriet, drawing her chair closer to that of Mrs. Pullen, "we can do very well without her. I don't think she's very nice, do you?"

"You must not speak of Miss Leyton like that to me, Miss Brandt," remonstrated Margaret, gently, "because —she is a great friend of our family."

She had been going to say, "Because she will be my sister-in-law before long," but remembered Elinor's request in time, and substituted the other sentence.

"I don't think she's very kind, though," persisted the other.

"It is only her manner, Miss Brandt! She does not mean anything by it!"

"But you are so different," said the girl as she crept still closer, "I could see it when you smiled at me at dinner. I knew I should like you at once. And I want you to like me too—so much! It has been the dream of my life to have some friends. That is why I would not stay in Jamaica. I don't like the people there! I want friends—real friends!"

"But you must have had plenty of friends of your own age in the Convent."

"That shows you don't know anything about a convent! It's the very last place where they will let you make a friend—they're afraid lest you should tell each other too much! The convent I was in was an Ursuline order, and even the nuns were obliged to walk three and three, never two, together, lest they should have secrets between them. As for us girls, we were never left alone for a single minute! There was always a sister with us, even at night, walking up and down between the rows of beds, pretending to read her prayers, but with her eyes on us the whole time and her ears open to catch what we said. I suppose they were afraid we should talk about lovers. I think girls do talk about

them when they can, more in convents than in other
places, though they have never had any. It would be
so dreadful to be like the poor nuns, and never have a
lover to the end of one's days, wouldn't it?"

"You would not fancy being a nun then, Miss Brandt!"

"*I*—Oh! dear no! I would rather be dead, twenty
times over! But they didn't like my coming out at all.
They did try so hard to persuade me to remain with
them for ever! One of them, Sister Féodore, told me I
must never talk even with gentlemen, if I could avoid it
—that they were all wicked and nothing they said was
true, and if I trusted them, they would only laugh at me
afterwards for my pains. But I don't believe that,
do you?"

"Certainly not!" replied Margaret warmly. "The
sister who told you so knew nothing about men. My
dear husband is more like an angel than a man, and
there are many like him. You mustn't believe such
nonsense, Miss Brandt! I am sure you never heard your
parents say such a silly thing!"

"O! my father and mother! I never remember hearing them say anything!" replied Miss Brandt. She had
crept closer and closer to Mrs. Pullen as she spoke, and
now encircled her waist with her arm, and leaned her
head upon her shoulder. It was not a position that
Margaret liked, nor one she would have expected from
a woman on so short an acquaintance, but she did not
wish to appear unkind by telling Miss Brandt to move
further away. The poor girl was evidently quite unused
to the ways and customs of Society, she seemed moreover very friendless and dependent—so Margaret laid
her solecism down to ignorance and let her head rest

where she had placed it, resolving inwardly meanwhile that she would not subject herself to be treated in so familiar a manner again.

"Don't you remember your parents then?" she asked her presently.

"Hardly! I saw so little of them," said Miss Brandt, "my father was a great doctor and scientist, I believe, and I am not quite sure if he knew that he had a daughter!"

"O! my dear, what nonsense!"

"But it is true, Mrs. Pullen! He was always shut up in his laboratory, and I was not allowed to go near that part of the house. I suppose he was very clever and all that—but he was too much engaged in making experiments to take any notice of me, and I am sure I never wanted to see him!"

"How very sad! But you had your mother to turn to for consolation and company, whilst she lived, surely?"

"O! my mother!" echoed Harriet, carelessly. "Yes! my mother! Well! I don't think I knew much more of her either. The ladies in Jamaica get very lazy, you know, and keep a good deal to their own rooms. The person there I loved best of all, was old Pete, the overseer!"

"The overseer!"

"Of the estate and niggers, you know! We had plenty of niggers on the coffee plantation, regular African fellows, with woolly heads and blubber lips, and yellow whites to their eyes. When I was a little thing of four years old, Pete used to let me whip the little niggers for a treat, when they had done anything wrong. It used to make me laugh to see them wriggle their legs under the whip and cry!"

"O! don't, Miss Brandt!" exclaimed Margaret Pullen, in a voice of pain.

"It's true, but they deserved it, you know, the little wretches, always thieving or lying or something! I've seen a woman whipped to death, because she wouldn't work. We think nothing of that sort of thing, over there. Still—you can't wonder that I was glad to get out of the Island. But I loved old Pete, and if he had been alive when I left, I would have brought him to England with me. He used to carry me for miles through the jungle on his back,—out in the fresh mornings and the cool, dewy eves. I had a pony to ride, but I never went anywhere, without his hand upon my bridle rein. He was always so afraid lest I should come to any harm. I don't think anybody else cared. Pete was the only creature who ever loved me, and when I think of Jamaica, I remember my old nigger servant as the one friend I had there!"

"It is very, very sad!" was all that Mrs. Pullen could say.

She had become fainter and fainter, as the girl leaned against her with her head upon her breast. Some sensation which she could not define, nor account for—some feeling which she had never experienced before—had come over her and made her head reel. She felt as if something or someone, were drawing all her life away. She tried to disengage herself from the girl's clasp, but Harriet Brandt seemed to come after her, like a coiling snake, till she could stand it no longer, and faintly exclaiming:

"Miss Brandt! let go of me, please! I feel ill!" she rose and tried to make her way between the crowded tables, towards the open air.   As she stumbled along, she came against (to her great relief) her friend, Elinor Leyton.

"O! Elinor!" she gasped, "I don't know what is the matter with me! I feel so strange, so light-headed! Do take me home!"

Miss Leyton dragged her through the audience, and made her sit down on a bench, facing the sea.

"Why! what's the matter?" demanded Harriet Brandt, who had made her way after them, "is Mrs. Pullen ill?"

"So it appears," replied Miss Leyton, coldly, "but how it happened, you should know better than myself! I suppose it is very warm in there!"

"No! no! I do not think so," said Margaret, with a bewildered air, "we had chairs close to the side.   And Miss Brandt was telling me of her life in Jamaica, when such an extraordinary sensation came over me! I can't describe it! it was just as if I had been scooped hollow!"

At this description, Harriet Brandt burst into a loud laugh, but Elinor frowned her down.

"It may seem a laughing matter to you, Miss Brandt," she said, in the same cold tone, "but it is none to me. Mrs. Pullen is far from strong, and her health is not to be trifled with.   However, I shall not let her out of my sight again."

"Don't make a fuss about it, Elinor," pleaded her friend, "it was my own fault, if anyone's.   I think there must be a thunderstorm in the air, I have felt so oppressed all the evening.   Or is the smell from the dunes

worse than usual? Perhaps I ate something at dinner
that disagreed with me!"

"I cannot understand it at all," replied Miss Leyton,
"you are not used to fainting, or being suddenly attacked
in any way. However, if you feel able to walk, let us
go back to the Hotel. Miss Brandt will doubtless find
someone to finish the evening with!"

Harriet was just about to reply that she knew no one
but themselves, and to offer to take Mrs. Pullen's arm
on the other side, when Elinor Leyton cut her short.

"No! thank you, Miss Brandt! Mrs. Pullen would,
I am sure, prefer to return to the Hotel alone with me!
You can easily join the Vieuxtemps or any other of the
visitors to the Lion d'Or. There is not much ceremony
observed amongst the English at these foreign places.
It would be better perhaps if there were a little more!
Come, Margaret, take my arm, and we will walk as
slowly as you like! But I shall not be comfortable until
I see you safe in your own room!"

So the two ladies moved off together, leaving Harriet
Brandt standing disconsolately on the Digue, watching
their departure. Mrs. Pullen had uttered a faint Good-
night to her, but had made no suggestion that she
should walk back with them, and it seemed to the girl
as if they both, in some measure, blamed her for the
illness of her companion. What had she done, she
asked herself, as she reviewed what had passed between
them, that could in any way account for Mrs. Pullen's
illness? She liked her so much—so very much—she
had so hoped she was going to be her friend—she would
have done anything and given anything sooner than put
her to inconvenience in any way. As the two ladies

moved slowly out of sight, Harriet turned sadly and walked the other way. She felt lonely and disappointed. She knew no one to speak to, and there was a cold empty feeling in her breast, as though, in losing her hold on Margaret Pullen, she had lost something on which she had depended. Something of her feeling must have communicated itself to Margaret Pullen, for after a minute or two she stopped and said,

"I don't half like leaving Miss Brandt by herself, Elinor! She is very young to be wandering about a town by night and alone!"

"Nonsense!" returned Miss Leyton, shortly, "a young lady who can make the voyage from Jamaica to Heyst on her own account, knocking about in London for a week on the way, is surely competent to walk back to the Hotel without your assistance. I should say that Miss Brandt was a very independent young woman!"

"Perhaps, by nature, but she has been shut up in a convent for the best part of her life, and that is not considered to be a good preparation for fighting one's way through the world!"

"She'll be able to fight her own battles, never fear!" was Elinor's reply.

Just then they encountered Bobby Bates, who lifted his cap as he hurried past them.

"Where are you going so fast, Mr. Bates?" said Elinor Leyton.

"I am going back to the Hotel to fetch Mamma's fur boa!" he answered.

They were passing a lighted lamp at the time, and she noticed that the lad's eyes were red, and his features bore traces of distress.

"Are you ill?" she enquired quickly, "or in any trouble?"

He halted for a minute in his stride.

"No! no! not exactly," he said in a low voice, and then, as if the words came from him against his will, he went on, "But O! I do wish someone would speak to Mamma about the way she treats me. It's cruel—to strike me with her stick before all those people, as if I were a baby, and to call me such names! Even the servant William laughs at me! Do all mothers do the same, Miss Leyton? Ought a man to stand it quietly?"

"Decidedly not!" cried Elinor, without hesitation.

"O! Elinor! remember, she is his mother," remonstrated Margaret, "don't say anything to set him against her!"

"But I was nineteen last birthday," continued the lad, "and sometimes she treats me in such a manner, that I can't bear it! The Baron dare not say a word to her! She swears at him so. Sometimes, I think I will run away and go to sea!"

"No! no! you mustn't do that!" called Miss Leyton after him, as he quickened his footsteps in the direction of the Lion d'Or.

"What an awful woman!" sighed Mrs. Pullen. "Fancy! striking her own son in public, and with that thick stick too. I believe he had been crying!"

"I am *sure* he had," replied her friend, "you can see the poor fellow is half-witted, and very weakly into the bargain. I suppose she has beaten his brains to a pap. What a terrible misfortune to have such a mother! You should hear some of the stories Madame Lamont has to tell of her!"

"But how does she hear them?"

"Through the Baron's servant William, I suppose. He says the Baroness has often taken her stick to him and the other servants, and thinks no more of swearing at them than a trooper! They all hate her. One day, she took up a kitchen cleaver and advanced upon her coachman with it, but he seized her by both arms and sat her down upon the fire, whence she was only rescued after being somewhat severely burned!"

"It served her right!" exclaimed Margaret, laughing at the ludicrous idea, "but what a picture she must have presented, seated on the kitchen range! Where can the woman have been raised? What sort of a person can she be?"

"Not what she pretends, Margaret, you may be sure of that! All her fine talk of lords and ladies is so much bunkum. But I pity the poor little Baron, who is, at all events, inoffensive. How can he put up with such a wife! He must feel very much ashamed of her sometimes!"

"And yet he seems devoted to her! He never leaves her side for a moment. He is her walking stick, her fetcher and carrier, and her scribe. I don't believe she can write a letter!"

"And yet she was talking at the *table d'hôte* yesterday of the Duke of This and the Earl of That, and hinting at her having stayed at Osborne and Windsor. Of course they are falsehoods! She has never. seen the inside of a palace unless it was in the capacity of a charwoman! Have you observed her hair? It is as coarse as a horse-tail? And her hands! Bobby informed me the other day that his Mamma took nines in gloves! She's not a woman, my dear! She's a female elephant!"

3*

Margaret was laughing still, when they reached the steps of the Lion d'Or.

"You are very naughty and very scandalous, Elinor," she said, "but you have done me a world of good. My unpleasant feelings have quite gone. I am quite capable of continuing our walk if you would like to do so."

"No such thing, Madam," replied Miss Leyton. "I am responsible for your well-doing in Arthur's absence. Upstairs and into bed you go, unless you would like a cup of coffee and a chasse first. That is the only indulgence I can grant you."

But Mrs. Pullen declined the proffered refreshment, and the two ladies sought their rooms in company.

CHAPTER III.

THE next morning dawned upon a perfect August day. The sun streamed brightly over every part of Heyst, turning the loose dry yellow sand (from end to end of which not a stone or boulder was to be seen), into a veritable cloth of gold. The patient asses, carrying their white-covered saddles, and tied to stakes, were waiting in a row for hire, whilst some dozen Rosinantes, called by courtesy, horses, were also of the company. The sands were already strewn with children, their short petticoats crammed into a pair of bathing-drawers, and their heads protected by linen hats or bonnets, digging away at the dry sand as if their lives depended on their efforts. The bathing-machines, painted in gay stripes of green, red, blue, or orange, were hauled down, ready for action, and the wooden tents, which can be hired for the season at any foreign watering place, were being swept out and arranged for the day's use.

Some of the more pretentious ones, belonging to private families, were surmounted by a gilt coronet, the proud possession of the Comte Darblaye, or the Herr Baron Grumplestein—sported flags moreover of France or Germany, and were screened from the eyes of the vulgar, by lace or muslin curtains, tied up with blue ribbons. On the balcony of the Lion d'Or, where the visitors always took their breakfast, were arranged tables, piled with dishes of crevettes, fresh from the sea, pistolets, and beautiful butter as white and tasteless as cream. It was a delight to breakfast on the open balcony, with the sea breeze blowing in one's face, and in the intervals of eating prawns and bread and butter, or perusing the morning papers, to watch the cheerful scene below.

The Baroness was there, early of course. She, and her husband, and the ill-used Bobby, occupied a table to themselves, whence she addressed her remarks to whomever she chose, whether they wished to listen, or not, and the Baron shelled her crevettes and buttered her pistolets for her. Margaret and Elinor were rather later than usual, for Mrs. Pullen had not passed a good night, and Miss Leyton would not have her disturbed.

Harriet Brandt was there as they appeared, and beside her, a pale, unhealthy-looking young woman, whom she introduced as her friend, and travelling companion, Olga Brimont.

"Olga did not wish to come down. She thought she would lie another day in bed, but I made her get up and dress, and I was right, wasn't I, Mrs. Pullen?"

"I think the fresh air will do Mademoiselle Brimont

more good than the close bedroom, if she is strong
enough to stand it!" replied Margaret, with a smile. "I
am afraid you are still feeling weak," she continued, to
the new-comer.

"I feel better than I did on board the steamer, or
in London," said Mademoiselle Brimont. She was an
under-sized girl with plain features, and did not shew off
to advantage beside her travelling companion.

"Did you suffer so much from sea-sickness? I can
sympathise with you, as I am a very bad sailor myself!"

"O! no! Madame, it was not the *mal de mer*. I
can hardly tell you what it was. Miss Brandt and I
occupied a small cabin together, and perhaps, it was
because it was so small, but I did not feel as if I could
breathe there—such a terrible oppression as though some
one were sitting on my chest—and such a general feeling of emptiness. It was the same in London, though
Miss Brandt did all she could for me, indeed she sat up
with me all night, till I feared she would be ill herself—
but I feel better now! Last night I slept for the first
time since leaving Jamaica!"

"That is right! You will soon get well in this lovely
air!"

They all sat down at the same table, and commenced
to discuss their rolls and coffee. Margaret Pullen, glancing up once, was struck by the look with which Harriet
Brandt was regarding her—it was so full of yearning
affection—almost of longing to approach her nearer, to
hear her speak, to touch her hand! It amused her to
observe it! She had heard of cases, in which young un-
sophisticated girls had taken unaccountable affections for
members of their own sex, and trusted she was not

going to form the subject for some such experience on Miss Brandt's part. The idea made her address her conversation more to Mademoiselle Brimont, than to her companion of the evening before.

"I suppose you and Miss Brandt were great friends in the Convent," she said.

"O! no, Madame, we hardly ever saw each other whilst there, except in chapel. There is so much difference in our ages, I am only seventeen, and was in the lower school, whilst Miss Brandt did hardly any lessons during the two last years she spent there. But I was very glad to have her company across to England. My brother would have sent for me last year, if he could have heard of a lady to travel with me!"

"Are you going on to join your brother soon?"

"He says he will fetch me, Madame, as soon as he can be spared from his business. He is my only relation. My parents died, like Miss Brandt's, in the West Indies."

"Well! you must be sure and get your looks back before he arrives!" said Margaret, kindly.

The head waiter now appeared with the letters from England, amongst which was one for Miss Leyton in a firm, manly handwriting, with a regimental crest in blue and gold upon the envelope. Her face did not change in the least as she broke the seal, although it came from her *fiancé*, Captain Ralph Pullen. Elinor Leyton's was an exceptionally cold face, and it matched her disposition. She had attractive features;—a delicate nose, carved as if in ivory—brown eyes, a fair rose-tinted complexion, and a small mouth with thin, firmly closed lips. Her hair was bronze-coloured, and it was always dressed to perfection. She had a good figure too, with small hands and feet—and she was robed in excellent taste. She was pre-eminently a woman for a man to be proud of as the mistress of his house, and the head of his table. She might be trusted never to say or do an unladylike thing—before all, she was cognisant of the obligations which devolved upon her as the daughter of Lord Walthamstowe and a member of the British aristocracy. But in disposition she was undoubtedly cold, and her *fiancé* had already begun to find it out. Their engagement had come about neither of them quite knew how, but he liked the idea of being connected with an aristocratic family, and she was proud of having won a man, for whom many caps had been pulled in vain. He was considered to be one of the handsomest men of his generation, and she was what people called an unexceptional match for him. She was fond of him in her way, but her way was a strange one. She called the attitude she assumed towards him, a proper and ladylike reserve, but impartial spectators, with stronger feelings, would have deemed it indifference.

However, like the proverbial dog in the manger, whether she valued her rights in Captain Pullen or not, Miss Leyton had no intention of permitting them to be interfered with. She would have died sooner than admit that he was necessary to her happiness,—at the same time she considered it due to her dignity as a woman, never to give in to his wishes, when they opposed her own, and often when they did not.

She displayed no particular enthusiasm when they met, nor distress when they parted—neither was she ever troubled by any qualms lest during their frequent separations, he should meet some woman whom he might perchance prefer to herself. They were engaged, and when the proper time came they would marry—meanwhile their private affairs concerned no one but themselves. In short, Elinor Leyton was not what is termed "a man's woman"—all her friends (if she had any) were of her own sex.

Having perused her letter, she refolded and replaced it in its envelope without a glance in the direction of Mrs. Pullen. Margaret thought she had a right to be informed of her brother-in-law's movements. She had invited Miss Leyton to accompany her to Heyst at his request, and any preparations which might be requisite before he joined them, would have to be made by herself.

"Is that from Ralph? What does he say?" she enquired in a low voice.

"Nothing in particular!"

"But when may we expect him at Heyst?"

"Next week, he says, in time for the *Bataille des Fleurs!*"

"Are you not pleased?"

"Of course I am!" replied Elinor, but without a sparkle or blush.

"O! if it were only my Arthur that were coming!" exclaimed Margaret, fervently, "I should go mad with joy!"

"Then it is just as well perhaps that it is *not* your Arthur!" rejoined her companion, as she put the letter into her pocket.

"Now, Bobby," announced the strident tones of the Baroness Gobelli from the other side of the balcony, "leave off picking the shrimps! You've 'ad more than enough! Ain't bread and butter good enough for you? What'll you want next?"

"But, Mamma," pleaded the youth, "I've only had a few! I've been shelling Papa's all this time!"

"Put 'em down at once, I say!" reiterated the Baroness, "'ere William, take Bobby's plate away! He's 'ad plenty for this morning!"

"But I haven't begun yet. I'm hungry!" remonstrated Bobby.

"Take 'is plate away!" roared the Baroness. "'Ang it all! Can't you 'ear what I say?"

"Mein tear! mein tear!" ejaculated the Herr Baron in a subdued voice.

"Leave me alone, Gustave! Do you suppose I can't manage my own son? He ain't yours! 'E'd make 'imself ill if I didn't look after him. Take 'is plate away, at once!"

The man-servant William lifted the plate of peeled shrimps and bread and butter from the table, whilst Bobby with a very red face rose from his seat and rushed down the steps to the beach.

"He! he! he!" cackled the Baroness, "that'll teach 'im not to fiddle with 'is food another time! Bobby don't care for an empty belly!"

"What a shame!" murmured Margaret, who was nothing if she was not a mother, "now the poor boy will go without his breakfast."

Presently, William was to be seen sneaking past the Hotel with a parcel in his hands. The Baroness pounced upon him like a cat upon a mouse.

"William!" she cried from the balcony, "what 'ave you got in your 'and?"

"Summat of my own, my lady!"

"Bring it 'ere!"

The man mounted the steps and stood before his mistress. He held a parcel in his hands, wrapped up in a table napkin.

"Open that parcel!" said the Baroness.

"Indeed, my lady, it's only the shrimps as Master Robert left behind him and I thought they would make me a little relish on the sands, my lady!"

"Open that parcel!"

William obeyed, and disclosed the rolls and butter and peeled shrimps just as Bobby had left them.

"You were going to take 'em down to Bobby on the beach!"

"No, indeed, my lady!"

"Confound you, Sir, don't you lie to me!" exclaimed the Baroness, shaking her stick in his face, "I've ways and means of finding out things that you know nothing of! Throw that stuff into the road!"

"But, my lady——"

"Throw it into the road at once, or you may take your month's warning! 'Ang it all! are you the mistress, or am I?"

The servant threw a glance of enquiry in the direction of the Herr Baron but the Herr Baron kept his face well down in his plate, so after a pause, he walked to the side, and shook the contents of the napkin upon the Digue.

"And now don't you try any more of your tricks upon me or I'll thrash you till your own mother won't know you! You leave Bobby alone for the future, or it'll be the worst day's work you ever did! Remember that!"

"Very good, my lady!" replied William, but as he left the balcony he gave a look at the other occupants, which well conveyed his feelings on the subject.

"I should not be surprised to hear that that woman had been murdered by her servants some day!" said Margaret to Elinor Leyton.

"No! and I should not be sorry! I feel rather like murdering her myself. But let us go down to the sands, Margaret, and try to find the disconsolate Bobby! I'm not afraid of his mother if William is, and if he wants something to eat, I shall give it him!"

They fetched their hats and parasols, and having left the Hotel by a side entrance, found their way down to the sands. It was a pretty sight there, and in some cases, a comical one. The bathing-machines were placed some sixty or more feet from the water, according to the tide, and their occupants, clad in bathing-costumes, had to run the gauntlet of all the eyes upon the beach, as they traversed that distance in order to reach the sea. To some visitors, especially the English ones, this ordeal was rather trying. To watch them open a crevice of the machine door, and regard the expectant crowd with horror;—then after some hesitation, goaded on by the cries of the bathing women that the time was passing, to see them emerge with reluctant feet, sadly conscious of their unclothed condition, and of the unsightly corns and bunions which disfigured their feet—to say nothing of the red and blue tint which their skin had suddenly assumed—was to find it almost impossible to refrain from laughter. The very skinny and knuckle-kneed ones; the very fat and bulging ones; the little fair men who looked like Bobby's peeled shrimps, and the muscular black and hairy ones who looked like bears escaped from a menagerie,—these types and many others, our ladies could not help being amused at, though they told each other it was very improper all the time. But everybody had to pass through the same ordeal and everybody submitted to it, and tried to laugh off their own humiliation by ridiculing the appearance of their neighbours. Margaret and Elinor were never tired of watching the antics of the Belgians and Germans whilst they were (what they called) bathing. The fuss they made over entering two feet of water—the way in which they gasped and puffed as they caught it up in their hands and rubbed their backs and chests with it—the reluctance with which the ladies were dragged by their masculine partners into the briny, as if they expected to be overwhelmed and drowned by the tiny waves which rippled over their toes, and made them catch their breath. And lastly, when they were convinced there was no danger, to see them, men and women, fat and thin, take hands and dance round in a ring as if they were playing at "Mulberry Bush" was too delightful. But if one bather, generally an Englishman, more daring than his fellows, went in for a good swim, the coast-guardsmen ran along the breakwater, shouting "Gare, gare!" until he came out again.

"They are funnier than ever to-day," remarked Margaret, after awhile, "I wonder what they will say when they see Ralph swimming out next week. They will be frightened to death. All the Pullens are wonderful swimmers. I have seen Anthony Pennell perform feats in the water that made my blood run cold! And Ralph is famous for his diving!"

The topic did not appear to interest Elinor. She reverted to the subject of Anthony.

"Is that the literary man—the cousin?"

"Yes! Have you not met him?"

"Never!"

"I am sure you would like him! He is such a fine fellow! Not such a 'beauty man' as Ralph, perhaps, but quite as tall and stalwart! His last book was a tremendous success!"

"Ralph has never mentioned him to me, though I knew he had a cousin of that name!"

"Well!—if you won't be offended at my saying so— Ralph has always been a little jealous of Anthony, at least so Arthur says. He outstripped him at school and college, and the feeling had its foundation there. And anyone might be jealous of him now! He has shewn himself to be a genius!"

"I don't like geniuses as a rule," replied Elinor, "they are so conceited. I believe that is Bobby Bates sitting out there on the breakwater! I will go and see if he is still hungry!"

"Give the poor boy a couple of francs to get himself a breakfast in one of the restaurants," said Margaret, "he will enjoy having a little secret from his terrible Mamma!"

She had not been alone long before the nurse came up to her, with the perambulator, piled up with toys, but no baby. Margaret's fears were excited at once.

"Nurse! nurse, what is the matter? Where is the baby?" she exclaimed in tones of alarm.

"Nothing's the matter, Ma'am! pray don't frighten yourself!" replied the servant, "it's only that the young ladies have got baby, and they've bought her all these toys, and sent me on to tell you that they would be here directly!"

The perambulator was filled with expensive play-things useless for an infant of six months' old. Dolls, woolly sheep, fur cats, and gaily coloured balls with a huge box of chocolates and caramels, were piled one on the top of the other. But Mrs. Pullen's face expressed nothing but annoyance.

"You had no right to let them take her, Nurse—you had no right to let the child out of your sight! Go back at once and bring her here to me! I am exceedingly annoyed about it!"

"Here are the young ladies, Ma'am, and you had better lay your orders on them, yourself, for they wouldn't mind me," said the nurse, somewhat sullenly.

In another minute Harriet Brandt, and Olga Brimont had reached her side, the former panting under the weight of the heavy infant, but with her face scarlet with the excitement of having captured her.

"O! Miss Brandt!" cried Margaret, "you have given me such a fright! You must never take baby away from her nurse again, please! As I told you last night, she is afraid of strangers, and generally cries when they try to take her! Come to me, my little one!" she continued, holding out her arms to the child, "come to mother and tell her all about it!"

But the baby seemed to take no notice of the fond appeal. It had its big eyes fixed upon Miss Brandt's face with a half-awed, half-interested expression.

"O! no! don't take her away!" said Harriet, eagerly, "she is so good with me! I assure you she is not frightened in the least bit, are you, my little love?" she added, addressing the infant. "And nurse tells me her name is Ethel, so I have ordered them to make her a little gold bangle with 'Ethel' on it, and she must wear it for my sake, darling little creature!"

"But, Miss Brandt, you must not buy such expensive things for her, indeed. She is too young to appreciate them, besides I do not like you to spend so much money on her!"

"But why shouldn't I? What am I to do with my money, if I may not spend it on others?"

"But, such a quantity of toys! Surely, you have not bought all these for my baby!"

"Of course I have! I would have bought the whole shop if it would have pleased her! She likes the colours! Little darling! look how earnestly she gazes at me with her lovely grey eyes, as if she knew what a little beauty I think her! O! you pretty dear! you sweet pink and white baby!"

Mrs. Pullen felt somewhat annoyed as she saw the dolls and furry animals which were strewn upon the sands, at the same time she was flattered by the admiration exhibited of her little daughter, and the endearments lavished upon her. She considered them all well deserved (as what mother would not?)—and it struck her that Harriet Brandt must be a kindhearted, as well as a generous girl to spend so much money on a stranger's child.

"She certainly does seem wonderfully good with you," she observed presently, "I never knew her so quiet with anybody but her nurse or me, before. Isn't it marvellous, Nurse?"

"It is, Ma'am! Baby do seem to take surprisingly to the young lady! And perhaps I might go into the town, as she is so quiet, and get the darning-wool for your stockings!"

"O! no! no! We must not let Miss Brandt get tired of holding her. She is too heavy to be nursed for long!"

"Indeed, indeed she is not!" cried Harriet, "do let me keep her, Mrs. Pullen, whilst nurse goes on her errand. It is the greatest pleasure to me to hold her. I should like never to give her up again!"

Margaret smiled.

"Very well, Nurse, since Miss Brandt is so kind, you can go!"

As the servant disappeared, she said to Harriet,

"Mind! you give her to me directly she makes your arm ache! I am more used to the little torment than you are."

"How can you call her by such a name, even in fun? What would I not give to have a baby of my very own to do what I liked with? I would never part with it, night nor day, I would teach it to love me so much, that it should never be happy out of my sight!"

"But that would be cruel, my dear! Your baby might have to part with you, as you have had to part with your mother!"

At the mention of her mother, something came into Miss Brandt's eyes, which Margaret could not define. It was not anger, nor sorrow, nor remorse. It was a kind of sullen contempt. It was something that made Mrs. Pullen resolve not to allude to the subject again.

The incident made her examine Harriet's eyes more closely than she had done before. They were beautiful in shape and colour, but they did not look like the eyes of a young girl. They were deeply, impenetrably black —with large pellucid pupils, but there was no sparkle nor brightness in them, though they were underlaid by smouldering fires which might burst forth into flame at any moment, and which seemed to stir and kindle and then go out again, when she spoke of anything that interested her. There was an attraction about the girl, which Mrs. Pullen acknowledged, without wishing to give in to. She could not keep her eyes off her! She seemed to hypnotise her as the snake is said to hypnotise the bird, but it was an unpleasant feeling, as if the next moment the smouldering fire would burst forth into flame and overwhelm her. But watching her play with, and hearing her talk to, her baby, Margaret put the idea away from her, and only thought how kindly natured she must be, to take so much trouble for another woman's child. It was not long before Miss Leyton found her way back to them, and as her glance fell upon Harriet Brandt and the baby, she elevated her eyebrows.

"Where is the nurse?" she demanded curtly.

"She has gone to the shops to see if she can get some darning-wool, and Miss Brandt was kind enough to offer to keep baby for her till she returns. And O! Elinor, look what beautiful toys Miss Brandt has bought her! Isn't she too kind?"

"Altogether too kind!" responded Elinor. "By the way, Margaret, I found our friend and transacted the little business we spoke of! But he says his Mamma has ordered him to remain here, till she comes down to see him bathe, and dry him, I suppose, with her own hands! And do I not descry her fairy feet indenting the sands at this very moment, and bearing down in our direction?"

"You could hardly mistake her for anything else!" replied Mrs. Pullen.

In another minute the Baroness was upon them.

"Hullo," she called out, "you're just in time to see Gustave bathe! He looks lovely in his bathing costume! His legs are as white as your baby's, Mrs. Pullen, and twice as well worth looking at!"

"Mein tear! mein tear!" remonstrated the Baron.

"Don't be a fool, Gustave! You know it's the truth! And the loveliest feet, Miss Leyton! Smaller than yours, I bet. Where's that devil, Bobby? I'm going to give 'im a dousing for his villainy this morning, I can tell you! Once I get 'is 'ead under water, it won't come up again in a hurry! I expect 'e's pretty 'ungry by this time! But 'e don't get a centime out of me for cakes to-day. I'll teach 'im not to stuff 'imself like a pig again. Come, Gustave! 'ere's a machine for you! Get me a chair that I may sit outside it! Now, we'll 'ave some fun," she added, with a wink at Mrs. Pullen.

"Let us move on to the breakwater!" said Margaret to Elinor Leyton, and the whole party got up and walked some little distance off.

"Ah! you don't hoodwink me!" screamed the Baroness after them. "You've got glasses with you, and you're going to 'ave a good squint at Gustave's legs through 'em, I know! You'd better 'ave stayed 'ere, like honest women, and said you enjoyed the sight!"

4*

"O! Margaret!" said Miss Leyton, with a look of horror, "if it had not been for the *Bataille de Fleurs* and . . . . the other thing . . . . I should have said, for goodness' sake, let us move on to Ostende or Blankenburghe, with the least possible delay. That woman will be the death of me yet! I'm sure she will!"

Notwithstanding which, they could not help laughing in concert, a little later on, to see the unwilling Bobby dragged down by William to bathe, and as he emerged from his machine, helpless and half naked, to watch his elephantine mother chase him with her stout stick in hand, and failing to catch him in time, slip on the wet sand and flounder in the waves herself, from which plight, it looked very much as though her servant instead of rescuing her, did his best to push her further in, before he dragged her, drenched and disordered, on dry land again.

CHAPTER IV.

THE Baroness Gobelli's temperament was as inconsistent as her dress. Under the garb of jocose good-humour, which often degenerated to horse-play, she concealed a jealous and vindictive disposition, which would go any lengths, when offended, to revenge itself. She was wont to say that she never forgot, nor forgave an injury, and that when she had her knife (as she termed it) in a man, she knew how to bide her time, but that when the time came, she turned it. These bloodthirsty sentiments, coupled with an asseveration which was constantly on her lips, that when she willed the death of anyone, he died, and that she had powers at her command of which no one was aware but herself, frightened many timid and ignorant people into trying to propitiate so apparently potent a mortal, and generally kow-tooing before her. To such votaries, so long as they pleased her, Madame Gobelli was used to shew her favour by various gifts of dresses, jewelry, or money, according to their circumstances, for in some cases she was lavishly generous, but she soon tired of her acquaintances and replaced them by fresh favourites.

The hints that she gave forth, regarding herself and her antecedents, were too extraordinary to gain credence except from the most ignorant of her auditors, but the Baroness always spoke in parables, and left no proof of what she meant, to be brought up against her. This proved that if she were clever, she was still more cunning. The hints she occasionally gave of being descended from Royal blood, though on the wrong side of the blanket, and of the connection being acknowledged privately, if not publicly, by the existing members of the reigning family, were received with open mouths by people of her own class, but rejected with scorn by such as were acquainted with those whom she affected to know. It was remarkable also, and only another proof that, whatever her real birth and antecedents, the Baroness Gobelli was unique, that, notwithstanding her desire to be considered noble by birth if not by law, she never shirked the fact that the Baron was in trade —on the contrary she rather made a boast of it, and used to relate stories bringing it into ridicule with the greatest gusto. The fact being that Baron Gobelli was ihe head of a large firm of export bootmakers, trading in London under the name of Fantaisie et Cie, the boots and shoes of which, though professedly French, were all manufactured in Germany, where the firm maintained an enormous factory. The Baroness could seldom be in the company of anyone for more than five minutes without asking them where they bought their boots and shoes, and recommending them to Fantaisie et Cie as the best makers in London. She wanted to be first in everything—in popularity, in notice, and in conversation—if she could not attract attention by her personality, she startled people by her vulgarity—if she could not reign supreme by reason of her supposed birth, she would do so by boots and shoes, if nothing else—and if anybody slighted her or appeared to discredit her statements, he or she was immediately marked down for retaliation.

Harriet Brandt had not been many days in Heyst before the Baroness had become jealous of the attention which she paid Mrs. Pullen and her child. She saw that the girl was attractive, she heard that she was rich, and she liked to have pretty and pleasant young people about her when at home—they drew men to the house and reflected a sort of credit upon herself—and she determined to get Harriet away from Margaret Pullen and chain her to her own side instead. The Baroness hated Miss Leyton quite as much as Elinor hated her. She was quick of hearing and very intuitive—she had caught more than one of the young lady's uncomplimentary remarks upon herself, and had divined still more than she had heard. She had observed her sympathy with Bobby also, and that she encouraged him in his boyish rebellion. For all these reasons, she "had her knife" into Miss Leyton, and was waiting her opportunity to turn it. And she foresaw—with the assistance perhaps of the Powers of Darkness, of whose acquaintance she was so proud—that she would be enabled to take her revenge on Elinor Leyton through Harriet Brandt.

But her first advances to the latter were suavity itself. She was not going to frighten the girl by shewing her claws, until she had stroked her down the right way with her *pattes de velours*.

She came upon her one morning, as she sat upon the sands, with little Ethel in her arms. The nurse was within speaking distance, busy with her needlework, and the infant seemed so quiet with Miss Brandt and she took such evident pleasure in nursing it, that Mrs. Pullen no longer minded leaving them together, and had gone for a stroll with Miss Leyton along the Digue. So the Baroness found Harriet, comparatively speaking, alone.

"So you're playing at nursemaid again!" she commenced in her abrupt manner. "You seem to have taken a wonderful fancy to that child!"

"She is such a good little creature," replied Harriet, "she is no trouble whatever. She sleeps half the day!"

Miss Brandt had a large box of chocolates beside her, into which she continually dipped her hand. Her mouth, too, was stained with the delicate sweetmeat—she was always eating, either fruit or bonbons. She handed the box now, with a timid air, to the Baroness. "Do you care for chocolate, Madame?" she asked.

The Baroness did not like to be called "Madame" according to the French fashion. She thought it derogated from her dignity. She wished everyone to address her as "my lady," and considered she was cheated out of her rights when it was omitted. But she liked chocolate almost as well as Harriet did.

"Thank you! I'll 'ave a few!" she said, grabbing about a dozen in her huge hand at the first venture. "What a liking for candies the Amurricans seem to 'ave introduced into England! I can remember the time when you never saw such a thing as sweets in the palace —I don't think they were allowed—and now they're all over the place. I shouldn't wonder if Her Majesty hasn't a box or two in her private apartments, and as for the Princesses, well!—"

"The Palace!—Her Majesty!"—echoed Miss Brandt, opening her dark eyes very wide.

"As I tell 'em," continued the Baroness, "they won't 'ave a tooth left amongst the lot of 'em soon! What are you staring at?"

"But—but—do you go to the Queen's palace?" demanded Harriet, incredulously, as well she might.

"Not unless I'm sent for, you may take your oath! I ain't fond enough of 'em for all that; besides, Windsor's 'orribly damp and don't suit me at all. But you mustn't go and repeat what I tell you, in the Hotel. It might give offence in high places if I was known to talk of it. You see there's some of 'em has never seen me since I married the Baron! Being in trade, they thought 'e wasn't good enough for me! I've 'eard that when Lady Morton—the dowager Countess, you know—was asked if she 'ad seen me lately, she called out loud enough for the whole room to 'ear, 'Do you mean the woman that married the boot man? No! I 'aven't seen 'er, and I don't mean to either!' Ha! ha! ha! But I can afford to laugh at all that, my dear!"

"But—I don't quite understand!" said Harriet Brandt, with a bewildered look.

"Why! the Baron deals in shoe-leather! 'Aven't you 'eard it? I suppose we've got the largest manufactory in Germany! Covers four acres of ground, I give you my word!"

"Shoe-leather!" again ejaculated Harriet Brandt, not knowing what to say.

"Why, yes! of course all the aristocracy go in for trade now-a-days! It's the fashion! There's the Viscountess Gormsby keeps a bonnet-shop, and Lord Charles Snowe 'as a bakery, and Lady Harrison 'as an old curiosity-shop, and stands about it, dusting tables and chairs, all day! But how can you know anything about it, just coming from the West Indies, and all those 'orrid blacks! Ain't you glad to find yourself amongst Christians again?"

"This is the first time I ever left Jamaica," said Miss Brandt, "I was born there."

"But you won't die there, or I'm much mistaken! You're too good to be wasted on Jamaica! When are you going back to England?"

"Oh! I don't know! I've hardly thought about it yet! Not while Mrs. Pullen stays here, though!"

"Why! you're not tied to 'er apron-string, surely! What's she to you?"

"She is very kind, and I have no friends!" replied Miss Brandt.

The Baroness burst into a coarse laugh.

"You won't want for friends, once you shew your face in England, I can tell you. I'd like to 'ave you at our 'ouse, the Red 'Ouse, we call it. Princess—but there, I mustn't tell you 'er name or it'll go through the

Hotel, and she says things to me that she never means
to go further—but she said the other day that she preferred the Red 'Ouse to Windsor! And for comfort,
and cheerfulness, so she may!"

"I suppose it is very beautiful then!" observed Harriet.

"You must judge for yourself," replied the Baroness,
with a broad smile, "when you come to London. You'll
be your own mistress there, I suppose, and not so tied
as you are here! I call it a shame to keep you dancing
attendance on that brat, when there's a nurse whose
business it is to look after 'er!"

"O! but indeed it is my own wish!" said the girl,
as she cuddled the sleeping baby to her bosom, and
laid her lips in a long kiss upon its little mouth. "I asked
leave to nurse her! She loves me and even Nurse cannot
get her off to sleep as I can! And it is so beautiful to
have something to love you, Madame Gobelli! In the
Convent I felt so cold—so lonely! If ever I took a
liking to a girl, we were placed in separate rooms! It is
what I have longed for—to come out into the world and
find someone to be a friend, and to love me, only me,
and all for myself!"

Madame Gobelli laughed again.

"Well! you've only got to shew those eyes of yours,
to get plenty of people to love you, and let you love
them in return—that is, if the men count in your estimation of what's beautiful!"

Harriet raised her eyes and looked at the woman
who addressed her!

There was the innocence of Ignorance in them as
yet, but the slumbering fire in their depths proved of
what her nature would be capable, when it was given

the opportunity to shew itself. Hers was a passionate temperament, yearning to express itself—panting for the love which it had never known—and ready to burst forth like a tree into blossom, directly the sun of Desire and Reciprocity shone upon it. The elder woman, who had not been without her little experiences in her day, recognised the feeling at once, and thought that she would not give a fig for the virtue of any man who was subjected to its influence.

"I don't think that you'll confine your attentions to babies long!" quoth the Baroness, as she encountered that glance.

"How do you know?" said her young companion.

"Ah! it's enough that I *do* know, my dear! I 'ave ways and means of knowing things that I keep to myself! I 'ave friends about me too, who can tell me everything—who can 'elp me, if I choose, to give Life and Fortune to one person, and Trouble and Death to another—and woe to them that offend me, that's all!"

But if the Baroness expected to impress Miss Brandt with her hints of terror, she was mistaken. Harriet did not seem in the least astonished. She had been brought up by old Pete and the servants on her father's plantation to believe in witches, and the evil eye, and "Obeah" and the whole cult of Devil worship.

"I know all about that," she remarked presently, "but you can't do me either good or harm. I want nothing from you and I never shall!"

"Don't you be too sure of that!" replied Madame Gobelli, nodding her head. "I've brought young women more luck than enough with their lovers before now— yes! and married women into the bargain! If it 'adn't

been for me, Lady—there! it nearly slipped out, didn't
it?—but there's a certain Countess who would never
'ave been a widow and married for the second time to
the man of 'er 'eart, if I 'adn't 'elped 'er, and she knows
it too! By the way, 'ow do you like Miss Leyton?"

"Not at all," replied Harriet, quickly, "she is not a
bit like Mrs. Pullen—so cold and stiff and disagreeable!
She hardly ever speaks to me! Is it true that she's the
daughter of a lord, as Madame Lamont says, and is it
that makes her so proud?"

"She's the daughter of Lord Walthamstowe, but
that's nothing. They've got no money. 'Er people live
down in the country, quite in a beggarly manner. A gal
with a fortune of 'er own, would rank 'eads and 'eads
above 'er in Society. There's not much thought of beside money, nowadays, I can tell you!"

"Why does she stay with Mrs. Pullen then? Are
they any relation to each other?" demanded Harriet.

"Relation, no! I expect she's just brought 'er 'ere
out of charity, and because she couldn't afford to go to
the seaside by 'erself!"

She had been about to announce the projected relationship between the two ladies, when a sudden thought
struck her. Captain Ralph Pullen was expected to arrive in Heyst in a few days—thus much she had ascertained through the landlady of the Lion d'Or. She knew
by repute that he was considered to be one of the handsomest and most conceited men in the Limerick Rangers,
a corps which was noted for its good-looking officers. It
might be better for the furtherance of her plans against
the peace of Miss Leyton's mind, she thought, to keep
her engagement to Captain Pullen a secret—at all events,

no one could say it was her business to make it public. She looked in Harriet Brandt's yearning, passionate eyes, and decided that it would be strange if any impressionable young man could be thrown within their influence, without having his fidelity a little shaken, especially if affianced to such a cold, uninteresting "bit of goods" as Elinor Leyton. Like the parrot in the story, though she said nothing, she "thought a deal" and inwardly rumbled with half-suppressed laughter, as she pictured the discomfiture of the latter young lady, if by any chance she should find her *fiancé's* attentions transferred from herself to the little West Indian.

"You seem amused, Madame!" said Harriet presently.

"I was thinking of you, and all the young men who are doomed to be slaughtered by those eyes of yours," said the Baroness. "You'd make mischief enough amongst *my* friends, I bet, if I 'ad you at the Red 'Ouse!"

Harriet felt flattered and consciously pleased. She had never received a compliment in the Convent—no one had ever hinted that she was pretty, and she had had no opportunity of hearing it since.

"Do you think I am handsome then?" she enquired with a heightened colour.

"I think you're a deal worse! I think you're dangerous!" replied her new friend, "and I wouldn't trust you with the Baron any further than I could see you!"

"O! how can you say so?" exclaimed the girl, though she was pleased all the same to hear it said.

"I wouldn't, and that's the truth! Gustave's an awful fellow after the gals. I 'ave to keep a tight 'old on 'im, I can tell you, and the more you keep out of 'is way, the better I shall be pleased! You'll make a grand match some day, if you're only sharp and keep your eyes open."

"What do you call a grand match?" asked Harriet, as she let the nurse take the sleeping child from her arms without remonstrance.

"Why! a Lord or an Honourable at the very least! since you 'ave money of your own. It's money they're all after in these times, you know—why! we 'ave dooks and markisses marrying all sorts of gals from Amurrica —gals whose fathers made their money in oil, or medicine, or electricity, or any other dodge, so long as they made it! And why shouldn't you do the same as the Amurrican gals? You have money, I know—and a goodish lot, I fancy—" added the Baroness, with her cunning eyes fixed upon the girl as if to read her thoughts.

"O! yes!" replied Harriet, "Mr. Trawler, my trustee, said it was too much for a young woman to have under her own control, but I don't know anything about the value of money, never having had it to spend before. I am to have fifteen hundred pounds every year. Is that a good deal?"

"Quite enough to settle you in life, my dear!" exclaimed the Baroness, who immediately thought what a good thing it would be if Miss Brandt could be persuaded to sink her capital in the boot trade, "and all under your own control too! You are a lucky young woman! I know 'alf-a-dozen lords,—not to say Princes —who would jump at you!"

"Princes!" cried Harriet, unable to believe her ears.

"Certainly! Not English ones of course, but German, which are quite as good after all, for a Prince is a Prince any day! There's Prince Adalbert of Waxsquiemer, and Prince Harold of Muddlesheim, and Prince Loris of Taxelmein, and ever so many more, and they're in and out of the Red 'Ouse, twenty times a day! But don't you be in an 'urry! Don't take the first that offers, Miss Brandt! Pick and choose! Flirt with whom you like and 'ave your fun, but wait and look about you a bit before you decide!"

The prospect was too dazzling! Harriet Brandt's magnificent eyes were opened to their widest extent—her cheeks flushed with expectation—both life and light had flashed into her countenance. Her soul was expanding, her nature was awakening—it shone through every feature—the Baroness had had no idea she was so beautiful! And the hungry, yearning look was more accentuated than before.—it seemed as if she were on the alert, watching for something, like a panther awaiting the advent of its prey. It was a look that women would have shrunk from, and men welcomed and eagerly responded to.

"I should like to go and see you when I go to England—very much!" she articulated slowly.

"And so you shall, my dear! The Baron and me will be very glad to 'ave you on a visit. And you mustn't let that capital of yours lie idle, you know! If it's in your own 'ands, you must make it yield double to what it does now! You consult Gustave! 'E's a regular business man and knows 'ow many beans make five! 'E'll tell you what's best to be done with it—'e'll be a

good friend to you, and you can trust 'im with everything!"

"Thank you!" replied the girl, but she still seemed
to be lost in a kind of reverie. Her gaze was fixed—
her full crimson lips were slightly parted—her slender
hands kept nervously clasping and unclasping each other.

"Well, you are 'andsome and no mistake!" exclaimed the Baroness. "You remind me a little of the
Duchess of Bewlay before she was married! The first
wife, I mean—the second is a poor, pale-faced, sandy-
'aired creature. ('Ow the Dook can stomach 'er after
the other, I can't make out!) The first Duchess's mother
was a great flame of my grandfather, the Dook of—however, I mustn't tell you that! It's a State secret, and I
might get into trouble at Court! You'd better not say
I mentioned it."

But Harriet Brandt was not in a condition to remember or repeat anything. She was lost in a dream
of the possibilities of the Future.

The bell for *déjeuner* roused them at last, and
brought them to their feet. They resembled each other
in one particular . . . . they were equally fond of the
pleasures of the table.

The little Baron appeared dutifully to afford his
clumsy spouse the benefit of his support in climbing the
hillocks of shifting sand, which lay between them and
the hotel, and Miss Brandt sped swiftly on her way
alone.

"I've been 'aving a talk with that gal Brandt,"
chuckled the Baroness to her husband, "she's a regular
green-'orn and swallows everything you tell 'er. I've
been stuffing 'er up, that she ought to marry a Prince,

with 'er looks and money, and she quite believes it.
But she ain't bad-looking when she colours up, and I expect she's rather a warm customer, and if she takes a
fancy to a man, 'e won't well know 'ow to get out of it!
And if he tries to, she'll make the fur fly. Ha! ha! ha!"

"Better leave it alone, better leave it alone!" said
the stolid German, who had had more than one battle
to fight already, on account of his wife's match-making
propensities, and considered her quite too clumsy an
artificer to engage in so delicate a game.

CHAPTER V.

THERE was a marked difference observable in the
manner of Harriet Brandt after her conversation with the
Baroness. Hitherto she had been shy and somewhat
diffident—the seclusion of her conventual life and its
religious teachings had cast a veil, as it were, between
her and the outer world, and she had not known how
to behave, nor how much she might venture to do, on
being first cast upon it. But Madame Gobelli's revelations concerning her beauty and her prospects, had torn
the veil aside, and placed a talisman in her hands,
against her secret fear.

She was beautiful and dangerous—she might become
a Princess if she played her cards well—the knowledge
changed the whole face of Nature for her. She became
assured, confident, and anticipatory. She began to frequent the company of the Baroness, and without neglect-
ing her first acquaintances, Mrs. Pullen and her baby,
spent more time in the Gobelli's private sitting-room

than in the balcony, or public salon, a fact for which Margaret did not hesitate to declare herself grateful.

"I do not know how it is," she confided to Elinor Leyton, "I rather like the girl, and I would not be unkind to her for all the world, but there is something about her that oppresses me. I seem never to have quite lost the sensation she gave me the first evening that she came here. Her company enervates me—I get neuralgia whenever we have been a short time together —and she leaves me in low spirits and more disposed to cry than laugh!"

"And no wonder," said her friend, "considering that she has that detestable school-girl habit of hanging upon one's arm and dragging one down almost to the earth! How you have stood it so long, beats me! Such a delicate woman as you are too. It proves how selfish Miss Brandt must be, not to have seen that she was distressing you!"

"Well! it will take a large amount of expended force to drag Madame Gobelli to the ground," said Margaret, laughing, "so I hope Miss Brandt will direct that portion of her attention to her, and leave me only the residue. Poor girl! she seems to have had so few people to love, or to love her, during her lifetime, that she is glad to practise on anyone who will reciprocate her affection. Did you see the Baroness kissing her this morning?"

"I saw the Baroness scrubbing her beard against Miss Brandt's cheek, if you call that 'kissing'?" replied Elinor. "The Baroness never kisses! I have noticed her salute poor Bobby in the morning exactly in the same manner. I have a curiosity to know if it hurts."

"Why don't you try it?" said Margaret.

"No, thank you! I am not so curious as all that! But the Gobellis and Miss Brandt have evidently struck up a great friendship. She will be the recipient of the Baroness's cast-off trinkets and laces next!"

"She is too well off for that, Elinor! Madame Lamont told me she has a fortune in her own right, of fifteen hundred a year!"

"She will want it all to gild herself with!" said Elinor.

Margaret Pullen looked at Miss Leyton thoughtfully. Did she really mean what she said, or did her jealousy of the West Indian heiress render her capable of uttering untruths? Surely, she must see that Harriet Brandt was handsome—growing handsomer indeed, every day, with the pure sea air tinting her cheeks with a delicate flush like the inside of a shell—and that her beauty, joined to her money, would render her a tempting morsel for the men, and a formidable rival for the women.

"I do not think you would find many people to agree with your opinion, Elinor!" she said after a pause, in answer to Miss Leyton's last remark.

"Well! I think she's altogether odious," replied her friend with a toss of her head, "I thought it the first time I saw her, and I shall think it to the last!"

It was the day that Captain Ralph Pullen was expected to arrive in Heyst and the two ladies were preparing to go to the station to meet him.

"The Baroness has at all events done you one good turn," continued Miss Leyton, "she has delivered you for a few hours from your 'Old Man of the Sea.' What have you been doing with yourself all the morning! I expected you to meet me on the sands, after I had done bathing!"

"I have not stirred out, Elinor. I am uneasy about baby! She does not seem at all well. I have been waiting your return to ask you whether I had not better send for a doctor to see her. But I am not sure if there is such a thing in Heyst!"

"Sure to be, but don't send unless it is absolutely necessary. What is the matter with her?"

The nurse was sitting by the open window with little Ethel on her lap. The infant looked much the same as usual—a little paler perhaps, but in a sound sleep and apparently enjoying it.

"She does not seem ill to me," continued Elinor, "is she in any pain?"

"Not at all, Miss," said the nurse, "and begging the mistress's pardon, I am sure she is frightening herself without cause. Baby is cutting two more teeth, and she feels the heat. That's all!"

"Why are you frightened, Margaret?" asked Miss Leyton.

"Because her sleep is unnatural, I am sure of it," replied Mrs. Pullen, "she slept all yesterday, and has hardly opened her eyes to-day. It is more like torpor than sleep. We can hardly rouse her to take her bottle and you know what a lively, restless little creature she has always been."

"But her teeth," argued Elinor Leyton, "surely her teeth account for everything! I know my sister, Lady Armisdale, says that nothing varies so quickly as teething children—that they're at the point of death one hour and quite well the next, and she has five, so she ought to know!"

"That's quite right, Miss," interposed the nurse, respectfully, "and you can hardly expect the dear child to be lively when she's in pain. She has a little fever on her too! If she were awake, she would only be fretful! I am sure that the best medicine for her is sleep!"

"You hear what Nurse says, Margaret, but if you are nervous, why not send for a doctor to see her! We can ask Madame Lamont as we go downstairs who is the best here, and call on him as we go to the station, or we can telegraph to Bruges for one, if you think it would be better!"

"O! no! no! I will not be foolish! I will try and believe that you and Nurse know better than myself. I will wait at all events until to-morrow."

"Where has baby been this morning?"

"She was with Miss Brandt on the sands, Miss!" replied the nurse.

"Since you are so anxious about Ethel, Margaret, I really wonder that you should trust her with a stranger like Miss Brandt! Perhaps she let the sun beat on her head."

"O! no, Elinor, Nurse was with them all the time. I would not let Miss Brandt or anyone take baby away alone. But she is so good-natured and so anxious to have her, that I don't quite know how to refuse."

"Perhaps she has been stuffing the child with some of her horrid chocolates or caramels. She is gorging them all day long herself!"

"I know my duty too well for that, Miss!" said the nurse resentfully, "I wouldn't have allowed it! The dear baby did not have anything to eat at all."

"Well! you're both on *her* side evidently, so I will say no more," concluded Miss Leyton, "At the same time if *I* had a child, I'd sooner trust it to a wild beast than the tender mercies of Miss Brandt. But it's past four o'clock, Margaret! If we are to reach the *entrepôt* in time we must be going!"

Mrs. Pullen hastily assumed her hat and mantle, and prepared to accompany her friend. They had opened the door, and were about to leave the room when a flood of melody suddenly poured into the apartment. It proceeded from a room at the other end of the corridor and was produced by a mandoline most skilfully played. The silvery notes in rills and trills and chords, such as might have been evolved from a fairy harp, arrested the attention of both Miss Leyton and Mrs. Pullen. They had scarcely expressed their wonder and admiration to each other, at the skilful manipulation of the instrument (which evinced such art as they had never heard before except in public) when the strings of the mandoline were accompanied by a young, fresh contralto voice.

"O! hush! hush!" cried Elinor, with her finger on her lip, as the rich mellow strains floated through the corridor, "I don't think I ever heard such a lovely voice before. Whose on earth can it be?"

The words of the song were in Spanish, and the only one they could recognise was the refrain of, "Seralie! Seralie!" But the melody was wild, pathetic, and passionate, and the singer's voice was touching beyond description.

"Some professional must have arrived at the Hotel," said Margaret, "I am sure that is not the singing of an amateur. But I hope she will not practise at night, and keep baby awake!"

Elinor laughed.

"O! you mother!" she said, "I thought you were lamenting just now that your ewe lamb slept too much! For my part, I should like to be lulled to sleep each night by just such strains as those. Listen, Margaret! She has commenced another song. Ah! Gounod's delicious 'Ave Maria.' How beautiful!"

"I don't profess to know much about music," said Margaret, "but it strikes me that the charm of that singing lies more in the voice than the actual delivery. Whoever it is, must be very young!"

"Whoever it proceeds from, it is charming," repeated Elinor. "How Ralph would revel in it! Nothing affects him like music. It is the only thing which makes me regret my inability to play or sing. But I am most curious to learn who the new arrival is. Ah! here is Mademoiselle Brimont!" she continued, as she caught sight of Olga Brimont, slowly mounting the steep staircase, "Mademoiselle, do you happen to know who it is who owns that lovely voice? Mrs. Pullen and I are perfectly enchanted with it!"

Olga Brimont coloured a little. She had never got over her shyness of the English ladies, particularly of the one who spoke so sharply. But she answered at once,

"It is Harriet Brandt! Didn't you know that she sang?"

Miss Leyton took a step backward. Her face expressed the intensest surprise—not to say incredulity.

"Harriet Brandt! Impossible!" she ejaculated.

"Indeed it is she," repeated Olga, "she always sang the solos in the Convent choir. They used to say she had the finest voice in the Island. O! yes, it is Harriet, really."

And she passed on to her own apartment.

"Do *you* believe it?" said Elinor Leyton, turning almost fiercely upon Mrs. Pullen.

"How can I do otherwise," replied Margaret, "in the face of Mademoiselle Brimont's assertion? But it is strange that we have heard nothing of Miss Brandt's talent before!"

"Has she ever mentioned the fact to you, that she could sing?"

"Never! but there has been no opportunity. There is no instrument here, and we have never talked of such a thing! Only fancy her possessing so magnificent a voice! What a gift! She might make her fortune by it if she needed to do so."

"Well! she ought to be able to sing with that mouth of hers," remarked Miss Leyton almost bitterly, as she walked into the corridor. She was unwilling to accord Harriet Brandt the possession of a single good attribute. As the ladies traversed the corridor, they perceived that others had been attracted by the singing as well as themselves, and most of the bedroom doors were open. Mrs. Montague caught Margaret by the sleeve as she passed.

"O! Mrs. Pullen, what a heavenly voice! Whose is it? Fred is just mad to know!"

"It's only that girl Brandt!" replied Elinor roughly, as she tried to escape further questioning.

"Miss Brandt! what, the little West Indian! Mrs. Pullen, is Miss Leyton jesting?"

"No, indeed, Mrs. Montague! Mademoiselle Brimont was our informant," said Margaret.

But at that moment their attention was diverted by

the appearance of Harriet Brandt herself. She looked brilliant. In one hand she carried her mandoline, a lovely little instrument, of sandal-wood inlaid with mother-of-pearl,—her face was flushed with the exertion she had gone through, and her abundant hair was somewhat in disorder. Mrs. Montague pounced on her at once.

"O! Miss Brandt! you are a sly puss! We have all been delighted—enchanted! What do you mean by ·hiding your light under a bushel in this way? Do come in here for a minute and sing us another song! Major Montague is in ecstasies over your voice!"

"I can't stop, I can't indeed!" replied Miss Brandt, evidently pleased with the effect she had produced, "because I am on my way down to dear Madame Gobelli. I promised to sing for her this afternoon. I was only trying my voice to see if it was fit for anything!"

She smiled at Mrs. Pullen as she spoke and added,

"I hope I have not disturbed the darling baby! I thought she would be out this lovely afternoon!"

"O! no! you did not disturb her. We have all been much pleased, and surprised to think that you have never told us that you could sing!"

"How could I tell that anyone would care about it?" replied Harriet, indifferently, with a shrug of her shoulders. "But the Baron is very musical! He has a charming tenor voice. I have promised to accompany him! I mustn't delay any longer! Good afternoon!"

And she flew down the stairs with her mandoline.

"It is all the dear Baroness and the dear Baron now, you perceive," remarked Elinor to Mrs. Pullen, as they walked together to the railway-station, "you and the baby are at a discount. Miss Brandt is the sort of young lady, I fancy, who will follow her own interests wherever they may lead her!"

"You should be the last to complain of her for that, Elinor, since you have tried to get rid of her at any cost," replied her friend.

Captain Ralph Pullen arrived punctually by the train which he had appointed, and greeted his sister-in-law and *fiancée* with marked cordiality.

He was certainly a man to be proud of, as far as outward appearance went. He was acknowledged, by general consent, to be one of the handsomest men in the British Army, and he was fully aware of the fact. He was tall and well built, with good features, almost golden hair; womanish blue eyes, and a long drooping moustache, which he was always caressing with his left hand. He regarded all women with the same languishing, tired-to-death glance, as if the attentions shewn him by the *beau sexe* had been altogether too much for him, and the most he could do now was to regard them with an indolent, worn-out favour, which had had all the excitement, and freshness, and flavour taken out of it long before. Most women would have considered his method of treatment as savouring little short of insult, but Elinor Leyton's nature did not make extravagant demands upon her lover, and so long as he dressed and looked well and paid her the courtesies due from a gentleman to a gentlewoman, she was quite satisfied. Margaret, on the other hand, had seen through her brother-in-law's affectations from the first, and despised him for them. She thought him foolish, vain, and uncompanionable, but she bore with him for Arthur's sake. She would have welcomed his cousin Anthony Pennell, though, with twice the fervour.

Ralph was looking remarkably well. His light grey suit of tweed was fresh and youthful looking, and the yellow rose in his buttonhole was as dainty as if he had just walked out of his Piccadilly club. He was quite animated (for him) at the idea of spending a short time in Heyst, and actually went the length of informing Elinor that she looked "very fit", and that if it was not so public a place he should kiss her. Miss Leyton coloured faintly at the remark, but she turned her head away and would not let him see that she was sorry the place was so public.

"Heyst seems to have done you both a lot of good," Captain Pullen went on presently, "I am sure you are fatter, Margaret, than when you were in Town. And, by the way, how is the daughter?"

"Not very well, I am sorry to say, Ralph! She is cutting more teeth. Elinor and I were consulting whether we should send for a doctor to see her, only this afternoon."

"By the way, I have good news for you, or you will consider it so. Old Phillips is coming over to join us next week."

"Doctor Phillips, my dear old godfather!" exclaimed Margaret, "O! I *am* glad to hear it! He will set baby to rights at once. But who told you so, Ralph?"

"The old gentleman himself! I met him coming out of his club the other day and told him I was coming over here, and he said he should follow suit as soon as ever he could get away, and I was to tell you to get a room for him by next Monday!"

"I shall feel quite happy about my baby now," said Mrs. Pullen, "I have not much faith in Belgian doctors. Their pharmacopœia is quite different from ours, but Doctor Phillips will see if there is anything wrong with her at once!"

"I hope you will not be disappointed with the Hotel visitors, Ralph," said Elinor, "but they are a terrible set of riff-raff. It is impossible to make friends with any one of them. They are such dreadful people!"

"O! you mustn't class them all together, Elinor," interposed Margaret, "I am sure the Montagues and the Vieuxtemps are nice enough! And *du reste*, there is no occasion for Ralph even to speak to them."

"Of course not," said Captain Pullen, "I have come over for the sake of your company and Margaret's, and have no intention of making the acquaintance of any strangers. When is the *Bataille de Fleurs?* Next week? that's jolly! Old Phillips will be here by that time, and he and Margaret can flirt together, whilst you and I are billing and cooing, eh, Elinor?"

"Don't be vulgar, Ralph," she answered, "you know how I dislike that sort of thing! And we have had so much of it here!"

"What, billing and cooing?" he questioned. But Elinor disdained to make any further remark on the subject.

The appearance of Ralph Pullen at the *table d'hôte* dinner naturally excited a good deal of speculation. The English knew that Mrs. Pullen expected her brother-in-law to stay with her, but the foreigners were all curious to ascertain who the handsome, well-groomed, military-looking stranger might be, who was so familiar with

Mrs. Pullen and her friend. The Baroness was not behind the rest in curiosity and admiration. She was much before them in her determination to gratify her curiosity and make the acquaintance of the new-comer, whose name she guessed, though no introduction had passed between them. She waited through two courses to see if Margaret Pullen would take the initiative, but finding that she addressed all her conversation to Captain Pullen, keeping her face, meanwhile, pertinaciously turned from the party sitting opposite to her, she determined to force her hand.

"Mrs. Pullen!" she cried, in her coarse voice, "when are you going to introduce me to your handsome friend?"

Margaret coloured uneasily and murmured,

"My brother-in-law, Captain Pullen—Madame Gobelli."

"Very glad to see you, Captain," said the Baroness, as Ralph bowed to her in his most approved fashion, "your sister thought she'd keep you all to 'erself, I suppose! But the young ladies of Heyst would soon make mincemeat of Mrs. Pullen if she tried that little game on them. We 'aven't got too many good-looking young men 'ereabouts, I can tell you. Are you going to stay long?"

Captain Pullen murmured something about "uncertain" and "not being quite sure", whilst the Baroness regarded him full in the face with a broad smile on her own. She always had a keen eye for a handsome young man!

"Ah! you'll stay as long as it suits your purpose, won't you? I expect you 'ave your own little game to play, same as most of us! And it's a pretty little game, too, isn't it, especially when a fellow's young and good-looking and 'as the chink-a-chink, eh?

"I fancy I know some of your brother officers, Mr. Naggett, and Lord Menzies, they belong to the Rangers, don't they?" continued Madame Gobelli, "Prince Adalbert of Waxsquiemer used to bring 'em to the Red 'Ouse! By the way I 'aven't introduced you to my 'usband, Baron Gobelli! Gustave, this is Captain Ralph Pullen, the Colonel's brother, you know. You must 'ave a talk with 'im after dinner! You two would 'it it off first-rate together! Gustave's in the boot trade, you know, Captain Pullen! We trade under the name of Fantaisie et Cie! The best boots and shoes in London, and the largest manufactory, I give you my word! You should get your boots from us. I know you dandy officers are awfully particular about your tootsies. If you'll come and see me in London, I'll take you over the manufactory, and give you a pair. You'll never buy any others, once you've tried 'em!"

Ralph Pullen bowed again, and said he felt certain that Madame was right and he looked forward to the fulfilment of her promise with the keenest anticipation.

Harriet Brandt meanwhile, sitting almost opposite to the stranger, was regarding him from under the thick lashes of her slumbrous eyes, like a lynx watching its prey. She had never seen so good-looking and aristocratic a young man before. His crisp golden hair and droop-ing moustaches, his fair complexion, blue eyes and chiselled features, were a revelation to her. Would the Princes whom Madame Gobelli had promised she should meet at her house, be anything like him, she wondered—could they be as handsome, as perfectly dressed, as fashionable, as completely at their ease, as the man before her? Every other moment, she was stealing a veiled glance at him—and Captain Pullen was quite aware of the fact. What young man, or woman, is not aware when they are being furtively admired? Ralph Pullen was one of the most conceited of his sex, which is not saying a little—he was *accomblé* with female attentions wherever he went, yet he was not *blasé* with them, so long as he was not called upon to reciprocate in kind. Each time that Harriet's magnetic gaze sought his face, his eyes by some mystical chance were lifted to meet it, and though all four lids were modestly dropped again, their owners did not forget the effect their encounter had left behind it.

"'Ave you been round Heyst yet, Captain Pullen," vociferated Madame Gobelli, "and met the Procession? I never saw such rubbish in my life. I laughed fit to burst myself! A lot of children rigged out in blue and white, carrying a doll on a stick, and a crowd of fools following and singing 'ymns. Call that Religion? It's all tommy rot. Don't you agree with me, Mrs. Pullen?"

"I cannot say that I do, Madame! I have been taught to respect every religion that is followed with sincerity, whether I agree with its doctrine or not. Besides, I thought the procession you allude to a very pretty sight. Some of the children with their fair hair and wreaths of flowers looked like little angels!"

"O! you're an 'umbug!" exclaimed the Baroness, "you say that just to please these Papists. Not that I wouldn't just as soon be a Papist as a Protestant, but I 'ate cant. I wouldn't 'ave Bobby 'ere, brought up in any religion. Let 'im choose for 'imself when 'e's a

man, I said, but no cant, no 'umbug! I 'ad a governess
for 'im once, a dirty little sneak, who thought she'd get
the better of me, so she made the boy kneel down each
night and say, 'God bless father and mother and all
kind friends, and God bless my enemies.' I came on
'em one evening and I 'ad 'im up on his legs in a
moment. I won't 'ave it, Bobby, I said, I won't 'ave
you telling lies for anyone, and I made 'im repeat after
me, 'God bless father and mother and all kind friends,
and d—n my enemies.'"

The governess was so angry with me, that she gave
warning, he! he! he! But I 'ad my way, and Bobby
'asn't said a prayer since, 'ave you, Bobby?"

"Sometimes, Mamma!" replied the lad in a low voice.
Margaret Pullen's kind eyes sought his at once with an
encouraging smile.

"Well! you'd better not let me 'ear you, or I'll give
you 'what for'. I 'ate 'umbug, don't you, Captain
Pullen?"

"Unreservedly, Madame!" replied Ralph in a stifled
voice and with an inflamed countenance. He had been
trying to conceal his amusement for some time past,
greatly to the disgust of Miss Leyton, who would have
had him pass by his opposite neighbour's remarks in
silent contempt, and the effort had been rather trying.
As he spoke, his eyes sought those of Harriet Brandt
again, and discovered the sympathy with his distress,
lurking in them, coupled with a very evident look of
admiration for himself. He looked at her back again—
only one look, but it spoke volumes! Captain Pullen
had never given such a glance at his *fiancée,* nor received one from her! It is problematical if Elinor

Leyton *could* make a telegraph of her calm brown eyes—
if her soul (if indeed she had in that sense a soul at all)
ever pierced the bounds of its dwelling-place to look
through its windows. As the dessert appeared, Margaret
whispered to her brother-in-law,

"If we do not make our escape now, we may not
get rid of her all the evening," at which hint he rose
from table, and the trio left the *salle à manger* together.
As Margaret descended again, equipped for their evening
stroll, she perceived Harriet Brandt in the corridor also
ready, and waiting apparently for her. She took her
aside at once.

"I cannot ask you to join us in our walk this evening, Miss Brandt," she said, "because, as it is the first
day of my brother's arrival, we shall naturally have
many family topics to discuss together!"

For the first time since their acquaintance, she observed a sullen look creep over Harriet Brandt's features.

"I am going to walk with the Baron and Baroness,
thank you all the same!" she replied to Margaret's remark, and turning on her heel, she re-entered her room.
Margaret did not believe her statement, but she was
glad she had had the courage to warn her—she knew
it would have greatly annoyed Elinor if the girl she
detested had accompanied them on that first evening.
The walk proved after all to be a very ordinary one.
They paraded up and down the Digue, until they were
tired and then they sat down on green chairs and
listened to the orchestra whilst Ralph smoked his
cigarettes. Elinor was looking her best. She was
pleased and mildly excited—her costume became her—
and she was presumably enjoying herself, but as far as

her joy in Captain Pullen went, she might have been
walking with her father or her brother. The conscious
looks that had passed between him and Harriet Brandt
were utterly wanting.

They began by talking of home, of Elinor's family,
and the last news that Margaret had received from
Arthur—and then went on to discuss the visitors to the
Hotel. Miss Leyton waxed loud in her denunciation of
the Baroness and her familiar vulgarity—she deplored
the ill fate that had placed them in such close proximity
at the *table d'hôte*, and hoped that Ralph would not
hesitate to change his seat if the annoyance became too
great. She had warned him, she said, of what he might
expect by joining them at Heyst.

"My dear girl," he replied, "pray don't distress yourself! In the first place I know a great deal more about
foreign hotels than you do, and knew exactly what I
might expect to encounter, and in the second, I don't
mind it in the least—in fact, I like it, it amuses me, I
think the Baroness is quite a character, and look forward
to cultivating her acquaintance with the keenest anti-
cipations."

"O! *don't*, Ralph, pray don't!" exclaimed Miss
Leyton, fastidiously, "the woman is beneath contempt!
I should be exceedingly annoyed if you permitted her
to get at all intimate with you."

"Why not, if it amuses him?" demanded Margaret,
laughing, "for my part, I agree with Ralph, that her very
vulgarity makes her most amusing as a change, and it is
not as if we were likely to be thrown in her way when
we return to England!"

"She is a *rara avis*," cried Captain Pullen enthusiastically, "she certainly must know some good people if men like Naggett and Menzies have been at her house, and yet the way she advertises her boots and shoes is too delicious! O! dear yes! I cannot consent to cut the Baroness Gobelli! I am half in love with her already!"

Elinor Leyton made a gesture of disgust.

"And you—who are considered to be one of the most select and fastidious men in Town," she said, "I wonder at you!"

Then he made a bad matter worse, by saying,

"By the way, Margaret, who was that beautiful girl who sat on the opposite side of the table?"

"The *what*," exclaimed Elinor Leyton, ungrammatically, as she turned round upon the Digue and confronted him.

"He means Miss Brandt!" interposed Margaret, hastily, "many people think that she is handsome!"

"No one could think otherwise," responded Ralph. "Is she Spanish?"

"O! no; her parents were English. She comes from Jamaica!"

"Ah! a drop of Creole blood in her then, I daresay! You never see such eyes in an English face!"

"What's the matter with her eyes?" asked Elinor sharply.

"They're very large and dark, you know, Elinor!" said Mrs. Pullen, observing the cloud which was settling down upon the girl's face, "but it is not everybody who admires dark eyes, or you and I would come off badly!"

"Well, with all due deference to you, my fair sister-in-law," replied Ralph, with the stupidity of a selfish man who never knows when he is wounding his hearers,

6 *

"most people give the preference to dark eyes in women. Anyway Miss Brandt (if that is her name) is a beauty and no mistake!"

"I can't say that I admire your taste," said Elinor, "and I sincerely hope that Miss Brandt will not force her company upon us whilst you are here. Margaret and I have suffered more than enough already in that respect! She is only half educated and knows nothing of the world, and is altogether a most uninteresting companion. I dislike her exceedingly!"

"Ah! don't forget her singing!" cried Margaret, unwittingly.

"Does she sing?" demanded the Captain.

"Yes! and wonderfully well for an amateur! She plays the mandoline also. I think Elinor is a little hard on her! Of course she is very young and unformed, but she has only just come out of a convent where she has been educated for the last ten years. What can you expect of a girl who has never been out in Society? I know that she is very good-natured, and has waited on baby as if she had been her servant!"

"Don't you think we have had about enough of Miss Harriet Brandt?" said Elinor, "I want to hear what Ralph thinks of Heyst, or if he advises our going on to Ostende. I believe Ostende is much gayer and brighter than Heyst!"

"But we must wait now till Doctor Phillips joins us," interposed Margaret.

"He could come after us, if Ralph preferred Ostende or Blankenburghe," said Elinor eagerly.

"My dear ladies," exclaimed Captain Pullen, "allow me to form an opinion of Heyst first, and then we will

talk about other places. This seems pleasant enough in all conscience to me now!"

"O! you two are bound to think any place pleasant," laughed Margaret, "but I think I must go in to my baby! I do not feel easy to be away from her too long, now that she is ailing. But there is no need for you to come in, Elinor! It is only just nine o'clock!"

"I would rather accompany you," replied Miss Leyton, primly.

"No! no! Elinor, stay with me! If you are tired we can sit in the balcony. I have seen nothing of you yet!" remonstrated her lover.

She consented to sit in the balcony with him for a few minutes, but she would not permit his chair to be placed too close to hers.

"The waiters pass backward and forward," she said, "and what would they think?"

"The deuce take what they think," replied Captain Pullen, "I haven't seen you for two months, and you keep me at arms' length as if I should poison you! What do you suppose a man is made of?"

"My dear Ralph, you know it is nothing of the kind, but it is quite impossible that we can sit side by side like a pair of turtle doves in a public Hotel like this!"

"Let us go up to your room then?"

"To my bedroom?" she ejaculated with horror.

"To Margaret's room then! she won't be so prudish, I'm sure! Anywhere where I can speak to you alone!"

"The nurse will be in Margaret's room, with little Ethel!"

"Hang it all, then, come for another walk! Let us

go away from the town, out on those sand hills. I'm sure no one will see us there!"

"Dear Ralph, you must be reasonable! If I were seen walking about Heyst alone with you at night, it would be all over the town to-morrow."

"Let it be! Where's the harm?"

"But I have kept our engagement most scrupulously secret! No one knows anything, but that you are Margaret's brother-in-law! You don't know how they gossip and chatter in a place like this. I could never consent to appear at the public *table d'hôte* again, if I thought that all those vulgarians had been discussing my most private affairs!"

"O! well! just as you choose!" replied Ralph Pullen discontentedly, "but I suppose you will not object to *my* taking another turn along the Digue before I go to bed! Here, garçon, bring me a chasse! Good-night, then, if you will not stay!"

"It is not that I *will* not—it is that I *cannot*, Ralph!" said Miss Leyton, as she gave him her hand. "Good-night! I hope you will find your room comfortable, and if it is fine to-morrow, we will have a nice walk in whichever direction you prefer!"

"And much good that will be!" grumbled the young man, as he lighted his cigarette and strolled out again upon the Digue.

As he stood for a moment looking out upon the sea, which was one mass of silvery ripples, he heard himself called by name. He looked up. The Gobellis had a private sitting-room facing the Digue on the ground floor, and the Baroness was leaning out of the open window, and beckoning to him.

"Won't you come in and 'ave a whiskey and soda?"
she asked. "The Baron 'as 'is own whiskey 'ere, real
Scotch, none of your nasty Belgian stuff, 'alf spirits of
wine and 'alf varnish! Come along! We've got a jolly
little parlour, and my little friend 'Arriet Brandt shall
sing to you! Unless you're off on some lark of your
own, eh?"

"No! indeed," replied Ralph, "I was only wondering
what I should do with myself for the next hour. Thank
you so much! I'll come with pleasure."

And in another minute he was seated in the company of the Baron and Baroness and Harriet Brandt.

CHAPTER VI.

THE day had heralded in the *Bataille de Fleurs* and
all Heyst was *en fête*. The little furnished villas, hired
for the season, were all built alike, with a balcony, on
the ground floor, which was transformed into a veritable
bower for the occasion. Villa Imperatrice vied with Villa
Mentone and Villa Sebastien, as to which decoration
should be the most beautiful and effective, and the result
was a long line of arbours garlanded with every sort of
blossom. From early morning, the occupants were busy,
entwining their pillars with evergreens, interspersed with
flags and knots of ribbon, whilst the balustrades were
laden with growing flowers and the tables inside bore
vases of severed blooms. One balcony was decorated
with corn, poppies and *bluets,* whilst the next would display pink roses mixed with the delicate blue of the sea-
nettle, and the third would be all yellow silk and white
marguerites. The procession of *charrettes,* and the *Ba-*

taille itself was not to commence till the afternoon, so the visitors crowded the sands as usual in the morning, leaving the temporary owners of the various villas, to toil for their gratification, during their absence. Margaret Pullen felt sad as she sat in the hotel balcony, watching the proceedings on each side of her. She had intended her baby's perambulator to take part in the procession of *charrettes,* and had ordered a quantity of white field-lilies with which to decorate it. It was to be a veritable triumph—so she and Miss Leyton had decided between themselves—and she had fondly pictured how lovely little Ethel would look with her fluffy yellow hair, lying amongst the blossoms, but now baby was too languid and ill to be taken out of doors, and Margaret had given all the flowers to the little Montagues, who were trimming their mail-cart with them, in their own fashion. As she sat there, with a pensive, thoughtful look upon her face, Harriet Brandt, dressed in a costume of grass-cloth, with a broad-brimmed hat, nodding with poppies and green leaves, that wonderfully became her, on her head, entered the balcony with an eager, excited appearance.

"O! Mrs. Pullen! have you seen the Baroness?" she exclaimed. "We are going to bathe this morning. Aren't you coming down to the sands?"

"No! Miss Brandt, not to-day. I am unhappy about my dear baby! I am sure you will be sorry to hear that she has been quite ill all night—so restless and feverish!"

"O! she'll be all right directly her teeth come through!" replied Harriet indifferently, as her eyes scanned the scene before them. "There's the Baroness! She's beckoning to me! Good-bye!" and without a word of sympathy or comfort, she rushed away to join her friends.

"Like the way of the world!" thought Margaret, as she watched the girl skimming over the sands, "but somehow—I didn't think she would be so heartless!"

Miss Leyton and her *fiancé* had strolled off after breakfast to take a walk, and Mrs. Pullen went back to her own room, and sat down quietly to needlework. She was becoming very anxious for Doctor Phillips' arrival; had even written to England to ask him to hurry it if possible—for her infant, though not positively ill, rejected her food so often that she was palpably thinner and weaker.

After she had sat there for some time, she took up her field glasses, to survey the bathers on the beach. She had often done so before, when confined to the hotel—it afforded her amusement to watch their faces and antics. On the present occasion, she had no difficulty in distinguishing the form of the Baroness Gobelli, looking enormous as, clad in a most conspicuous bathing costume, she waddled from her machine into the water, loudly calling attention to her appearance, from all assembled on the sands, as she went. The Baron, looking little less comical, advanced to conduct his spouse down to the water, whilst after them flew a slight boyish figure in yellow, with a mane of dark hair hanging down her back, which Margaret immediately recognised as that of Harriet Brandt.

She was dancing about in the shallow water, shrieking whenever she made a false step, and clinging hold of the Baron's hand, when Margaret saw another gentleman come up to them, and join in the ring. She turned the glasses upon him and saw to her amazement that it was her brother-in-law. Her first feeling was that of annoyance. There was nothing extraordinary or improper, in his joining the Baroness's party—men and women bathed promiscuously in Heyst, and no one thought anything of it. But that Ralph should voluntarily mix himself up with the Gobellis, after Elinor's particular request that he should keep aloof from them, was a much more serious matter. And by the way, that reminded her, where was Elinor the while? Margaret could not discern her anywhere upon the sands, and wondered if she had also been persuaded to bathe. She watched Captain Pullen, evidently trying to induce Miss Brandt to venture further into the water, holding out both hands for her protection,—she also saw her yield to his persuasion, and leaving go of her hold on the Herr Baron, trust herself entirely to the stranger's care. Mrs. Pullen turned from the window with a sigh. She hoped there were not going to be any "ructions" between Ralph and Elinor—but she would not have liked her to see him at that moment. She bestowed a silent benediction, "not loud but deep" on the foreign fashion of promiscuous bathing, and walked across the corridor to her friend's room, to see if she had returned to the Hotel. To her surprise, she found Miss Leyton dismantled of her walking attire, soberly seated at her table, writing letters.

"Why! Elinor," she said, "I thought you were out with Ralph!"

The young lady was quite composed.

"So I was," she answered, "until half an hour ago! But as he then expressed his determination to bathe, I left him to his own devices and came back to write my letters."

"Would he not have preferred your waiting on the sands till he could join you again?"

"I did not ask him! I should think he would hardly care for me to watch him whilst bathing, and I am sure I should not consent to do so!"

"But everybody does it here, Elinor, and if you did not care to go down to the beach, you might have waited for him on the Digue."

"My dear Margaret, I am not in the habit of dancing attendance upon men. It is their business to come after me! If Ralph is eager for another walk after his dip, he can easily call for me here!"

"True! and he can as easily go for his walk with any stray acquaintance he may pick up on the sands!"

"O! if he should prefer it, he is welcome to do so," replied Elinor, resuming her scribbling.

"My dear Elinor, I don't think you quite understand Ralph! He has been terribly spoilt, you know, and when men have been accustomed to attention they will take it wherever they can get it! He has come over here expressly to be with you, so I think you should give him every minute of your time. Men are fickle creatures, my dear! It will take some time yet to despoil them of the idea that women were made for their convenience."

"I am afraid the man is not born yet for whose convenience I was made!"

"Well! you know the old saying: 'Most women can catch a man, but it takes a clever woman to keep him.' I don't mean to insinuate that you are in any danger of losing Ralph, but I think he's quite worth keeping, and, I believe, you think so too!"

"And I mean to keep him!" replied Miss Leyton, as she went on writing.

Margaret did not venture to give her any further hints, but returned to her own room, and took another look through her spyglass.

The bathers in whom she was interested had returned to their machines by this time, and presently emerged, "clothed and in their right minds," Miss Brandt looking more attractive than before, with her long hair hanging down her back to dry. And then, that occurred which she had been anticipating. Captain Pullen, having taken a survey of the beach, and seeing none of his own party there, climbed with Harriet Brandt to where they were high and dry above the tide, and threw himself down on the hot, loose sand by her side, whilst the Baron and Baroness with a laughing injunction to the two young people, to take care of themselves, toiled up to the Digue and walked off in another direction.

When they all met at *déjeuner,* she attacked her brother-in-law on the subject.

"Have you been bathing all this while?" she said to him, "you must have stayed very long in the water!"

"O! dear no!" he replied, "I wasn't in above a quarter of an hour!"

"And what have you been doing since?"

"Strolling about, looking for you and Elinor!" said Captain Pullen. "Why the dickens didn't you come out this lovely morning?"

"I could not leave baby!" cried Margaret shortly.

"And I was writing," chimed in Elinor.

"Very well, ladies, if you prefer your own company to mine, of course I have nothing to say against it! But I suppose you are not going to shut yourselves up this afternoon!"

"O! no. It is a public duty to attend the *Bataille de Fleurs*. Have you bought any confetti, Ralph?"

"I have! Miss Brandt was good enough to show me where to get them, and we are well provided. There is to be a race between lady jockeys at the end of the Digue too, I perceive!"

"What, with horses?"

"I conclude so. I see they have railed in a portion of ground for the purpose," replied Captain Pullen.

"'Ow could they race without 'orses?" called out the Baroness.

Harriet Brandt did not join in the conversation, but she was gazing all the while at Ralph Pullen—not furtively as she had done the day before, but openly, and unabashedly, as though she held a proprietary right in him. Margaret noticed her manner at once and interpreted it aright, but Miss Leyton, true to her principles, never raised her eyes in her direction and ignored everything that came from that side of the table.

Mrs. Pullen was annoyed; she knew how angry Elinor would be if she intercepted any telegraphic communication between her lover and Miss Brandt; and she rose from the table as soon as possible, in order to avert such a catastrophe. She had never considered her brother-in-law a very warm wooer, and she fancied that his manner towards Miss Leyton was more indifferent than usual. She took one turn with them along the Digue to admire the flower-bedecked villas, which were

in full beauty, and then returned to her nursery, glad of
an excuse to leave them together, and give Elinor a
chance of becoming more cordial and affectionate to
Ralph, than she had yet appeared to be. The lovers
had not been alone long, however, before they were
waylaid, to the intense disgust of Elinor, by Harriet
Brandt and her friend, Olga Brimont.

Still further to her annoyance, Captain Pullen seemed
almost to welcome the impertinent interference of the
two girls, who could scarcely have had the audacity to
join their company, unless he had invited them to do so.

"The *charrettes* are just about to start!" exclaimed
Harriet. "O! they are lovely, and such dear little children!
I am so glad that the *Bataille de Fleurs* takes place to-
day, because my friend's brother, Alfred Brimont, is
coming to take her to Brussels the day after to-morrow!"

"Brussels is a jolly place. Mademoiselle Brimont
will enjoy herself there," said Ralph. "There are theatres,
and balls and picture-galleries, and every pleasure that
a young lady's heart can desire!"

"Have you been to Brussels?" asked Harriet.

"Yes! when I was a nasty little boy in jacket and
trousers. I was placed at Mr. Jackson's English school
there, in order that I might learn French, but I'm afraid
that was the last thing I acquired. The Jackson boys
were known all over the town for the greatest nuisances
in it!"

"What did you do?"

"What did we *not* do? We tore up and down the
rue Montagne de la Cour at all hours of the day, shouting and screaming and getting into scrapes. We ran
up bills at the shops which we had no money to pay—

we appeared at every place of amusement—and we made love to all the school-girls, till we had become a terror to the school-mistresses."

"What naughty boys!" remarked Miss Brandt, with a side glance at Miss Leyton. She did not like to say all she thought before this very stiff and proper young English lady. "But Captain Pullen," she continued, "where are the confetti? Have you forgotten them? Shall I go and buy some more?"

"No! no! my pockets are stuffed with them," he said, producing two bags, of which he handed Harriet one. Her thanks were conveyed by throwing a large handful of tiny pieces of blue and white and pink paper (which do duty for the more dangerous chalk sugar-plums) at him and which covered his tweed suit and sprinkled his fair hair and moustaches. He returned the compliment by flying after her retreating figure, and liberally showering confetti upon her.

"O! Ralph! I do hope you are not going to engage in this horse-play," exclaimed Elinor Leyton, "because if so I would rather return to the Hotel. Surely, we may leave such vulgarities to the common people, and— Miss Harriet Brandt!"

"What nonsense!" he replied. "It's evident you've never been in Rome during the Carnival! Why, every-one does it! It's the national custom. If you imagine I'm going to stand by, like a British tourist and stare at everything, without joining in the fun, you're very much mistaken!"

"But is it fun?" questioned Miss Leyton.

"To me it is! Here goes!" he cried, as he threw

a handful of paper into the face of a passing stranger, who gave him as good as she had got, in return.

"I call it low—positively vulgar," said Miss Leyton, "to behave so familiarly with people one has never seen before—of whose antecedents one knows nothing! I should be very much surprised if the mob behaved in such a manner towards me. Oh!"

The exclamation was induced by the action of some young *épicier*, or hotel *garçon*, who threw a mass of confetti into her face with such violence as almost for the moment to blind her.

"Ha! ha! ha!" roared Ralph Pullen with his healthy British lungs, as he saw her outraged feelings depicted in her countenance.

"I thought you'd get it before long!" he said, as she attempted to brush the offending paper off her mantle.

"It has not altered my opinion of the indecency of the custom!" she replied.

"Never mind!" he returned soothingly. "Here come the *charrettes.*"

They were really a charming sight. On one cart was drawn a boat, with little children dressed as fishermen and fisherwomen—another represented a harvest-field, with the tiny haymakers and reapers—whilst a third was piled with wool to represent snow, on the top of which were seated three little girls attired as Esquimaux. The mail-carts, and perambulators belonging to the visitors to Heyst were also well represented, and beautifully trimmed with flowers. The first prize was embowered in lilies and white roses, whilst its tiny inmate was seated in state as the Goddess Flora, with a wreath twined in her golden curls. The second was taken by a gallant Neapolitan fisherman of about four years old, who wheeled a mail cart of pink roses, in which sat his little sisters, dressed as angels with large white wings. The third was a wheel-barrow hidden in moss and narcissi, on which reposed a Sleeping Beauty robed in white tissue, with a coronal of forget-me-nots.

Harriet Brandt fell into ecstasies over everything she saw. When pleased and surprised, she expressed herself more like a child than a young woman, and became extravagant and ungovernable. She tried to kiss each baby that took part in the procession, and thrust coins into their chubby hands to buy bonbons and confetti with. Captain Pullen thought her conduct most natural and unaffected; but Miss Leyton insisted that it was all put on for effect. Olga Brimont tried to put in a good word for her friend.

"Harriet is very fond of children," she said, "but she has never seen any—there were no children at the Convent under ten years of age, so she does not know how to make enough of them when she meets them. She wants to kiss every one. Sometimes, I tell her, I think she would like to eat them. But she only means to be kind!"

"I am sure of that!" said Captain Pullen.

"But she should be told," interposed Elinor, "that it is not the custom in civilised countries for strangers to kiss every child they meet, any more than it is to speak before being introduced, or to bestow their company where it is not desired. Miss Brandt has a great deal to learn in that respect before she can enter English Society!"

As is often the case when a woman becomes unjust

in abusing another, Miss Leyton made Captain Pullen say more to cover her discourtesy, than, in other circumstances, he would have done.

"Miss Brandt," he said slowly, "is so beautiful, that she will have a great deal forgiven her, that would not be overlooked in a plainer woman."

"That may be *your* opinion, but it is not mine," replied Miss Leyton.

Her tone was so acid, that it sent him flying from her side, to battle with his confetti against the tribe of Montagues, who fortunately for the peace of all parties, joined their forces to theirs, and after some time spent on the Digue, they returned, a large party, to the Hotel.

It was not until they had sat down to dinner, that they remembered they had never been to see the lady jockey race.

"He! he! he!" laughed Madame Gobelli, "but *I* did, and you lost something, I can tell you! We 'ad great difficulty to get seats, but when we did, it was worth it, wasn't it, Gustave?"

"*You* said so, mein tear!" replied the Baron, gravely.

"And you *thought* so, you old rascal! don't you tell me! *I* saw your wicked eyes glozing at the gals in their breeches and boots! There weren't any 'orses, after all, Captain Pullen, but sixteen gals with different-coloured jackets on and top boots and tight white breeches—such a sight you never saw! Gustave 'ere did 'ave a treat! As for Bobby, when I found we couldn't get out again, because of the crowd, I tied my 'andkerchief over 'is eyes, and made him put 'is 'ead in my lap!"

"Dear! dear!" cried Ralph, laughing, "was it as bad as that, Madame?"

"Bad! my dear boy! It was as bad as it could be! It's a mercy you weren't there, or we shouldn't 'ave seen you 'ome again so soon! There were the sixteen gals, with their tight breeches and their short racing jackets, and a fat fellow dressed like a huntsman whipping 'em round and round the ring, as if they were so much cattle! You should 'ave seen them 'op, when he touched 'em up with the lash of 'is whip. I expect they've never 'ad such a tingling since the time their mothers smacked 'em! There was a little fat one, there! I wish you could 'ave seen 'er, when 'e whipped 'er to make 'er 'urry! It was comical! She 'opped like a kangaroo!"

"And what was the upshot of it all? Who won?" asked Ralph.

"O! I don't know! I got Gustave out as soon as I could! I wasn't going to let 'im spend the whole afternoon, watching those gals 'opping. There were 'is eyes goggling out of 'is 'ead, and his lips licking each other, as if 'e was sucking a sugar-stick—"

"Mein tear! mein tear!" interposed the unfortunate Baron.

"You go on with your dinner, Gustave, and leave me alone! *I* saw you! And no more lady jockey races do you attend, whilst we're in this Popish country. They ain't good for you."

"I'm very thankful that I have been saved such a dangerous experiment," said Captain Pullen, "though if I thought that you would tie your handkerchief over my eyes, and put my head in your lap, Madame, I should feel tempted to try it as soon as dinner is over!"

"Go along with you, you bad boy!" chuckled the

Baroness, "there's something else to see this evening! They are going to 'ave a procession of lanterns as soon as it's dark!"

"And it is to stop in front of every hotel," added Harriet, "and the landlords are going to distribute bon-bons and gâteaux amongst the lantern-bearers."

"O! we must not miss that on any account!" replied Captain Pullen, addressing himself to her in reply.

Margaret and Elinor thought, when the time came, that they should be able to see the procession of lanterns just as well from the balcony as when mingled with the crowd, so they brought their work and books down there, and sat with Ralph, drinking coffee and conversing of all that had occurred. The Baroness had disappeared, and Harriet Brandt had apparently gone with her—a fact for which both ladies were inwardly thankful.

Presently, as the dusk fell, the procession of lanterns could be seen wending its way from the further end of the Digue. It was a very pretty and fantastical sight. The bearers were not only children—many grown men and women took part in it, and the devices into which the Chinese lanterns had been formed were quaint and clever. Some held a ring around them, as milkmaids carry their pails—others held crosses and banners designed in tiny lanterns, far above their heads. One, which could be seen topping all the rest, was poised like a skipping-rope over the bearer's shoulders, whilst the coloured lanterns swung inside it, like a row of bells. The members of the procession shouted, or sang, or danced, or walked steadily, as suited their temperaments, and came along, a merry crowd, up and down the Digue, stopping at the various hotels for largesse in the shape of cakes and sugar-plums.

Ralph Pullen found his eyes wandering more than once in the direction of the Baroness's sitting-room, to see if he could catch a glimpse of her or her *protégée* (as Harriet Brandt seemed to be now universally acknowledged to be), but he heard no sound, nor caught a glimpse of them, and concluded in consequence that they had left the hotel again.

"Whoever is carrying that skipping-rope of lanterns seems to be in a merry mood," observed Margaret after awhile, "for it is jumping up and down in the most extravagant manner! She must be dancing! Do look, Elinor!"

"I see! I suppose this sort of childish performance amuses a childish people, but for my own part, I think once of it is quite enough, and am thankful that we are not called upon to admire it in England!"

"O! I think it is rather interesting," remarked Margaret, "I only wish my dear baby had been well enough to enjoy it! How she would have screamed and cooed at those bright-coloured lanterns! But when I tried to attract her attention to them just now, she only whined to be put into her cot again. How thankful I shall be to see dear Doctor Phillips to-morrow!"

The procession had reached the front of the Hotel by this time, and halted there for refreshment. The waiters, Jules and Phillippe and Henri, appeared with plates of dessert and cakes and threw them indiscriminately amongst the people. One of the foremost to jump and scramble to catch the falling sweetmeats was the girl who carried the lantern-skipping rope above

her head, and in whom Ralph Pullen, to his astonishment, recognised Harriet Brandt.   There she was, fan-
tastically dressed in a white frock, and a broad yellow
sash, with her magnificent hair loose and wreathed with
scarlet flowers.   She looked amazingly handsome, like
a Bacchante, and her appearance and air of abandon,
sent the young man's blood into his face and up to the
roots of his fair hair.

"Surely!" exclaimed Margaret, "that is never Miss
Brandt!"

"Yes! it is," cried Harriet, "I'm having the most
awful fun! Why don't you come too? I've danced the
whole way up the Digue, and it is so warm! I wish the
waiters would give us something to drink! I've eaten so
many bonbons I feel quite sick!"

"What will you take, Miss Brandt?" asked Captain
Pullen eagerly, "*limonade* or soda water?"

"A *limonade*, please! You *are* good!" she replied,
as he handed her the tumbler over the balcony balustrades.   "Come along and dance with me!"

"I cannot! I am with my sister and Miss Leyton!"
he replied.

"O! pray do not let *us* prevent you," said Elinor
in her coldest voice; "Margaret was just going upstairs
and I am quite ready to accompany her!"

"No, no, Elinor," whispered Mrs. Pullen with a shake
of her head, "stay here, and keep Ralph company!"

"But it is nearly ten o'clock," replied Miss Leyton,
consulting her watch, "and I have been on my feet all
day! and feel quite ready for bed. Good-night, Ralph!"
she continued, offering him her hand.

"Well! if you two are really going to bed, I shall go

too," said Captain Pullen, rising, "for there will be nothing for me to do here after you're gone!"

"Not even to follow the procession?" suggested Miss Leyton, with a smile.

"Don't talk nonsense!" he rejoined crossly. "Am I the sort of man to go bobbing up and down the Digue amongst a parcel of children?"

He shook hands with them both, and walked away rather sulkily to his own quarter of the hotel. But he did not go to bed. He waited until some fifteen minutes had elapsed, and then telling himself that it was impossible to sleep at that hour, and that if Elinor chose to behave like a bear, it was not his fault, he came downstairs again and sauntered out on the sea front.

It was very lonely there at that moment. The procession had turned and gone down to the other end again, where its lights and banners could be seen, waving about in the still summer air.

"Why shouldn't the girl jump about and enjoy herself if she chooses," thought Ralph Pullen. "Elinor makes no allowances for condition or age, but would have everyone as prim and old-maidish as herself. I declare she gets worse each time I see her! A nice sort of wife she will make if this kind of thing goes on! But by Jingo! if we are ever married, I'll take her prudery out of her, and make her—what? The woman who commences by pursing her mouth up at everything, ends by opening it wider than anybody else! There's twice as much harm in a prude as in one of these frank open-hearted girls, whose eyes tell you what they're thinking of, the first time you see them!"

He had been strolling down the Digue as he pondered thus, and now found himself meeting the procession again.

"Come and dance with me," cried Harriet Brandt, who, apparently as fresh as ever, was still waving her branch of lanterns to the measure of her steps. He took her hand and tried to stop her.

"Haven't you had about enough of this?" he said, "I'm sure you must be tired. Here's a little boy without a lantern! Give him yours to hold, and come for a little walk with me!"

The touch of his cool hand upon her heated palm, seemed to rouse all the animal in Harriet Brandt's blood. Her hand, very slight and lissom, clung to his with a force of which he had not thought it capable, and he felt it trembling in his clasp.

"Come!" he repeated coaxingly, "you mustn't dance any more or you will overtire yourself! Come with me and get cool and rest!"

She threw her branch of lanterns to the boy beside her impetuously.

"Here!" she cried, "take them! I don't want them any more! And take me away," she continued to Ralph, but without letting go of his hand. "You are right! I want—I want—rest!"

Her slight figure swayed towards him as he led her out of the crowd, and across a narrow street, to where the road ran behind all the houses and hotels, and was dark and empty and void. The din of the voices, and the trampling of feet, and the echo of the songs still reached them, but they could see nothing—the world was on the Digue, and they were in the dusk and quietude together—and alone.

Ralph felt the slight form beside him lean upon his shoulder till their faces almost touched. He threw his arm about her waist. Her hot breath fanned his cheek.

"Kiss me!" she murmured in a dreamy voice.

Captain Pullen was not slow to accept the invitation so confidingly extended. What Englishman would be? He turned his face to Harriet Brandt's, and her full red lips met his own, in a long-drawn kiss, that seemed to sap his vitality. As he raised his head again, he felt faint and sick, but quickly recovering himself, he gave her a second kiss more passionate, if possible, than the first. Then the following whispered conversation ensued between them.

"Do you know," he commenced, with his head close to hers, "that you are the very jolliest little girl that I have ever met!"

"And you—you are the man I have dreamt of, but never seen till now!"

"How is that? Am I so different from the rest of my sex?"

"Very—very different! So strong and brave and beautiful!"

"Dear little girl! And so you really like me?"

"I love you," said Harriet feverishly, "I loved you the first minute we met."

"And I love you! You're awfully sweet and pretty, you know!"

"Do you really think so? What would Mrs. Pullen say if she heard you?"

"Mrs. Pullen is not the keeper of my conscience. But she must not hear it."

"O! no! nor Miss Leyton either!"

"Most certainly not Miss Leyton. She is a terrible prude! She would be awfully shocked!"

"It must be a secret,—just between you and me!" murmured the girl.

"Just so! A sweet little secret, all our own, and nobody else's!"

And then the fair head and the dark one came again in juxtaposition, and the rest was lost in—Silence!

CHAPTER VII.

DOCTOR PHILLIPS had not been in the Hôtel Lion d'Or five minutes before Margaret Pullen took him up-stairs to see her baby. She was becoming terribly anxious about her. They encountered Captain Ralph Pullen on the staircase.

"Hullo! young man, and what have *you* been doing to yourself?" exclaimed the doctor.

He was certainly looking ill. His face was chalky white, and his eyes seemed to have lost their brightness and colour.

"Been up racketing late at night?" continued Doctor Phillips. "What is Miss Leyton about, not to look after you better?"

"No, indeed, Doctor," replied the young man with a smile, "I am sure my sister-in-law will testify to the good hours I have kept since here. But I have a headache this morning—a rather bad one," he added, with his hand to the nape of his neck.

"Perhaps this place doesn't agree with you—it was always rather famous for its smells, if I remember aright!

However, I am going to see Miss Ethel Pullen now, and when I have finished with her, I will look after you!"

"No, thank you, Doctor," said Ralph laughing, as he descended the stairs. "None of your nostrums for me! Keep them for the baby!"

"He is not looking well," observed Doctor Phillips to Margaret, as they walked on together.

"I don't think he is, now you point it out to me, but I have not noticed it before," replied Margaret. "I am sure he has been living quietly enough whilst here!"

The infant was lying as she had now done for several days past—quite tranquil and free from pain, but inert and half asleep. The doctor raised her eyelids and examined her eyeballs—felt her pulse and listened to her heart—but he did not seem to be satisfied.

"What has this child been having?" he asked abruptly.

"Having, Doctor? Why! nothing, of course, but her milk, and I have always that from the same cow!"

"No opium—no soothing syrup, nor quackeries of any kind?"

"Certainly not! You know how often you have warned me against anything of the sort!"

"And no one has had the charge of her, except you and the nurse here? You can both swear she has never been tampered with?"

"O! I think so, certainly, yes! Baby has never been from under the eye of one or the other of us. A young lady resident in the hotel—a Miss Brandt—has often nursed her and played with her, but one of us has always been there at the time."

"A Miss—what did you say?" demanded the doctor, sharply.

"A Miss Brandt—a very good-natured girl, who is fond of children!"

"Very well then! I will go at once to the pharmacien's, and get a prescription made up for your baby, and I hope that your anxiety may soon be relieved!"

"O! thank you, Doctor, so much!" exclaimed Margaret. "I knew you would do her good, as soon as you saw her!"

But the doctor was not so sure of himself. He turned the case over and over in his mind as he walked to the chemist's shop, wondering how such a state of exhaustion and collapse could have been brought about.

The baby had her first dose and the doctor had just time to wash and change his travelling suit before they all met at the dinner-table.

Here they found the party opposite augmented by the arrival of Monsieur Alfred Brimont, a young Brussels tradesman, who had come over to Heyst to conduct his sister home. He was trying to persuade Harriet Brandt to accompany Olga and stay a few days with them, but the girl—with a long look in the direction of Captain Pullen—shook her head determinedly.

"O! you might come, Harriet, just for a few days," argued Olga, "now that the *Bataille de Fleurs* is over, there is nothing left to stay for in Heyst, and Alfred says that Brussels is such a beautiful place."

"There are the theatres, and the Parc, and the Quinçonce, and Wauxhall!" said young Brimont, persuasively. "Mademoiselle would enjoy herself, I have no doubt!"

But Harriet still negatived the proposal.

"Why shouldn't we make up a party and all go to-gether," suggested the Baroness, "me and the Baron and Bobby and 'Arriet? You would like it then, my dear, wouldn't you?" she said to the girl, "and you really should see Brussels before we go 'ome! What do you say, Gustave? We'd go to the Hôtel de Saxe, and see everything! It wouldn't take us more than a week or ten days."

"Do as you like, mein tear," acquiesced the Baron.

"And why shouldn't you come with us, Captain?" continued Madame Gobelli to Ralph. "You don't look quite the thing to me! A little change would do you good. All work and no play makes Jack a dull boy! 'Ave you been to Brussels?"

"I lived there for years, Madame, and know every part of it!" he replied.

"Come and renew your acquaintance then, and take me and 'Arriet about!! The Baron isn't much good when it comes to sight-seeing, are you, Gustave? 'E likes 'is pipe and 'is slippers too well! But you're young and spry! Well! is it a bargain?"

"I really could not decide in such a hurry," said Ralph, with a glance at Margaret and Elinor, "but we might all go on to Brussels perhaps, a little later on."

"I don't think you must buoy up the hopes of the Baroness and Miss Brandt with that idea," remarked Miss Leyton, coldly, "because I am sure that Mrs. Pullen has no intention of doing anything of the sort. If you wish to accompany Madame Gobelli's party, you had better make your arrangements without any reference to us!"

"All right! If you prefer it, I will," he answered in the same indifferent tone.

"*Who* is that young lady sitting opposite, with the dark eyes?" demanded Doctor Phillips of Mrs. Pullen.

"The same I spoke to you of, upstairs, as having been kind to baby—Miss Harriet Brandt!"

"I knew a Brandt once," he answered. "Has she anything to do with the West Indies?"

"O! yes! she comes from Jamaica! She is an orphan, the daughter of Doctor Henry Brandt, and has been educated in the Ursuline Convent there! She is a young lady with an independent fortune, and considered to be quite a catch in Heyst!"

"And you and Miss Leyton are intimate with her?"

"She has attached herself very much to us since coming here. She has few friends, poor girl!"

"Will you introduce me?"

"Miss Brandt, my friend, Doctor Phillips, wishes for an introduction to you."

The usual courtesies passed between them, and then the doctor said,

"I fancy I knew your father, Miss Brandt, when I was quartered in Jamaica with the Thirteenth Lances. Did he not live on the top of the Hill, on a plantation called Helvetia?"

"That was the name of our place," replied Harriet, "but I left it when I was only eleven. My trustee, Mr. Trawler, lives there now!"

"Ah! Trawler the attorney! I have no doubt he made as much out of the property as he could squeeze."

"Do you mean that he cheated me?" asked Harriet, naïvely.

"God forbid! my dear young lady. But he was a great crony of your father's, and a d—d sharp lawyer, and those sort of gentry generally feather their own nest pretty well, in payment of their friendship."

"He can't do me any harm now," said Harriet, "for I have my property in my own hands!"

"Quite right! quite right! that is, if you're a business woman," rejoined the doctor. "And are you travelling all by yourself?"

Harriet was about to answer in the affirmative, when the Baroness took the words out of her mouth.

"No, Sir, she ain't! She came over with her friend, Mademoiselle Brimont, and now she's under my chaperonage. She's a deal too 'andsome, ain't she? to be travelling about the world alone, with her money-bags under her arm. My name's the Baroness Gobelli,—this is my 'usband, Baron Gustave Gobelli, and this is my little boy, Bobby Bates—by my first 'usband, you'll understand—and when you return to London, if you like to come and see Miss Brandt at our 'ouse—the Red 'Ouse, 'Olloway, we shall be very pleased to see you!"

"I am sure, Madame, you are infinitely kind," replied Doctor Phillips gravely.

"Not at all! You'll meet no end of swells there, Prince Loris of Taxelmein, and Prince Adalbert of Waxsquiemer, and 'eaps of others. But all the same we're in trade, the Baron and I—and we're not ashamed of it either. We make boots and shoes! Our firm is Fantaisie et Cie, of Oxford Street, and though I say it, you won't find better boots and shoes in all London than ours. No brown paper soles, and rotten uppers! Not a bit of it! It's all genuine stuff with us. You can take any boot out of the shop and rip it to pieces, and prove what I say! The best materials, and the best workmen, that's our principle, and it answers. We can't make 'em fast enough!"

"I have no doubt of it," again gravely responded the old doctor.

"Ah! you might send some of your patients to us, Doctor, and we'll pay back by recommending you to our friends. Are you a Gout man? Prince Adalbert 'as the gout awfully! I've rubbed 'is feet with Elliman's Embrocation, by the hour together, but nothing gives 'im relief! Now if you could cure 'im your fortune would be made! 'E says it's all the English climate, but *I* say it's over-eating, and 'e'd attend more to a medical man, if 'e told 'im to diet, than 'e will to me!"

"Doubtless, doubtless!" said the Doctor, in a dreamy manner. He seemed to be lost in a reverie, and Margaret had to touch his arm to remind him that the meal was concluded.

She wanted him to join the others in a promenade and see the beauties of Heyst, but he was strangely eager in declining it.

"No! no! let the youngsters go and enjoy themselves, but I want to speak to you, *alone.*"

"My dear doctor, you frighten me! Nothing about baby, I hope!"

"Not at all! Don't be foolish! But I want to talk to you where we cannot be overheard."

"I think we had better wait till the rest have dispersed then, and go down upon the sands. It is almost impossible to be private in a hotel like this!"

"All right! Get your hat and we will stroll off together."

As soon as they were out of earshot, he commenced abruptly,

"It is about that Miss Brandt! You seem pretty intimate with her! You must stop it at once. You must have nothing more to do with her."

Margaret's eyes opened wide with distress.

"But, Doctor Phillips, for what reason? I don't see how we could give her up now, unless we leave the place."

"Then leave the place! You mustn't know her, neither must Miss Leyton. She comes of a terrible parentage. No good can ever ensue of association with her."

"You must tell me more than this, Doctor, if you wish me to follow your advice!"

"I will tell you all I know myself! Some twelve or thirteen years ago I was quartered in medical charge of the Thirteenth Lances, and stationed in Jamaica, where I knew of, rather than knew, the father of this girl, Henry Brandt. You called him a doctor—he was not worthy of the name. He was a scientist perhaps—a murderer certainly!"

"How horrible! Do you really mean it?"

"Listen to me! This man Brandt matriculated in the Swiss hospitals, whence he was expelled for having caused the death of more than one patient by trying his scientific experiments upon them. The Swiss laboratories are renowned for being the foremost in Vivisection and other branches of science that gratify the curiosity and harden the heart of man more than they confer any lasting benefit on humanity. Even there,

Henry Brandt's barbarity was considered to render him unfit for association with civilised practitioners, and he was expelled with ignominy. Having a private fortune he settled in Jamaica, and set up his laboratory there, and I would not shock your ears by detailing one hundredth part of the atrocities that were said to take place under his supervision, and in company of this man Trawler, whom the girl calls her trustee, and who is one of the greatest brutes unhung."

"Are you not a little prejudiced, dear Doctor?"

"Not at all! If when you have heard all, you still say so, you are not the woman I have taken you for. Brandt did not confine his scientific investigations to the poor dumb creation. He was known to have decoyed natives into his Pandemonium, who were never heard of again, which raised, at last, the public feeling so much against him, that I am glad to say that his negroes revolted, and after having murdered him with appropriate atrocity, set fire to his house and burned it and all his property to the ground. Don't look so shocked! I repeat that I am *glad* to say it, for he richly deserved his fate, and no torture could be too severe for one who spent his worthless life in torturing God's helpless animals!"

"And his wife—" commenced Margaret.

"He had no wife! He was never married!"

"Never married! But this girl Harriet Brandt—"

"Has no more right to the name than you have! Henry Brandt was not the man to regard the laws, either of God or man. There was no reason why he should not have married—for that very cause, I suppose, he preferred to live in concubinage."

"Poor Harriet! Poor child! And her mother, did you know her?"

"Don't speak to me of her mother. She was not a woman, she was a fiend, a fitting match for Henry Brandt! To my mind she was a revolting creature. A fat, flabby half-caste, who hardly ever moved out of her chair but sat eating all day long, until the power to move had almost left her! I can see her now, with her sensual mouth, her greedy eyes, her low forehead and half-formed brain, and her lust for blood. It was said that the only thing which made her laugh, was to watch the dying agonies of the poor creatures her brutal protector slaughtered. But she thirsted for blood, she loved the sight and smell of it, she would taste it on the tip of her finger when it came in her way. Her servants had some story amongst themselves to account for this lust. They declared that when her slave mother was pregnant with her, she was bitten by a Vampire bat, which are formidable creatures in the West Indies, and are said to fan their victims to sleep with their enormous wings, whilst they suck their blood. Anyway the slave woman did not survive her delivery, and her fellows prophecied that the child would grow up to be a murderess. Which doubtless she was in heart, if not in deed!"

"What an awful description! And what became of her?"

"She was killed at the same time as Brandt, indeed the natives would have killed her in preference to him, had they been obliged to choose, for they attributed all the atrocities that went on in the laboratory to her influence. They said she was 'Obeah' which means diabolical witchcraft in their language. And doubtless their

8*

unfortunate child would have been slaughtered also, had
not the overseer of the plantation carried her off to his
cabin, and afterwards, when the disturbance was quelled,
to the Convent, where, you say, she has been educated."

"But terrible as all this is, dear Doctor, it is not the
poor girl's fault. Why should we give up her acquaintance for that?"

"My dear Margaret, are you so ignorant as not to
see that a child born under such conditions cannot turn
out well? The bastard of a man like Henry Brandt, cruel,
dastardly, Godless, and a woman like her terrible mother,
a sensual, self-loving, crafty and bloodthirsty half-caste
—what do you expect their daughter to become? She
may seem harmless enough at present, so does the tiger
cub as it suckles its dam, but that which is bred in
her will come out sooner or later, and curse those with
whom she may be associated. I beg and pray of you,
Margaret, not to let that girl come near you, or your
child, any more. There is a curse upon her, and it will
affect all within her influence!"

"You have made me feel very uncomfortable, Doctor,"
replied Mrs. Pullen. "Of course if I had known all this
previously, I would not have cultivated Miss Brandt's
acquaintance, and now I shall take your advice and
drop her as soon as possible! There will be no difficulty
with Miss Leyton, for she has had a strange dislike to
the girl ever since we met, but she has certainly been
very kind to my baby—"

"For Heaven's sake don't let her come near your
baby any more!" cried Doctor Phillips, quickly.

"Certainly I will not, and perhaps it would be as
well if we moved on to Ostende or Blankenburghe, as

we have sometimes talked of doing. It would sever the acquaintance in the most effectual way!"

"By all means do so, particularly if the young lady does not go to Brussels, as that stout party was proposing at dinner time. What an extraordinary person she appears to be! Quite a character!"

"That is just what she is! But, Doctor, there is another thing I should like to speak to you about, concerning Miss Brandt, and I am sure I may trust you to receive it in the strictest confidence. It is regarding my brother-in-law, Ralph Pullen. I am rather afraid, from one or two things I have observed, that he likes Miss Brandt—O! I don't mean anything particular, for (as you know) he is engaged to be married to Elinor Leyton and I don't suspect him of wronging her, only—young men are rather headstrong you know and fond of their own way, and perhaps if you were to speak to Ralph—"

"Tell me plainly, has he been carrying on with this girl?"

"Not in the sense you would take it, Doctor, but he affects her company and that of the Gobellis a good deal. Miss Brandt sings beautifully, and Ralph loves music, but his action annoys Elinor, I can see that, and since you think we should break off the intimacy——"

"I consider it most imperatively necessary, for many reasons, and especially in the case of a susceptible young man like Captain Pullen. She has money, you say—"

"Fifteen hundred a year, so I am told!"

"And Miss Leyton has nothing, and Ralph only his pay! O! yes! you are quite right, such an acquaintanceship is dangerous for him. The sense of honour is not so strong now, as it was when I was a boy, and gold is a powerful bait with the rising generation. I will take an early opportunity of talking to Captain Pullen on the subject."

"You will not wound his feelings, Doctor, nor betray me?"

"Trust me for doing neither! I shall speak from my own experience, as I have done to you. If he will not take my advice, you must get someone with more influence to caution him about it. I hardly know how to make my meaning clear to you, Margaret, but Miss Brandt is a *dangerous* acquaintance, for all of you. We medical men know the consequences of heredity, better than outsiders can do. A woman born in such circumstances—-bred of sensuality, cruelty, and heartlessness— cannot in the order of things, be modest, kind, or sympathetic. And she probably carries unknown dangers in her train. Whatever her fascinations or her position may be, I beg of you to drop her at once and for ever!"

"Of course I will, but it seems hard upon her! She has seemed to crave so for affection and companionship."

"As her mother craved for food and blood; as her father craved for inflicting needless agony on innocent creatures, and sneered meanwhile at their sufferings! I am afraid I should have little faith in Miss Brandt craving for anything, except the gratification of her own senses!"

They were seated on the lower step of the wooden flight that led from the Digue to the sands, so that whilst they could see what went on above them, they were concealed from view themselves.

Just then, Harriet Brandt's beautiful voice, accompanied by the silvery strains of the mandoline, was heard to warble Gounod's "Marguerite" from the open window of the Baroness's sitting-room. Margaret glanced up. The apartment was brilliantly lighted—on the table were bottles of wine and spirits, with cakes and fruit, and Madame Gobelli's bulky form might be seen leaning over the dishes. She had assembled quite a little party there that night. The two Brimonts were present, and Captain Pullen's tall figure was distinctly visible under the lamplight. Harriet was seated on the sofa, and her full voice filled the atmosphere with melody.

"There's something like a voice!" remarked the old doctor.

"That is the very girl we have been talking of!" replied Mrs. Pullen. "I told you she had a lovely voice, and was an accomplished musician."

"Is that so?" said Doctor Phillips, "then she is still more dangerous than I imagined her to be! Those tones would be enough to drag any man down to perdition, especially if accompanied by such a nature as I cannot but believe she must have inherited from her progenitors!"

"And see, Doctor, there is Ralph," continued Margaret, pointing out her brother-in-law! "I left him with Miss Leyton. He must have got rid of her by some means and crept up to the Gobellis. He cannot go for *them*. He is so refined, so fastidious with regard to people in general, that a woman like the Baroness must grate upon his feelings every time she opens her mouth, and the Baron never opens his at all. He can only frequent their company for the sake of Harriet Brandt!

I have seen it for some time past and it has made me very uneasy."

"He shall know everything about her to-morrow, and then if he will not hear reason—" Doctor Phillips shrugged his shoulders and said no more.

"But surely," said his companion, "you do not think for a moment that Ralph could ever seriously contemplate breaking his engagement with Elinor Leyton for the sake of this girl! O! how angry Arthur would be if he suspected his brother could be guilty of such a thing—*he*, who considers that a man's word should be his bond!"

"It is impossible to say, Margaret—I should not like to give an opinion on the subject. When young men are led away by their passions, they lose sight of everything else—and if this girl is anything like her mother, she must be an epitome of lust!"

"O! you will speak to Ralph as soon as ever you can," cried Margaret, in a tone of distress. "You will put the matter as strongly before him as possible, will you not?"

"You may depend on my doing all I can, Margaret, but as there seems no likelihood of my being able to interview the young gentleman to-night, suppose you and I go to bed! I feel rather tired after my passage over, and you must want to go back to your baby!"

"Doctor," said Margaret, in a timid voice, as they ascended the hotel staircase together, "you don't think baby *very* ill, do you?"

"I think she requires a great deal of care, Margaret!"

"But she has always had that!"

"I don't doubt it, but I can't deny that there are symptoms about her case that I do not understand. She seems to have had all her strength drawn out of her. She is in the condition of a child who has been exercised and excited and hurried from place to place, far beyond what she is able to bear. But it may arise from internal causes. I shall be better able to judge to-morrow when my medicine has had its effect. Goodnight, my dear, and don't worry. Please God, we will have the little one all right again in a couple of days."

But he only said the words out of compassion. In his own opinion, the infant was dying.

Meanwhile, Harriet having finished her songs, was leaning out of the window with Ralph Pullen by her side. She wore an open sleeve and as he placed his hand upon her bare arm, the girl thrilled from head to foot.

"And so you are determined *not* to go to Brussels," he whispered in her ear.

"Why should I go? You will not be there! The Baroness wants to stay for a week! What would become of me all that time, moping after you?"

"Are you sure that you *would* mope? Monsieur Brimont is a nice young man, and seems quite ready to throw himself at your feet! Would he not do as well, *pro tem?*"

Harriet's only answer was to cast her large eyes upwards to meet his own.

"Does that mean, 'No'?" continued Captain Pullen. "Then how would it do, if *I* joined you there, after a couple of days? Would the Baroness be complaisant, do you think, and a little short-sighted, and let us go about together, and show each other the sights of the town?"

"O! I'm sure she would!" cried Harriet, all the blood in her body flying into her face, "she is so very kind to me! Madame Gobelli!" she continued, turning from the window to the light, "Captain Pullen says that if you will allow him to show us the lions of Brussels, he will come and join us there in a couple of days—"

"If I find I can manage it!" interposed Ralph, cautiously.

"Manage it! Why, of course you can manage it," said the Baroness. "What's to 'inder a young man like you doing as 'e chooses? You're not tied to your sister's apron-string, are you? Now mind! we shall 'old you to it, for I believe it's the only thing that will make 'Arriet come, and I think a week in Brussels will do us all good! You're not looking well yourself, you know, Captain Pullen! You're as white as ashes this evening, and if I didn't know you were such a good boy, I should say you'd been dissipating a bit lately! He! he! he!"

"The only dissipating I have indulged in, is basking in the sunshine of your eyes, Madame!" replied Ralph gallantly.

"That's a good 'un!" retorted the Baroness, "it is more likely you've been looking too much in the eyes of my little friend 'ere. You're a couple of foxes, that's what you are, and I expect it would take all my time to be looking after you both! And so I suppose it's settled, Miss 'Arriet, and you'll come with us to Brussels after all!"

"Yes, Madame, if you'll take charge of me!" said Miss Brandt.

"We'll do that for a couple of days, and then we'll give over charge. Are we to engage a room for you, Captain, at the Hôtel de Saxe?"

"I had better see after that myself, Madame, as the date of my coming is uncertain," replied Ralph.

"But you *will* come!" whispered Harriet.

"Need you ask? Would I not run over the whole world, only to find myself by your side? ,Haven't you taken the taste out of everything else for me, Harriet?"

CHAPTER VIII.

DOCTOR PHILLIPS was a man of sixty, and a bachelor. He had never made any home ties for himself, and was therefore more interested in Margaret Pullen (whose father had been one of his dearest friends) than he might otherwise have been. He feared that a heavy trial lay before her and he was unwilling to see it aggravated by any misconduct on the part of her brother-in-law. He could see that the young man was (to say the least of it) not behaving fairly towards his *fiancée,* Elinor Leyton, and he was determined to open his eyes to the true state of affairs with regard to Harriet Brandt. He spent a sleepless night, his last visit to Margaret's suffering child having strengthened his opinion as to her hopeless condition, and he lay awake wondering how he should break the news to the poor young mother. He rose with the intention of speaking to Ralph without delay, but he found it more difficult to get a word with him than he had anticipated. The Gobelli party had decided to start with the Brimonts that afternoon, and

Captain Pullen stuck to them the entire morning, ostensibly to assist the Baroness in her preparations for departure, but in reality, as anyone could see, to linger by the side of Miss Brandt. Miss Leyton perceived her lover's defalcation as plainly as the rest, but she was too proud to make a hint upon the subject, even to Margaret Pullen. She sat alone in the balcony, reading a book, and gave no sign of annoyance or discomfiture. But a close observer might have seen the trembling of her lip when she attempted to speak, and the fixed, white look upon her face, which betrayed her inward anxiety. It made Margaret's kind heart ache to see her, and Dr. Phillips more indignant with Ralph Pullen than before.

The party for Brussels had arranged to travel by the three o'clock train, and at the appointed time the doctor was ready in the balcony to accompany them to the *entrepôt*. There were no cabs in Heyst, the station being in the town. Luggage was conveyed backwards and forwards in hand carts drawn by the porters, and travellers invariably walked to their destination. The Baroness appeared dressed for her journey, in an amazing gown of blue velvet, trimmed with rare Maltese lace, with a heavy mantle over it, and a small hat on her head, which made her round, flat, unmeaning face, look coarser than before. She used the Herr Baron as a walking-stick as usual, whilst Harriet Brandt, in a white frock and large hat shading her glowing eyes under a scarlet parasol, looked like a tropical bird skimming by her side, with Captain Pullen in close attendance, carrying a flimsey wrap in case she should require it before she reached her journey's end. The Brimonts, following in the rear, were of no account beside their more brilliant and important friends.

Ralph Pullen did not look pleased when he saw Doctor Phillips join the party.

"Are you also going to the *entrepôt?*" he exclaimed, "what can you find to interest you there?—a dirty little smutty place! I am going just to help the ladies over the line, as there is no bridge for crossing."

"Perhaps I am bent on the same errand," replied the doctor, "do you give me credit for less gallantry than yourself, Pullen?"

"That's right, Doctor," said the Baroness, "and I've no doubt you'll be very useful! My Bobby ain't any manner of good, and the Baron 'as so many traps to carry that 'e 'asn't got an arm to spare. I only wish you were coming with us! Why don't you make up your mind to come over with Captain Pullen the day after to-morrow, and 'ave a little 'oliday?"

"I was not aware that Captain Pullen *was* going to Brussels, madame! I fancy he will have to get Miss Leyton's consent first!"

At the mention of Miss Leyton's name in connection with himself, Ralph Pullen flushed uneasily, and Harriet Brandt turned a look of startled enquiry upon the speaker.

"O! 'ang Miss Leyton!" retorted the Baroness, graphically, "she surely wouldn't stop Captain Pullen's fun, just because 'e's staying with 'is sister-in-law! I should call that very 'ard. You can't always tie a young man to 'is relations' apron-strings, Doctor!"

"Not always, madame!" he replied, and dropped the subject.

"You wouldn't let Miss Leyton or Mrs. Pullen keep you from me!" whispered Harriet, to her cavalier.

"Never!" he answered emphatically.

They had reached the little station by this time, and the porters were calling out vociferously that the train was about to start for Brussels, so that in the hurry of procuring their tickets, and conveying the ladies and the luggage across the cinder-besprinkled line, to where the train stood puffing to be off, there was no more time to exchange sentimentalities, or excite suspicion. The party being safely stowed away in their carriage, Ralph Pullen and Doctor Phillips stood on the wooden platform with their hats off, bowing their farewells.

"Mind you don't put off your coming after Thursday!" screamed the Baroness to Ralph, as she filled up the entire window with her bulky person, "we shall expect you by dinner-time! And I shall bespeak a room for you, whether you will or no! 'Arriet 'ere will break 'er 'eart if you don't turn up, and I don't want the responsibility of 'er committing suicide on my 'ands!"

"All right! all right!" responded Ralph, pretending to turn it off as a joke, "None of you shall do that on my account, I promise you!"

"O! well! I 'ope you're going to keep your word, or we shall come back to 'Eyst in double quick time. Good-bye! Good-bye!" and kissing her fat hand to the two gentlemen, the Baroness was whisked out of Heyst.

Ralph looked longingly after the departing line of carriages for a minute, and then crossed the line again to the road beyond.

Doctor Phillips did not say a word till they were well clear of the station, and then he commenced,

"Of course you're not in earnest about following these people to Brussels."

"Why should I not be? I knew Brussels well as a lad, and I should enjoy renewing my acquaintance with the old town."

"In proper company perhaps, but you can hardly call that party a fit one for you to associate with!"

"You're alluding to the Baron and Baroness being in trade. Well! as a rule I confess that I do not care to associate intimately with bootmakers and their friends, but one does things abroad that one would not dream of doing in England. And for all her vulgarity, Madame Gobelli is very good-natured and generous, and I really don't see that I lower my dignity by being on friendly terms with her whilst here!"

"I was not alluding to Madame Gobelli, though I do not think that either she or the Brimonts are fit companions for a man who belongs to the Limerick Rangers, or is engaged to marry the daughter of Lord Walthamstowe. Neither do I admire the spirit which would induce you to hobnob with them in Heyst, when you would cut them in Bond Street. But as far as I know the Baron and his wife are harmless. It is Miss Harriet Brandt that I would caution you against!"

A quick resentment appeared on Ralph Pullen's features. His eyes darkened, and an ominous wrinkle stood out on his brow.

"And what may you have to say of Miss Brandt?" he demanded, coldly.

"A great deal more than you know, or can possibly imagine! She is not a fit person for Elinor Leyton to associate with, and consequently, one whom it is your duty to avoid, instead of cultivating."

"I think you exceed *your* duty, Doctor, in speaking to me thus!"

"I am sorry you should think so, Pullen, but your anger will not deter me from telling you what is in my mind. You must not forget how old a friend I am of both sides of your family. Your brother Arthur is one of my greatest chums, and his wife's father was, without exception, my dearest friend—added to this, I am on intimate terms with the Walthamstowes. Knowing what I do, therefore, I should hold myself criminal if I left you in ignorance of the truth concerning this young woman."

"Are you alluding, may I ask, to Miss Brandt?"

"I am alluding to the girl who calls herself by that name, but who is in reality only the bastard daughter of Henry Brandt, one of the most infamous men whom God ever permitted to desecrate this earth, and his half-caste mistress."

"Be careful what you say, Doctor Phillips!" said Ralph Pullen, with ill-suppressed wrath gleaming in his blue eyes.

"There is no need to be, my dear fellow, I can verify everything I say, and I fear no man's resentment. I was stationed in Jamaica with my regiment, some fifteen years ago, when this girl was a child of six years old, running half naked about her father's plantation, uncared for by either parent, and associating solely with the negro servants. Brandt was a brute—the perpetrator of such atrocities in vivisection and other scientific experiments, that he was finally slaughtered on his own plantation by his servants, and everyone said it served him right. The mother was the most awful woman I have ever seen, and my experience of the sex in back slums and alleys has not been small. She was the daughter of a certain Judge Carey of Barbadoes by one of his slave girls, and Brandt took her as his mistress before she was fourteen. At thirty, when I saw her, she was a revolting spectacle. Gluttonous and obese—her large eyes rolling and her sensual lips protruding as if she were always licking them in anticipation of her prey. She was said to be 'Obeah' too by the natives and they ascribed all the deaths and diseases that took place on the plantation, to her malign influence. Consequently, when they got her in their clutches, I have heard that they did not spare her, but killed her in the most torturing fashion they could devise."

"And did the British Government take no notice of the massacre?"

"There was an enquiry, of course, but the actual perpetrator of the murders could not be traced, and so the matter died out. The hatred and suspicion in which Brandt had been held for some time, had a great effect upon the verdict, for in addition to his terrible experiments upon animals—experiments which he performed simply for his own gratification and for no use that he made of them in treating his fellow creatures—he had been known to decoy diseased and old natives into his laboratory, after which they were never seen again, and it was the digging up of human bones on the plantation, which finally roused the negroes to such a pitch of indignation that they rose *en masse,* and after murdering both Brandt and his abominable mistress, they set fire to the house and burned it to the ground. There is no doubt but that, if the overseer of the plantation, an African negro named Pete, had not carried off the little girl, she would have shared the fate of her parents. And who can say if it would not have been as well if she had!"

"I really cannot see what right you have to give vent to such a sentiment!" exclaimed Captain Pullen. "What has this terrible story got to do with Miss Brandt?"

"Everything! 'When the cat is black, the kitten is black too!' It's the law of Nature!"

"I don't believe it! Miss Brandt bears no trace in feature or character of the parentage you ascribe to her!"

"Does she not? Your assertion only proves your ignorance of character, or characteristics. The girl is a quadroon, and she shews it distinctly in her long-shaped eyes with their blue whites and her wide mouth and blood-red lips! Also in her supple figure and apparently boneless hands and feet. Of her personal character, I have naturally had no opportunity of judging, but I can tell you by the way she eats her food, and the way in which she uses her eyes, that she has inherited her half-caste mother's greedy and sensual disposition. And in ten years' time she will in all probability have no figure at all! She will run to fat. I could tell that also at a glance!"

"And have you any more compliments to pay the young lady?" enquired Captain Pullen, sarcastically.

"I have this still to say, Pullen—that she is a woman whom you must never introduce to your wife, and that it is your bounden duty to separate her, as soon as possible, from your *fiancée* and your sister-in-law!"

"And what if I refuse to interfere in a matter which, as far as I can see, concerns no one but Miss Brandt herself?"

"In that case, I regret to say that I shall feel it *my* duty, to inform your brother Colonel Pullen and your future father-in-law, Lord Walthamstowe of what I have told you! Come, my dear boy, be reasonable! This girl has attracted you, I suppose! We are all subject to a woman's influence at times, but you must not let it go further. You must break it off, and this is an excellent opportunity to do so! Your sister's infant is, I fear, seriously ill. Take your party on to Ostende, and send the Baroness a polite note to say that you are prevented from going to Brussels, and all will be right! You will take my advice—will you not?"

"No! I'll be hanged if I will," exclaimed the young man, "I am not a boy to be ordered here and there, as if I were not fit to take care of myself. I've pledged my word to go to Brussels and to Brussels I shall go. If Miss Leyton doesn't like it, she must do the other thing! She does not shew me such a superfluity of affection as to prevent the necessity of my seeking for sympathy and friendship elsewhere."

"I am sorry to hear you speak like that, Pullen. It does not augur well for the happiness of your married life!"

"I have thought more than once lately, that I shall not be married at all—that is to Miss Leyton!"

"No! no! don't say so. It is only a passing infidelity, engendered by the attraction of this other girl. Consider what your brother would say, and what Lord Walthamstowe would think, if you committed the great mistake at this late hour, of breaking off your engagement!"

"I cannot see why my brother's opinion, or Lord Walthamstowe's thoughts, should interfere with the happiness of my whole life," rejoined Ralph, sullenly. "However, let that pass! The question on the *tapis* is, my acquaintance with Miss Brandt, which you consider should be put a stop to. For what reason? If what you bring against her is true, it appears to me that she has all the more need of the protection and loyalty of her friends. It would be cowardly to desert a girl, just because her father and mother happened to be brutes. It is not *her* fault!"

"I quite allow that! Neither is it the fault of a madman that his progenitors had lunacy in their blood, nor of a consumptive, that his were strumous. All the same the facts affect their lives and the lives of those with whom they come in contact. It is the curse of heredity!"

"Well! and if so, how can it concern anyone but the poor child herself?"

"O! yes, it can and it will! And if I am not greatly mistaken, Harriet Brandt carries a worse curse with her even than that! She possesses the fatal attributes of the Vampire that affected her mother's birth—that endued her with the thirst for blood, which characterised her life—that will make Harriet draw upon the health and strength of all with whom she may be intimately associated—that may render her love fatal to such as she may cling to! I must tell you, Pullen, that I fear we have already proofs of this in the illness of your little niece, whom, her mother tells me, was at one time scarcely ever out of Miss Brandt's arms. I have no other means of accounting for her sudden failure of strength and vitality. You need not stare at me, as if you thought I do not know what I am talking about! There are many cases like it in the world. Cases of persons who actually feed upon the lives of others, as the deadly upas tree sucks the life of its victim, by lulling him into a sleep from which he never wakens!"

"Phillips, you must be mad! Do you know that you are accusing Miss Brandt of murder—of killing the child to whom she never shewed anything but the greatest kindness. Why! I have known her carry little Ethel about the sands for a whole afternoon."

"All the worse for poor little Ethel! I do not say she does harm intentionally or even consciously, but that the deadly attributes of her bloodthirsty parents have descended on her in this respect, I have not a shadow of doubt! If you watch that young woman's career through life, you will see that those she apparently cares for most, and clings to most, will soonest fade out of existence, whilst she continues to live all the stronger that her victims die!"

"Rubbish! I don't believe it!" replied Ralph sturdily. "You medical men generally have some crotchet in your brains, but this is the most wonderful bee that ever buzzed in a bonnet! And all I can say is, that I should be quite willing to try the experiment!"

"You *have* tried it, Pullen, in a mild form, and it has had its effect on you! You are not the same fellow who came over to Heyst, though by all rules, you should be looking better and stronger for the change. And Margaret has already complained to me of the strange effect this girl has had upon her! But you must not breathe a suspicion to her concerning the child's illness, or I verily believe she would murder Miss Brandt!"

"Putting all this nonsense aside," said Ralph, "do you consider Margaret's baby to be seriously ill?"

"Very seriously. My medicines have not had the slightest effect upon her condition, which is inexplicable. Her little life is being slowly sapped. She may cease to breathe at any moment. But I have not yet had the courage to tell your sister the truth!"

"How disappointed poor Arthur will be!"

"Yes! but his grief will be nothing to the mother's. She is quite devoted to her child!"

By mutual consent, they had dropped the subject of Harriet Brandt, and now spoke only of family affairs. Ralph was a kind-hearted fellow under all his conceit, and felt very grave at the prospect held out in regard to his baby niece.

The fulfilment of the prophecy came sooner than even Doctor Phillips had anticipated. As they were all sitting at dinner that evening, Madame Lamont, her eyes over-brimming with tears, rushed unceremoniously into the *salle à manger*, calling to Margaret.

"Madame! Madame! please come up to your room at once! The dear baby is worse!"

Margaret threw one agonised glance at Doctor Phillips and rushed from the room, followed by himself and Elinor Leyton. The high staircase seemed interminable —more than once Margaret's legs failed under her and she thought she should never reach the top. But she did so all too soon. On the bed was laid the infant form, limp and lifeless, and Martin the nurse met them at the door, bathed in tears.

"Oh! Ma'am!" she cried, "it happened all of a minute! She was lying on my lap, pretty dear, just as usual, when she went off in a convulsion and died."

"Died, died!" echoed Margaret in a bewildered voice, "Doctor Phillips! *who* is it that has died?"

"The baby, Ma'am, the dear baby! She went off like a lamb, without a struggle! O! dear mistress, do try to bear it!"

"Is my baby—*dead?*" said Margaret in the same dazed voice, turning to the doctor who had already satisfied himself that the tiny heart and pulse had ceased to beat.

"No! my dear child, she is not dead—she is living —with God! Try to think of her as quite happy and free from this world's ill."

"O! but I *wanted* her so—I *wanted* her," exclaimed the bereaved mother, as she clasped the senseless form in her arms, "O! baby! baby! why did you go, before you had seen your father?"

And then she slid, rather than sank, from the bedside, in a tumbled heap upon the floor.

"It is better so—it will help her through it," said Doctor Phillips, as he directed the nurse to carry the dead child into Elinor Leyton's room, and placed Margaret on her own bed. "You will not object, Miss Leyton, I am sure, and you must not leave Mrs. Pullen to-night!"

"Of course I shall not," replied Elinor; "I have been afraid for days past that this would happen, but poor Margaret would not take any hints."

She spoke sympathetically, but there were no tears in her eyes, and she did not caress, nor attempt to console her friend. She did all that was required of her, but there was no spontaneous suggestion on her part, with regard either to the mother, or the dead child, and as Doctor Phillips noted her coolness, he did not wonder so much at Ralph's being attracted by the fervour and warmth of Harriet Brandt.

As soon as poor Margaret had revived and had her cry out, he administered a sleeping draught to her, and leaving her in charge of Elinor Leyton, he went down-stairs again to consult Captain Pullen as to what would be the best thing for them to do.

Ralph was very much shocked to hear of the baby's sudden death, and eager to do all in his power for his brother's wife. There was no Protestant cemetery in Heyst, and Doctor Phillips proposed that they should at once order a little shell, and convey the child's body either to Ostende or England, as Margaret might desire, for burial. The sooner she left the place where she had lost her child, he said, the better, and his idea was that she would wish the body to be taken to Devonshire and buried in the quiet country churchyard, where her hus-band's father and mother were laid to sleep. He left Ralph to telegraph to his brother in India and to any-one the news might concern in England—also to settle all hotel claims and give notice to the Lamonts that they would leave on the morrow.

"But supposing Margaret should object," suggested Ralph.

"She will not object!" replied the Doctor," she might if we were not taking the child's body with us, but as it is, she will be grateful to be thought, and acted, for. She is a true woman, God bless her! I only wish He had not seen fit to bring this heavy trial on her head!"

Not a word was exchanged between the two men about Harriet Brandt. Ralph, remembering the hint the doctor had thrown out respecting her being the ultimate cause of the baby's illness, did not like to bring up her name again—felt rather guilty with respect to it, indeed —and Doctor Phillips was only too glad to see the young man bestirring himself to be useful, and losing sight of his own worry in the trouble of his sister-in-law. Of course he could not have refused, or even demurred, at accompanying his party to England on so mournful an errand—and to do him justice, he did not wish it to be otherwise. Brussels, and its anticipated pleasures, had been driven clean out of his head by the little tragedy that had occurred in Heyst, and his attitude towards Margaret when they met again, was so quietly affectionate and brotherly that he was of infinite comfort to her. She quite acquiesced in Doctor Phillips' decision that her child should be buried with her father's family, and the mournful group with the little coffin in their midst, set out without delay for Devonshire.

CHAPTER IX.

HARRIET BRANDT set off for Brussels in the best of spirits. Captain Pullen had pledged himself to follow her in a couple of days, and had sketched with a free hand the pleasure they would mutually enjoy in each other's company, without the fear of Mrs. Pullen, or Miss Leyton, popping on them round the corner. Madame

Gobelli also much flattered her vanity by speaking of
Ralph as if he were her confessed lover, and prospective
fiancé, so that, what with the new scenes she was passing
through, and her anticipated good fortune, Harriet was
half delirious with delight, and looked as "handsome as
paint" in consequence.

Olga Brimont, on the contrary, although quietly
happy in the prospect of keeping house for her brother,
did not share in the transports of her Convent companion. Alfred Brimont, observed, more than once, that
she seemed to visibly shrink from Miss Brandt, and took
an early oportunity of asking her the reason why. But
all her answer was conveyed in a shrug of the shoulders,
and a request that he would not leave her at the Hotel
de Saxe with the rest of the party, but take her home
at once to the rooms over which she was to preside for
him. In consequence, the two Brimonts said good-bye
to the Gobellis and Harriet Brandt at the Brussels station,
and drove to their apartments in the rue de Vienne,
after which the others saw no more of them. The
Baroness declared they were "a good riddance of bad
rubbish," and that she had never liked that pasty-faced
Mademoiselle Brimont, and believed that she was jealous
of the brilliancy and beauty of her dear 'Arriet. The
Baroness had conceived one of her violent, and generally
short-lived, fancies for the girl, and nothing, for the time
being, was too good for her. She praised her looks and
her talents in the most extravagant manner, and told
everyone at the Hotel that the Baron and she had known
her from infancy—that she was their ward—and that
they regarded her as the daughter of the house, with
various other falsehoods that made Harriet open her

dark eyes with amazement, whilst she felt that she could not afford to put a sudden end to her friendship with Madame Gobelli, by denying them. Brussels is a very pretty town, full of modern and ancient interest, and there was plenty for them to see and hear during their first days there. But Harriet was resolved to defer visiting the best sights until Captain Pullen had joined them.

She went to the concerts at the Quinçonce and Wauxhall, and visited the Zoological Gardens, but she would not go to the Musée nor the Académie des Beaux Arts, nor the Cathedral of Sainte Gudule, whilst Ralph remained in Heyst. Madame Gobelli laughed at her for her reticence—called her a sly cat—said she supposed they must make up their minds to see nothing of her when the handsome Captain came to Brussels—finally sending her off in company of Bobby to walk in the Parc, or visit the Wiertz Museum. The Baroness was not equal to much walking at the best of times, and had been suffering from rheumatism lately, so that she and the Baron did most of their sight-seeing in a carriage, and left the young people to amuse themselves. Bobby was very proud to be elected Miss Brandt's cavalier, and get out of the way of his formidable Mamma, who made his *table-d'hôte* life a terror to him. He was a well-grown lad and not bad-looking. In his blue eyes and white teeth, he took after his mother, but his hair was fair, and his complexion delicate. He was an anæmic young fellow and very delicate, being never without a husky cough, which, however, the Baroness seemed to consider of no consequence. He hardly ever opened his mouth in the presence of his parents, unless it were to

remonstrate against the Baroness's strictures on his appearance, or his conduct, but Harriet Brandt found he
could be communicative enough, when he was alone with
her. He gave her lengthy descriptions of the Red House,
and the treasures which it contained—of his Mamma's
barouche lined with satin—of the large garden which
they had at Holloway, with its greenhouses and hot-
houses, and the numbers of people who came to visit
them there.

"O! yes!" rejoined Harriet, "the Baroness has told
me about them, Prince Adalbert and Prince Loris and
others! She said they often came to the Red House! I
should like to know them very much!"

The youth looked at her in a mysterious manner.

"Yes! they do come, very often, and plenty of other
people with them; the Earl of Watherhouse and Lord
Drinkwater, and Lady Mountacue, and more than I know
the names of. But—but—did Mamma tell you *why*
they come?"

"No! not exactly! To see her and the Baron, I
suppose!"

"Well! yes! for that too perhaps," stammered Bobby.
"But there is another reason. Mamma is very wonderful, you know! She can tell people things they never
knew before. And she has a room where—but I had
better not say any more. You might repeat it to her
and then she would be so angry.". The two were on
their way to the Wiertz Museum at the time, and Harriet's curiosity was excited.

"I will not, I promise you, Bobby," she said, "what
has the Baroness in that room?"

Bobby drew near enough to whisper, as he replied,

"O! I don't know, I daren't say, but horrible things go on there! Mamma has threatened sometimes to make me go in with her, but I wouldn't for all the world. Our servants will never stay with us long. One girl told me before she left that Mamma was a witch, and could raise up the dead. Do you think it can be true —that it is possible?"

"I don't know," said Harriet, "and I don't want to know! There are no dead that *I* want to see back again, unless indeed it were dear old Pete, our overseer. He was the best friend I ever had. One night our house was burned to the ground and lots of the things in it, and old Pete wrapped me up in a blanket and carried me to his cabin in the jungle, and kept me safe until my friends were able to send me to the Convent. I shall never forget that. I should like to see old Pete again, but I don't believe the Baroness could bring him back. It wants 'Obeah' to do that!"

"What is 'Obeah,' Miss Brandt?"

"Witchcraft, Bobby!"

"Is it wicked?"

"I don't know. I know nothing about it! But let us talk of something else. I don't believe your Mamma can do anything more than other people, and she only says it to frighten you. But you mustn't tell her I said so. Is this the Wiertz Museum? I thought it would be a much grander place!"

"I heard father say that it is the house Wiertz lived in, and he left it with all his pictures to the Belgian Government on condition they kept it just as it was."

They entered the gallery, and Harriet Brandt, although not a great lover of painting in general, stood enwrapt before most of the pictures. She passed over the "Bouton de Rose" and the sacred paintings with a cursory glance, but the representation of Napoleon in Hell, being fed with the blood and bones of his victims—of the mother in a time of famine devouring her child— and of the Suicide between his good and evil angels, appeared to absorb all her senses. Her eyes fixed themselves upon the canvasses, she stood before them, entranced, enraptured, and when Bobby touched her arm as a hint to come and look at something else, she drew a long breath as though she had been suddenly aroused from sleep. Again and again she returned to the same spot, the pictures holding her with a strange fascination, which she could not shake off, and when she returned to the Hotel, she declared the first thing she should do on the following morning, would be to go back to the Wiertz Museum and gaze once more upon those inimitable figures.

"But such 'orrid subjects, my dear," said the Baroness, "Bobby says they were all blood and bones!"

"But I like them—I *like* them!" replied Harriet, moving her tongue slowly over her lips, "they interest me! They are so life-like!"

"Well! to-morrow will be Thursday, you know, so I expect you will have somebody's else's wishes to consult! You will 'ave a letter by the early post, you may depend upon it, to say that the Captain will be with us by dinner-time!"

Harriet Brandt flushed a deep rose. It was when the colour came into her usually pale cheeks, and her eyes awakened from their slumbers and sparkled, that she looked beautiful. On the present occasion as she

glanced up to see Bobby Bates regarding her with steadfast surprise and curiosity, she blushed still more.

"You'll be 'aving a fine time of it together, you
two, I expect, continued the Baroness facetiously, and
Bobby, 'ere, will 'ave to content 'imself with me and his
Papa! But we'll all go to the theatre together to-morrow night. I've taken five seats for the Alcazar, which
the Captain said was the house he liked best in Brussels."

"How good you are to me!" exclaimed Harriet, as
she wound her slight arms about the uncouth form of
the Baroness.

"Good! Nonsense! Why! Gustave and I look upon
you as our daughter, and you're welcome to share everything that is ours. You can come and live altogether
at the Red 'Ouse, if you like! But I don't expect we
shall keep you long, though I must say I should be
vexed to see you throw yourself away upon an army
Captain before you have seen the world a bit!"

"O! don't talk of such a thing, pray don't!" said
the girl, hiding her face in the Baroness's ample bosom,
"you know there is nothing as yet—only a pleasant
friendship."

"He! he! he!" chuckled Madame Gobelli, "so that's
what you call a pleasant friendship, eh? I wonder
what Captain Pullen calls it! I expect we shall 'ear in
a few days. But what 'e thinks is of no consequence,
so long as *you* don't commit yourself, till you've looked
about you a little. I do want you to meet Prince
Adalbert! 'Is 'air's like flax—such a nice contrast to
yours. And you speaking French so well! You would
get on first-rate together!"

Bobby did not appear to like this conversation at all.

"I call Prince Adalbert hideous," he interposed. "Why! his face is as red as a tomato, and he drinks too much. I've heard Papa say so! I am sure Miss Brandt wouldn't like him."

"'Old your tongue," exclaimed the Baroness, angrily, "'Ow dare you interrupt when I'm speaking to Miss Brandt? A child like you! What next, I wonder! Just mind your own business, Bobby, or I'll send you out of the room. Go away now, do, and amuse yourself! We don't want any boys 'ere!"

"Miss Brandt is going into the Parc with me," said Bobby sturdily.

"Ah! well, if she is going to be so good, I 'ope you won't worry 'er, that's all! But if you would prefer to come out in the carriage with the Baron and me, my dear, we'll take a drive to the Bois de Cambres."

"All right, if Bobby can come too," acquiesced Harriet.

"Lor! whatever do you want that boy to come with us for? 'E'll only take up all the room with 'is long legs."

"But we mustn't leave him alone," said the girl, kindly, "I shouldn't enjoy my drive if we were to do so!"

The lad gave her a grateful glance through eyes that were already moist with the prospect of disappointment.

"Very well then," said Madame Gobelli, "if you will 'ave your own way, 'e may come, but you must take all the trouble of 'im, 'Arriet, mind that!"

Bobby was only too happy to accompany the party, even in these humiliating circumstances, and they all set out together for the Bois de Cambres. The next day was looked forward to by Harriet Brandt as one of certain happiness, but the morning post arrived without bringing the anticipated notice from Ralph Pullen that he should join them as arranged in the afternoon. The piteous eyes that she lifted to the Baroness's face as she discovered the defalcation, were enough to excite the compassion of anyone.

"It's all right!" said her friend, across the breakfast table, "'E said 'e would come, so there's no need of writing. Besides, it was much safer not! 'E couldn't stir, I daresay, without one of those two cats, Mrs. Pullen or Miss Leyton, at 'is elbow, so 'e thought they might find out what 'e was after, and prevent 'is starting. Say they wanted to leave 'Eyst or something, just to keep 'im at their side! You mark my words, I've means of finding out things that you know nothing of, and I've just seen it written over your 'ead that 'e'll be 'ere by dinner time, so you can go out for your morning's jaunt in perfect comfort!"

Harriet brightened up at this prophecy, and Bobby had never had a merrier time with her than he had that morning.

But the prophecy was not fulfilled. Ralph Pullen was by that time in England with his bereaved sister-in-law, and the night arrived without the people in Brussels hearing anything of him. He had not even written a line to account for his failure to keep his engagement with them. The fact is that Captain Pullen, although as a rule most punctilious in all matters of courtesy, felt so ashamed of himself and the folly into which he had been led, that he felt that silence would be the best explanation that he had decided to break off the acquaintanceship. He had no real feeling for Harriet Brandt or anybody (except himself)—with him "out of sight" was "out of mind"—and the sad occurrence which had forced him to return to England seemed an excellent opportunity to rid himself of an undesirable entanglement. But Harriet became frantic at the nonfulfilment of his promise. Her strong feelings could not brook delay. She wanted to rush back to Heyst to demand the reason of his defalcation—and in default of that, to write, or wire to him at once and ascertain what he intended to do. But the Baroness prevented her doing either.

"Look 'ere, Arriet!" she said to the girl, who was working herself up into a fever, "it's no use going on like this! 'Ell come or 'e won't come! Most likely you'll see 'im to-morrow or next day, and if not, it'll be because 'is sister won't let 'im leave 'er, and the poor young man doesn't know what excuse to make! Couldn't you see 'ow that Doctor Phillips was set against the Captain joining us? 'E went most likely and told Mrs. Pullen, and she 'as dissuaded her brother from coming to Brussels. It's 'ard for a man to go against 'is own relations, you know!"

"But he should have written," pleaded Harriet, "it makes me look a fool!"

"Not a bit of it! Captain Pullen thinks you no fool. 'E's more likely to be thinking 'imself one. And, after all, you know, we shall be going back to 'Eyst in a couple more days, and then you can 'ave 'im all to yourself in the evenings and scold 'im to your 'eart's content!"

But the girl was not made of the stuff that is

amenable to reason. She pouted and raved and de-
nounced Ralph Pullen like a fury, declaring she would
not speak to him when they met again,—yet lay awake
at night all the same, wondering what had detained him
from her side, and longing with the fierceness of a
tigress for blood, to feel his lips against her own and to
hear him say that he adored her. Bobby Bates stood
by during this tempestuous time, very sorrowful and
rather perplexed. He was not admitted to the confidence of his mother and her young friend, so that he
did not quite understand why Harriet Brandt should
have so suddenly changed from gay to grave, just because Captain Pullen was unable to keep his promise to
join them at Brussels. He had so enjoyed her company
hitherto and she had seemed to enjoy his, but now she
bore the gloomiest face possible, and it was no pleasure
to go out with her at all. He wondered if all girls were
so—as capricious and changeable! Bobby had not
seen much of women. He had been kept in the school-
room for the better part of his life, and his Mamma had
not impressed him with a great admiration for the sex.
So, naturally, he thought Harriet Brandt to be the most
charming and beautiful creature he had ever seen,
though he was too shy to whisper the truth, even to
himself. He tried to bring back the smiles to her face
in his boyish way, and the gift of an abnormally large
and long *sucre de pomme* really did achieve that object
better than anything else. But the defalcation of Captain Pullen made them all lose their interest in Brussels,
and they returned to Heyst a day sooner than they had
intended.

As the train neared the station, Harriet's forgotten

smiles began to dimple her face again, and she peered eagerly from the windows of the carriage, as if she expected Ralph Pullen to be on the platform to meet them. But from end to end, she saw only cinders, Flemish country women with huge baskets of fish or poultry on their arms, priests in their *soutanes* and broad-brimmed hats, and Belgians chattering and screaming to each other and their children, as they crossed the line. Still, she alighted with her party, expectant and happy, and traversed the little distance between the *entrepôt* and the Hotel, far quicker than the Baroness and her husband could keep up with her. She rushed into the balcony and almost fell into the arms of the *proprietaire*, Madame Lamont.

"Ah! Mademoiselle!" she cried, "welcome back to Heyst, but have you heard the desolating news?"

"What news?" exclaimed Harriet with staring eyes and a blanched cheek.

"Why! that the English lady, *cette Madame, si tranquille, si charmante,* lost her dear *bébé* the very day that Mademoiselle and Madame la Baronne left the Hotel!"

"Lost," repeated Harriet, "do you mean that the child is *dead?"*

"Ah! yes, I do indeed," replied Madame Lamont, "the dear *bébé* was taken with a fit whilst they were all at dinner, and never recovered again. *C'était une perte irréparable!* Madame was like a creature distracted whilst she remained here!"

"Where is she then? Where has she gone?" cried Harriet, excitedly.

"Ah! that I cannot tell Mademoiselle. The dear

bébé was taken away to England to be buried. Madame Pullen and Mademoiselle Leyton and Monsieur Phillippe and *le beau Capitaine* all left Heyst on the following day, that is Wednesday, and went to Ostende to take the boat for Dover. I know no more!"

"Captain Pullen has gone away—he is not here?" exclaimed Miss Brandt, betraying herself in her disappointment. "Oh! I don't believe it! It cannot be true! He has gone to Ostende to see them on board the steamer, but he will return—I am sure he will?"

Madame Lamont shrugged her shoulders.

"Monsieur paid everything before he went and gave *douceurs* to all the servants—I do not think he has any intention of returning!"

At that juncture the Baron and Baroness reached the hotel. Harriet flew to her friend for consolation.

"I cannot believe what Madame Lamont says," she exclaimed; "she declares that they are all gone for good, Mrs. Pullen and Miss Leyton and Captain Pullen and the doctor! They have returned to England. But he is sure to come back, isn't he? after all his promises to meet us in Brussels! He couldn't be so mean as to run off to England, without a word, or a line, unless he intended to come back."

She clung to Madame Gobelli with her eyes wide open and her large mouth trembling with agitation, until even the coarse fibre of the Baroness's propriety made her feel ashamed of the exhibition.

"'Ould up, 'Arriet!" she said, "you don't want the 'ole 'ouse to 'ear what you're thinking of, surely! Let me speak to Madame Lamont! What is all the row about, Madame?" she continued, turning to the *propriétaire.*

"There is no 'row' at all, Madame," was the reply, "I was only telling Mademoiselle Brandt of the sad event that has taken place here during your absence—that that *chère* Madame Pullen had the great misfortune to lose her sweet *bébé*, the very day you left Heyst, and that the whole party have quitted in consequence and crossed to England. I thought since Mademoiselle seemed so intimate with Madame Pullen and so fond of the dear child, that she would be *désolée* to hear the sad news, but she appears to have forgotten all about it, in her grief at hearing that the *beau Capitaine* accompanied his family to England where they go to bury the *petite.*"

And with rather a contemptuous smile upon her face, Madame Lamont re-entered the *salle à manger*.

"Now, 'Arriet, don't make a fool of yourself!" said the Baroness. "You 'eard what that woman said—she's laughing at you and your Captain, and the story will be all over the Hotel in half an hour. Don't make any more fuss about it! If 'e's gone, crying won't bring 'im back. It's much 'arder for Mrs. Pullen, losing her baby so suddenly! I'm sorry for 'er, poor woman, but as for the other, there's as good fish in the sea as ever came out of it!"

But Harriet Brandt only answered her appeal by rushing away down the corridor and up the staircase to her bedroom like a whirlwind. The girl had not the slightest control over her passions. She would listen to no persuasion, and argument only drove her mad. She tumbled headlong up the stairs, and dashing into her room, which had been reserved for her, threw herself tumultuously upon the bed. How lonely and horrible the corridor, on which her apartment opened, seemed. Olga Brimont, Mrs. Pullen, Miss Leyton, and Ralph, all gone! No one to talk to—no one to walk with—except the Baroness and her stupid husband! Of course this interpreted simply, meant that Captain Pullen had left the place without leaving a word behind him, to say the why or wherefore, or hold out any prospect of their meeting again. Of course it was impossible but that they must meet again—they *should* meet again, Harriet Brandt said to herself between her closed teeth—but meanwhile, what a wilderness, what a barren, dreary place this detestable Heyst would seem without him!

The girl put her head down on the pillow, and taking the corner of the linen case between her strong, white teeth, shook it and bit it, as a terrier worries a rat! But that did not relieve her feelings sufficiently, and she took to a violent fit of sobbing, hot, angry tears coursing each other down her cheeks, until they were blurred and stained, and she lay back upon the pillow utterly exhausted.

The first dinner bell rang without her taking any notice of it, and the second was just about to sound, when there came a low tap at her bedroom door. At first she did not reply, but when it was repeated, though rather timidly, she called out,

"Who is it? I am ill. I don't want any dinner! I cannot come down!"

A low voice answered.

"It is *I*, dear Miss Brandt, Bobby! May I come in? Mamma has sent me to you with a message!"

"Very well! You can enter, but I have a terrible headache!" said Harriet.

The door opened softly, and the tall lanky form of
Bobby Bates crept silently into the room. He held a
small bunch of pink roses in his hand, and he advanced
to the bedside and laid them without a word on the
pillow beside her hot, inflamed cheek. They felt delici-
ously cool and refreshing. Harriet turned her face towards them, and in doing so, met the anxious, perturbed
eyes of Bobby.

"Well!" she said smiling faintly, "and what is your
Mamma's message?"

"She wishes to know if you are coming down to
dinner. It is nearly ready!"

"No! no! I cannot! I am not hungry, and my eyes
are painful," replied Harriet, turning her face slightly
away.

The lad rose and drew down the blind of her window,
through which the setting sun was casting a stream of
light, and then captured a *flacon* of eau de Cologne
from her toilet-table, and brought it to her in his hand.

"May I sit beside you a little while in case you need
anything?" he asked.

"No! no! Bobby! You will want your dinner, and
your Mamma will want you. You had better go down
again at once, and tell her that if my head is better, I
will meet her on the Digue this evening!"

"I don't want any dinner, I could not eat it whilst
you lie here sick and unhappy. I want to stay, to see
if I can help you, or do you any good. I wish—I *wish*
I could!" murmured the lad.

"Your roses have done me good already," replied
Harriet, more brightly. "It was sweet of you to bring
them to me, Bobby."

"I wish I had ten thousand pounds a year," said Bobby feverishly, "that I might bring you roses, and everything that you like best!"

He laid his blonde head on the pillow by the side of hers and Harriet turned her face to his and kissed him.

The blood rushed into his face, and he trembled. It was the first time that any woman had kissed him. And all the feelings of his manhood rushed forth in a body to greet the creature who had awakened them.

As for Harriet Brandt, the boy's evident admiration flattered and pleased her. The tigress deprived of blood, will sometimes condescend to milder food. And the feelings with which she regarded Captain Pullen were such as could be easily replaced by anyone who evinced the same reciprocity. Bobby Bates was not a *beau sabreur,* but he was a male creature whom she had vanquished by her charms, and it interested her to watch his rising passion, and to know that he could never possibly expect it to be requited. She kissed and fondled him as he sat beside her with his head on the pillow— calling him every nice name she could think of, and caressing him as if he had been what the Baroness chose to consider him—a child of ten years old.

His sympathy and entreaties that she would make an effort to join them on the Digue, added to his love-lorn eyes, the clear childish blue of which was already becoming blurred with the heat of passion, convinced her that all was not lost, although Ralph Pullen *had* been ungrateful and impolite enough to leave Heyst without sending her notice, and presently she persuaded the lad to go down to his dinner, and inform the Baroness that she had ordered a cup of tea to be sent up to her bed-

room, and would try to rise after she had taken it, and
join them on the Digue.

"But you will keep a look-out for me, Bobby, won't
you?" she said in parting. "You will not let me miss
your party, or I shall feel so lonely that I shall come
straight back to bed!"

"Miss you! as if I would!" exclaimed the boy
fervently, "why, I shall not stir from the balcony until
you appear! O! Miss Brandt! I love you so. You cannot tell—you will never know—but you seem like part
of my life!"

"Silly boy!" replied Harriet, reproachfully, as she
gave him another kiss. "There, run away at once, and
don't tell your mother what we've been about, or she
will never let me speak to you again."

Bobby's eyes answered for him, that he would be
torn to pieces before he let their precious secret out of
his grasp, as he took his unwilling way down to the
table d'hôte.

"Well! you 'ave made a little fool of yourself, and
no mistake," was the Baroness's greeting, as Harriet
joined her in the balcony an hour later, "and a nice lot
of lies I've 'ad to tell about you to Mrs. Montague and
the rest. But luckily, they're all so full of the poor child's
death, and the coffin of white cloth studded with silver
nails that was brought from Bruges to carry the body to
England in, that they 'ad no time to spare for your
tantrums. Lor! that poor young man must 'ave 'ad
enough to do, I can tell you, from all accounts, without
writing to you! Everything was on 'is 'ands, for Mrs.
Pullen wouldn't let the doctor out of 'er sight! 'E 'ad
to fly off to Bruges to get the coffin and to wire half

over the world, besides 'aving the two women to tow about, so you mustn't be 'ard on 'im. 'E'll write soon, and explain everything, you may make sure of that, and if 'e don't, why, we shall be after 'im before long! Aldershot, where the Limerick Rangers are quartered, is within a stone's throw of London, and Lord Menzies and Mr. Nalgett often run over to the Red 'Ouse, and so can Captain Pullen, if he chooses! So you just make yourself 'appy, and it will be all right before long."

"O! I'm all right!" cried Harriet, gaily, "I was only a little startled at the news, so would anyone have been. Come along, Bobby! Let us walk over the dunes to the next town. This cool air will do my head good. Goodbye, Baroness! You needn't expect us till you see us! Bobby and I are going for a good long walk!"

And tucking the lad's arm under her own, she walked off at a tremendous pace, and the pair were soon lost to view.

"I wish that Bobby was a few years older," remarked the Baroness thoughtfully to her husband, as they were left alone, "she wouldn't 'ave made a bad match for him, for she 'as a tidy little fortune, and it's all in Consols. But perhaps it's just as well there's no chance of it! She ain't got much 'eart—I couldn't 'ave believed that she'd receive the news of that poor baby's death, without a tear or so much as a word of regret, when at one time she 'ad it always in 'er arms. She quite forgot all about it, thinking of the man. Drat the men! They're more trouble than they're worth, but 'e's pretty sure to come after 'er as soon as 'e 'ears she's at the Red 'Ouse!"

"But to what good, mein tear," demanded the Baron, "when you know he is betrothed to Miss Leyton?"

"Yes! and 'e'll marry Miss Leyton, too. 'E's not the sort of man to let the main chance go! And 'Arriet will console 'erself with a better beau. I can read all that without your telling me, Gustave. But Miss Leyton won't get off without a scratch or two, all the same, and that's what I'm aiming at. I'll teach 'er not to call me a female elephant! I've got my knife into that young woman, and I mean to turn it! Confound 'er impudence! What next?"

And having delivered herself of her feelings, the Baroness rose and proceeded to take her evening promenade along the Digue.

CHAPTER X.

THE Red House at Holloway was, like its owner, a contradiction and an anomaly. It had lain for many years in Chancery, neglected and uncared-for, and the Baroness had purchased it for a song. She was very fond of driving bargains, and sometimes she was horribly taken in. She had been known to buy a house for two thousand pounds for a mere caprice, and exchange it, six months afterwards, for a dinner service. But as a rule she was too shrewd to be cheated, for her income was not a tenth part of what she represented. When she had concluded her bargain for the Red House, which she did after a single survey of the premises, and entered on possession, she found it would take double the sum she had paid to put it into proper repair. It was a very old house of the Georgian, era standing in its own grounds of about a couple of acres, and containing thirty rooms, full of dust, damp, rats, and decay. The Baroness, however, having sent for a couple of workmen from the firm, to put the tangled wilderness which called itself a garden, into something like order, sent in all her household gods, and settled down there, with William and two rough maid servants, as lady of the Manor. The inside of the Red House presented an incongruous appearance. This extraordinary woman, who could not sound her aspirates and could hardly write her own name, had a wonderful taste for old china and pictures, and knew a good thing from a bad one. Her drawing-room was heaped with valuables, many of them piled on rickety tables which threatened every minute to overturn them upon the ground. The entrance hall was dingy, bare, and ill-lighted, and the breakfast-room to the side was furnished with the merest necessities. Yet the dressing-table in the Baroness's sleeping apartment was draped in ruby velvet, and trimmed with a flounce of the most costly Brussels lace, which a Princess might not have been ashamed to wear. The bed was covered with a *duvet* of the thickest satin, richly embroidered by her own hand, whilst the washing-stand held a set of the commonest and cheapest crockery. Everything about the house was on the same scale; it looked as though it belonged to people who had fallen from the utmost affluence to the depths of poverty. Harriet Brandt was terribly disappointed when she entered it, Bobby's accounts of the magnificence of his home having led her to expect nothing short of a palace.

The Baroness had insisted on her accompanying them to England. She had taken one of her violent fancies to the girl, and nothing would satisfy her but that Harriet should go back with her husband and herself to the Red House, and stay there as long as she chose.

"Now look 'ere," she said in her rough way, "you must make the Red 'Ouse your 'ome. Liberty 'All, as I call it! Get up and go to bed; go out and come in, just when you see fit—do what you like, see what you like, and invite your friends, as if the 'ouse was your own. The Baron and I are often 'alf the day at the boot shop, but that need make no difference to you. I daresay you'll find some way to amuse yourself. You're the daughter of the 'ouse, remember, and free to do as you choose!"

Harriet gladly accepted the offer. She had no friends of her own to go to, and the prospect of living by herself, in an unknown city, was rather lonely. She was full of anticipation also that by means of the Red House and the Baroness's influence, she would soon hear of, or see, Captain Pullen again—full of hope that Madame Gobelli would write to the young man and force him to fulfil the promises he had made to her. She did not want to know Prince Adalbert or Prince Loris—at the present moment, it was Ralph and Ralph only, and none other would fill the void she felt at losing him. She was sure there must be some great mistake at the bottom of his strange silence, and that they had but to meet, to see it rectified. She was only too glad then, when the day for their departure from Heyst arrived. Most of the English party had left the Lion d'Or by that time. The death of Mrs. Pullen's child seemed to have frightened them away. Some became nervous lest little Ethel had inhaled poisonous vapours from the drainage—others thought that the atmosphere was unhealthy, or that it was getting too late in the year for the seaside, and so the visitors dwindled, until the Baroness Gobelli found they were left alone with foreigners, and elected to return to England in consequence.

Harriet had wished to write to Captain Pullen and ask for an explanation of his conduct, but the Baroness conjured her not to do so, even threatened to withdraw her friendship, if the girl went against her advice. The probabilities were, she said, that the young man was staying with his sister-in-law wherever she might be, and that the letter would be forwarded to him from the Camp, and fall into the hands of Mrs. Pullen, or Miss Leyton. She assured Harriet that it would be safer to wait until she had ascertained his address, and was sure that any communication would reach him at first hand.

"A man's never the worse for being let alone, 'Arriet," she said. "Don't let 'im think 'e's of too much consequence and 'e'll value you all the more! Our fellows don't care for the bird that walks up to the gun. A little 'olesome indifference will do my gentleman all the good in the world!"

"O! but how *can* I be indifferent, when I am burning to see him again, and to hear why he never wrote to say that he could not come to Brussels," exclaimed Harriet, excitedly. "Do you think it was all falsehoods, Madame Gobelli? Do you think that he does not want to see me any more?"

Her eyes were flashing like diamonds—her cheeks and hands were burning hot. The Baroness chuckled over her ardour and anxiety.

"He! he! he! you little fool, no, I don't! Anyone could see with 'alf an eye, that he took a fancy for you! You're the sort of stuff to stir up a man and make 'im forget everything but yourself. Now don't you worry. 'E'll be at the Red 'Ouse like a shot, as soon as 'e 'ears we're back in London. Mark my words! it won't be long before we 'ave the 'ole lot of 'em down on us, like bees 'umming round a flower pot."

After this flattering tale, it was disheartening to arrive in town on a chilly September day, under a pouring rain, and to see the desolate appearance presented by the Red House.

It was seven in the evening before they reached Holloway, and drove up the dark carriage drive, clumped by laurels, to the hall door.

After the grand description given by Bobby of his Mamma's barouche lined with olive green satin, Harriet was rather astonished that they should have to charter cabs from the Victoria Station to Holloway, instead of being met by the Baroness's private carriage. But she discovered afterwards that though there was a barouche standing in the coach-house, which had been purchased in a moment of reckless extravagance by Madame Gobelli, there were no horses to draw it, and the only vehicle kept by the Baroness was a very much patched, not to say disreputable looking Victoria, with a spavined cob attached to it, in which William drove the mistress when she visited the boot premises.

The chain having been taken down, the hall door was opened to them by a slight, timid looking person, whom Harriet mistook for an upper housemaid.

"Well, Miss Wynward," exclaimed the Baroness, as she stumped into the hall, "'ere we are, you see!"

"Yes! my lady," said the person she addressed, "but I thought, from not hearing again, that you would travel by the night boat! Your rooms are ready," she hastened to add, "only—dinner, you see! I had no orders about it!"

"That doesn't signify," interrupted the Baroness, "send out for a steak and give us some supper instead! 'Ere William, where are you? Take my bag and Miss Brandt's up to our rooms, and, Gustave, you can carry the wraps! Where's that devil Bobby? Come 'ere at once and make yourself useful! What are you standing there, staring at 'Arriet for? Don't you see Miss Wynward? Go and say "ow d'ye do' to 'er?"

Bobby started, and crossing to where Miss Wynward stood, held out his hand. She shook it warmly.

"How are you, Bobby?" she said. "You don't look much stronger for your trip. I expected to see you come back with a colour!"

"Nonsense!" commenced the Baroness testily, "what rubbish you old maids do talk! What should you know about boys? 'Ow many 'ave *you* got? 'Ere, why don't you kiss 'im? You've smacked 'im often enough, *I* know!"

Miss Wynward tried to pass the coarse rejoinder off as a joke, but it was with a very plaintive smile that she replied,

"I think Bobby is growing rather too tall to be kissed, and he thinks so too, don't you, Bobby?"

Bobby was about to make some silly reply, when his Mamma interrupted him,

"Oh! does he? 'E'll be wanting to kiss the gals soon,

so 'e may as well practise on you first! Come! Bobby,
do you 'ear what I say? Kiss 'er!"

But Miss Wynward drew up her spare figure with
dignity.

"No! my lady!" she said quietly, "I do not wish it!"

"He! he! he!" giggled the Baroness, as she commenced to mount the stairs, "'e ain't old enough for you,
that's what's the matter! Come along, 'Arriet, my dear!
I'm dog-tired and I daresay you're much the same! Let
us 'ave some 'ot water to our rooms, Miss Wynward!"

Harriet Brandt was now ushered by her hostess into
a bedroom on the same floor as her own, and left to
unpack her bundles and boxes as she best might. It
was not a badly furnished room, but there was too much
pomp and too little comfort in it. The mantelshelf was
ornamented with some rare old Chelsea figures, and a
Venetian glass hung above them, but the carpet was
threadbare, and the dressing-table was inconveniently
small and of painted deal. But as though to atone for
these discrepancies, the hangings to the bed were of satin,
and the blind that shaded the window was edged with
Neapolitan lace. Harriet had not been used to luxuries
in the Convent, but her rooms in the Lion d'Or had
been amply provided with all she could need, and she
was a creature of sensual and indolent temperament,
who felt any rebuff, in the way of her comfort, terribly.

There was an un-homelike feeling in the Red House
and its furniture, and a coldness in their reception,
which made the passionate, excited creature feel inclined to sit down and burst into tears. She was on
the very brink of doing so, when a tap sounded on the
door, and Miss Wynward entered with a zinc can of hot

water, which she placed on the washing-stand. Then she stood for a moment regarding the girl as though she guessed what was in her mind, before she said,

"Miss Brandt, I believe! I am so sorry that the Baroness never wrote me with any certainty regarding her arrival, or things would have been more comfortable. I hope you had a good dinner on board!"

"No!" said Harriet, shaking her head, "I felt too ill to eat. But it does not signify, thank you!"

"But you are looking quite upset! Supper cannot be ready for another hour. I will go and make you a cup of tea!"

She hurried from the room again, and presently returned with a small tray on which was set a Sèvres cup and saucer and Apostle teaspoon, with an earthenware teapot that may possibly have cost sixpence. But Harriet was too grateful for the tea to cavil whence it came, and drinking it refreshed her more than anything else could have done.

"Thank you, thank you so much," she said to Miss Wynward, "I think the long journey and the boat had been too much for me. I feel much better now!"

"It is such a melancholy house to come to when one is out of sorts," observed her companion, "I have felt that myself! It will not give you a good impression of your first visit to London. Her ladyship wrote me you had just come from the West Indies," she added, timidly.

"Yes! I have not long arrived in Europe," replied Harriet. "But I thought—I fancied—the Baroness gave me the idea that the Red House was particularly gay and cheerful, and that so many people visited her here!"

"That is true! A great many people visit here! But

11 *

—not such people, perhaps, as a young lady would care for!"

"O! I care for every sort," said Harriet, more gaily, "and you,—don't you care for company, Miss Wynward?"

"I have nothing to do with it, Miss Brandt, beyond seeing that the proper preparations are made for receiving it. I am Bobby's governess, and housekeeper to the Baroness!"

"Bobby is getting rather tall for a governess!" laughed Harriet.

"He is, poor boy, but his education is very deficient. He ought to have been sent to school long ago, but her ladyship would not hear of it. But I never teach him now. He is supposed to be finished!"

"Why don't you find another situation then?" demanded Harriet, who was becoming interested in the ex-governess.

She was a fragile, melancholy looking woman of perhaps five-and-thirty, who had evidently been good-looking in her day and would have been so then but for her attenuation, and shabby dress. But she was evidently a gentlewoman, and far above the menial offices she appeared to fill in the Red House. She gazed at Harriet for a minute in silence after she had put the last question to her, and then answered slowly:

"There are reasons which render it unadvisable. But you, Miss Brandt, have you known the Baroness before?"

"I never saw her till we met at Heyst and she invited me here," replied the girl.

"O! why did you come? Why did you come?" exclaimed Miss Wynward, as she left the room.

Harriet stood gazing at the door as it closed behind her. *Why had she come?* What an extraordinary question to ask her! For the same reason that other people accepted invitations to them by their friends—because she expected to enjoy herself, and have the protection of the Baroness on first entering English society! But why should this governess—her dependant, almost her servant—put so strange a question to her? Why had she come? She could not get it out of her mind. She was roused from her train of speculation by hearing the Baroness thumping on the outside panels of her door with her stick.

"Come along," she cried, "never mind dressing! The supper's ready at last and I'm as 'ungry as an 'unter."

Hastily completing her toilet, Harriet joined her hostess, who conducted her down to a large dining-room, wrapt in gloom. The two dozen morocco chairs ranged against the wall, looked sepulchral by the light of a single lamp, placed in the centre of a long mahogany table, which was graced by a fried steak, a huge piece of cheese, bread and butter, and lettuces from the garden. Harriet regarded the preparations for supper with secret dismay. She was greedy by nature, but it was the love of good feeding, rather than a superfluity of food, that induced her to be so. However, when the Baron produced a couple of bottles of the very best Champagne to add to the meal, she felt her appetite somewhat revive, and played almost as good a knife and fork as the Baroness. Bobby and Miss Wynward, who as it appeared, took her meals with the family, were the only ones who did not do justice to the supper.

The lad looked worn-out and very pale, but when

Miss Wynward suggested that a glass of champagne might do him good, and dispel the exhaustion under which he was evidently labouring, his mother vehemently opposed the idea.

"Champagne for a child like 'im," she cried, "I never 'eard of such a thing. Do you want to make 'im a drunkard, Miss Wynward? No! thank you, there 'ave been no 'ard drinkers in *our* family, and 'e shan't begin it! 'Is father was one of the soberest men alive! 'E never took anything stronger than toast and water all the time I knew 'im."

"Of course not, your ladyship," stammered Miss Wynward, who seemed in abject fear of her employer, "I only thought as Bobby seems so very tired, that a little stimulant——"

"Then let 'im go to bed," replied Madame Gobelli. "Bed is the proper place for boys when they're tired! Come, Sir, off to bed with you, at once, and don't let me 'ear anything more of you till to-morrow morning!"

"But mayn't I have some supper?" pleaded Bobby.

"Not a bit of it!" reiterated the Baroness, "if you're so done up that you require champagne, your stomach can't be in a fit state to digest beef and bread! Be off at once, I say, or you'll get a taste of my stick."

"But, my lady——" said Miss Wynward, entreatingly.

"It's not a bit of good, Miss Wynward, I know more about boys' insides than you do. Sleep's the thing for Bobby. Now, no more nonsense, I say——"

But Bobby, after one long look at Harriet Brandt, had already quitted the room. This episode had the effect of destroying Miss Wynward's appetite. She sat gazing at her plate for a few minutes, and then with some murmured excuse of its being late, she rose and disappeared. The Baroness was some time over her meal, and Harriet had an opportunity to examine the apartment they sat in, as well as the dim light allowed her to do. The walls were covered with oil paintings and good ones, as she could see at a glance, whilst at the further end, where narrow shelves were fixed from the floor to the ceiling, was displayed the famous dinner service of Sèvres, for which the Baroness was said to have bartered the two thousand lease of her house.

Harriet glanced from the pictures and the china upon the walls to the steak and bread and cheese upon the table, and marvelled at the incongruity of the whole establishment. Madame Gobelli who, whilst at the Lion d'Or, had appeared to think nothing good enough for her, was now devouring fried steak and onions, as if they had been the daintiest of fare. But the champagne made amends, on that night at least, for the solids which accompanied it, and the girl was quite ready to believe that the poverty of the table was only due to the fact that they had arrived at the Red House unexpectedly. As they reached the upper corridor, her host and hostess parted with her, with much effusion, and passing into their own room, shut the door and locked it noisily. As Harriet gained hers, she saw the door opposite partly unclose to display poor Bobby standing there to see her once again.

He was clothed only in his long night-shirt, and looked like a lanky ghost, but he was too childish in mind to think for one moment that his garb was not a suitable one for a lover to accost his mistress in. She heard him whisper her name as she turned the handle of her own door.

"Why, Bobby," she exclaimed, "not in bed yet?"

"Hush! hush!" he said in a low voice, "or Mamma will hear you! I couldn't sleep till I had seen you again and wished you good-night!"

"Poor dear boy! Are you not very hungry?"

"No, thanks. Miss Wynward is very kind to me. She has seen after that. But to leave without a word to you. That was the hard part of it!"

"Poor Bobby!" ejaculated Harriet again, drawing nearer to him. "But you must not stay out of bed. You will catch your death of cold!"

"Kiss me then and I will go!"

He advanced his face to the opening of the door, and she put her lips to his, and drew his breath away with her own.

"Good-night! good-night!" murmured Bobby with a long sigh. "God bless you! good-night!" and then he disappeared, and Harriet entered her own room, and her eyes gleamed, as she recognised the fact that Bobby also was going to make a fool of himself for her sake.

The next morning she was surprised on going downstairs at about nine o'clock, to find a cloth laid over only part of the dining table, and breakfast evidently prepared for one person. She was still gazing at it in astonishment, and wondering what it meant, when Miss Wynward entered the room, to express a hope that Miss Brandt had slept well and had everything that she required.

"O! certainly yes! but where are we going to have breakfast?"

"Here, Miss Brandt, if it pleases you. I was just about to ask what you would like for your breakfast."

"But the Baron and Baroness—"

"O! they started for the manufactory two hours ago. Her ladyship is a very early riser when at home, and they have some four miles to drive."

"The manufactory!" echoed Harriet, "do you mean where they make the boots and shoes?"

"Yes! There is a manufactory in Germany, and another in England, where the boots and shoes are finished off. And then there is the shop in Oxford Street, where they are sold. The Baron's business is a very extensive one!"

"So I have understood, but what good can Madame Gobelli do there? What can a woman know about such things?"

Miss Wynward shrugged her shoulders.

"She looks after the young women who are employed, I believe, and keeps them up to their work. The Baroness is a very clever woman. She knows something about most things—and a good deal that were better left unknown," she added, with a sigh.

"And does she go there every morning?"

"Not always, but as a rule she does. She likes to have a finger in the pie, and fancies that nothing can go on properly without her. And she is right so far that she has a much better head for business than the Baron, who would like to be out of it all if he could!"

"But why can't he give it up then, since they are so very rich?" demanded Harriet.

Miss Wynward regarded her for a moment, as if she

wondered who had given her the information, and then
said quietly,

"But all this time we are forgetting your breakfast,
Miss Brandt! What will you take? An egg, or a piece
of bacon?"

"O! I don't care," replied Harriet, yawning, "I never
can eat when I am alone! Where is Bobby? Won't he
take his breakfast with me?"

"O! he had his long ago with his Mamma, but I daresay he would not mind a second edition, poor boy!"

She walked to the French windows which opened
from a rustic porch to the lawn, and called "Bobby!
Bobby!"

"Yes, Miss Wynward," replied the lad in a more
cheerful tone than Harriet remembered to have ever
heard him use before, "what is it?"

"Come in, my dear, and keep Miss Brandt company,
whilst she takes her breakfast!"

"Won't I!" cried Bobby, as he came running from
the further end of the disorderly garden, with a bunch
of flowers.

"They are for you!" he exclaimed, as he put them
into Harriet's hand, "I gathered them on purpose!"

"Thank you, Bobby," she replied. "It *was* kind of
you!"

She felt cheered by the simple attention. For her
hostess to have left her on the very first morning, without a word of explanation, had struck her as looking
very much (notwithstanding all the effusive flattery and
protestations of attachment with which she had been
laden) as if she were not wanted at the Red House.

But when her morning meal was over, and she had been introduced to every part of the establishment under the chaperonage of Bobby—to the tangled, overgrown garden, the empty stables, Papa's library, which was filled with French and German books, and Mamma's drawing-room, which was so full of valuable china that one scarcely dared move freely about it—the burning thirst to see, or hear something of Ralph Pullen returned with full force upon Harriet, and she enquired eagerly of Miss Wynward when her hostess might be expected to return.

Miss Wynward looked rather blank as she replied,

"Not till dinner time, I am afraid! I fancy she will find too much to enquire about and to do, after so long an absence from home. I am so sorry, Miss Brandt," she continued, noting the look of disappointment on the girl's face, "that her ladyship did not make this plain to you last night. Her injunctions to me were to see that you had everything you required, and to spare no trouble or expense on your account. But that is not like having her here, of course! Have you been into the library? There are some nice English works there, and there is a piano in the drawing-room which you might like to use. I am afraid it is not in tune, on account of the rain we have had, and that I have not opened it myself during the Baroness's absence, and indeed it is never used, except to teach Bobby his music lessons on, but it may amuse you in default of anything else."

"O! I daresay I shall find something to amuse myself with," replied Harriet rather sullenly, "I have my own instrument with me, and my books, thank you! But is no one likely to call this afternoon, do you think?"

"This afternoon," echoed Miss Wynward, "are you expecting any of your own friends to see you?"

"O! no! I have no friends in England,—none at least that know I have returned from Heyst. But the Baroness told me—she said the Red House was always full of guests—Prince Adalbert and Prince Loris, and a lot of others—do you think they may come to-day to see her?"

"O! not in September," replied her companion, "it is not the season now, Miss Brandt, and all the fashionable people are out of town, at the foreign watering-places, or shooting in the country. Her ladyship could never have intended you to understand that the people you have mentioned would come here at any time except between May and July! They *do* come here then —sometimes—but not I expect, as *you* think—not as friends, I mean!"

"Not as *friends!* What as, then?" demanded Harriet.

"Well!" returned Miss Wynward, dubiously, "many of them have business with her ladyship, and they come to see her upon it! I generally conduct them to her presence, and leave them alone with her, but that is all I see of them! They have never come here to a party, or dinner, to my knowledge!"

"How very extraordinary!" cried Harriet. "What do they come for then?"

"The Baroness must tell you that!" replied the other, gravely, "I am not in her confidence, and if I were, I should not feel justified in revealing it."

This conversation drove Harriet to her room to indite a letter to Captain Pullen. If she were to be deprived of the society of dukes and princes, she would at least secure the company of one person who could make the time pass pleasantly to her. As she wrote to him, rapidly, unadvisedly, passionately, her head burned ' and her heart was fluttering. She felt as if she had been deceived—cheated—decoyed to the Red House under false pretences, and she was in as much of a rage as her indolent nature would permit her to be. The revelations of Miss Wynward had sunk down into her very soul. No parties, no dinners, with princes handing her into the dining-room and whispering soft nothings into her ears all the time! Why had Madame Gobelli so often promised to console her for the loss of Captain Pullen by this very means, and it was a dream, a chimera, they only came to the Red House on business—business, horrid unromantic word—and were shut up with the Baroness. *What* business, she wondered! Could it be about boots and shoes, and if so, why did they not go to the shop, which surely was the proper place from which to procure them! The idea that she had been deceived in this particular, made her write far more warmly and pleadingly perhaps, than she would otherwise have done. A bird in the hand was worth two in the bush—Harriet was not conversant with the proverb, but she fully endorsed the sentiment. When her letter was written and addressed to the Camp at Aldershot, and she had walked out with Bobby to post it in the pillar box, she felt happier and less resentful. At all events she was her own mistress and could leave the Red House when she chose, and take up her abode elsewhere. A hot sun had dried the garden paths and grass, and she spent the rest of the afternoon wandering about the unshaven lawn with Bobby, and lingering on the rotten wooden benches under the trees, with the boy's arm round her waist, and his head drooping on her shoulder.

Bobby was blissfully happy, and she was content. If we cannot get caviare, it is wise to content ourselves with cod's roe. They spent hours together that afternoon, until the dusk had fallen and the hour of dining had drawn nigh. They talked of Heyst and the pleasures they had left behind them, and Harriet was astonished to hear how manly were some of Bobby's ideas and sentiments, when out of sight of his Mamma.

At last, the strident tones of the Baroness's voice were heard echoing through the grounds. Harriet and Bobby leaped to their feet in a moment.

"'Ere, 'Arriet! Bobby! where are you? You're a nice son and daughter to 'ide away from me, when I've been toiling for your benefit all the day."

She came towards them as she spoke, and when Harriet saw how fatigued she looked, she almost forgave her for leaving her in the lurch as she had done.

"I suppose you thought we were both dead, didn't you?" she continued. "Well, we are, almost. Never 'ad such a day's work in my life! Found everything wrong, of course! You can't turn your back for five minutes but these confounded workmen play old 'Arry with your business! I sent off ten fellows before I'd been in the factory ten minutes, and fined as many girls, and 'ave been running all over London since to replace 'em. It's 'ard work, I can tell you!"

She plumped down upon the rotten seat, nearly bringing it to the ground, as she spoke, and burst out laughing.

"You should 'ave seen one man, you would 'ave died of laughing! 'Get out,' I said to 'im, 'not another day's work do you do 'ere!' 'Get out of the factory where I've worked for twenty years?' 'e said, 'Well, then, I shan't, not for you! If the governor 'ad said so, it might be a different thing, but a woman 'as no right to come interfering in business as she knows nothing about!' 'That's the way the wind lies,' I replied, 'and you want a man to turn you out! We'll soon see if a woman can't do it!' and I took my stick and laid it on his back till he holload again. He was out of the place before you could say Jack Robinson! "Ow will that do?' I said to the others, 'who else wants a taste of my stick before 'e'll go!' But they all cleared out before I 'ad done speaking! I laughed till I was ill! But come along, children! It's time for dinner!" As they returned to the house, she accosted Harriet,

"I 'ope you've amused yourself to-day! You'll 'ave to look after yourself whenever I'm at the factory! But a 'andsome gal like you won't want long for amusement. We'll 'ave plenty of company 'ere, soon! Miss Wynward," she continued, as they entered the dining-room, "Mr. Milliken is coming to-morrow! See that 'is room is ready for 'im!"

"Very good, my lady!" replied Miss Wynward, but Harriet fancied she did not like the idea of Mr. Milliken staying with them.

The dinner proceeded merrily. It was more sumptuous than the day before, consisting of several courses, and the champagne flowed freely. Harriet, sitting at her ease and thoroughly enjoying the repast, thought that it atoned for all the previous inconvenience. But a strange incident occurred before the meal was over. The Baron, who was carver, asked Bobby twice if he would take some roast beef, and received no answer, which immediately aroused the indignation of the Baroness.

"Do you 'ear what your father is saying to you, Bobby?" she cried, shrilly. "Answer 'im at once or I'll send you out of the room! Will you 'ave some beef?"

But still there was no reply.

"My lady! I think that he is ill," said Miss Wynward in alarm.

"Ill! Rubbish!" exclaimed the Baroness. Being so coarse-fibred and robust a woman herself, she never had any sympathy with delicacy or illness, and generally declared all invalids to be humbugs, shamming in order to attract the more attention. She now jumped up from her seat, and going round to her son's chair, shook him violently by the shoulder.

"'Ere, wake up! what are you about?" she exclaimed, "if you don't sit up at once and answer your father's question, I'll lay my stick about your back!"

She was going to put her argument into effect, when Harriet prevented her.

"Stop! stop! Madame Gobelli!" she exclaimed; "can't you see, he has fainted!"

It was really true! Bobby had fainted dead away in his chair, where he lay white as a sheet, with closed eyes, and limp body. Miss Wynward flew to her pupil's assistance.

"Poor dear boy! I was sure he was not well directly he entered the house," she said.

"Not well!" replied the Baroness, "nonsense! what should ail 'im? 'Is father was one of the strongest men on God's earth! He never 'ad a day's illness in 'is life. 'Ow should the boy, a great 'ulking fellow like 'im, 'ave got ill?"

She spoke roughly, but there was a tremor in her voice as she uttered the words, and she looked at Bobby as though she were afraid of him.

But as he gradually revived under Miss Wynward's treatment, she approached nearer, and said with some tenderness in her tones,

"Well! Bobby, lad, and 'ow do you feel now?"

"Better, Mamma, thank you! only my head keeps going round!"

"Had I not better help him up to his bed, my lady?" asked Miss Wynward.

"O! yes! but I 'ope 'e isn't going to make a fool of 'imself like this again, for I don't 'old with boys fainting like hysterical gals!"

"I couldn't help it, Mamma!" said Bobby faintly.

"O! yes! you could, if you 'ad any pluck! You never saw *me* faint. Nor Gustave either! It's all 'abit! Trundle 'im off to bed, Miss Wynward. The sooner 'e's there, the better!"

"And I may give him a little stimulant," suggested Miss Wynward timidly, recalling the scene of the evening before, "a little champagne or brandy and water— I think he requires it, my lady!"

"O! yes! Coddle 'im to your 'eart's content, only don't let me 'ear of it! I 'ate a fuss! Good-night, Bobby! Mind you're well by to-morrow morning!"

And she brushed the lad's cheek with her bristly chin.

"Good-night!" replied Bobby, "good-night to all!"

as he was supported from the room on the arm of Miss Wynward.

The Baroness did not make any further remarks concerning her son, but Harriet noticed that her appetite disappeared with him, and declaring that she had tired herself too much to eat, she sat unoccupied and almost silent for the remainder of the meal.

CHAPTER XL.

MR. ALEXANDER MILLIKEN arrived punctually upon the morrow.

He was a tall, gaunt, weak-kneed man, with a prominent nose and eyes that required the constant use of glasses. Harriet Brandt could not at first determine his relationship to the Baroness, who received him with one of the rough kisses she was wont to bestow on Bobby and herself.

He established himself in the Red House as if he had been a member of the family, and Harriet frequently surprised him engaged in confidential talk with their hostess, which was immediately stopped on her arrival. She perceived that Miss Wynward had an evident dislike for the new-comer, and never addressed him but in the most formal manner and when it was strictly necessary. The Baroness did not go so often to the manufactory after Mr. Milliken's arrival, but often shut herself up with him in a room with locked doors, after which Mr. Milliken would be much occupied with secretarial work, writing letters with his short-sighted eyes held close to the paper. He was a source of much curiosity to Harriet Brandt, but he need not have been.

He was only that very common and unclean animal—
the jackal to Madame Gobelli's lion.

He was poor and she was rich, so he did all the
dirty work which she was unable, or afraid, to do for
herself. Mr. Milliken called himself an author and an
actor, but he was neither. On account of his accidental
likeness to a popular actor, he had once been engaged
to play the part of his double at a West-end theatre, but
with the waning of the piece, Mr. Milliken's fame evaporated, and he had never obtained an engagement since.
His assumed authòrship was built on the same scale.
He had occasionally penned anonymous articles for news-
papers, which had been inserted without pay, but no
one in the literary or any other world knew him by
name or by fame. Of late he had attached himself to
Madame Gobelli, writing her letters for her (of doing
which she was almost incapable), and occasionally dab-
bling in dirtier work, which she was too cunning to do
for herself. Miss Wynward could have told tales of
abusive epistles which had been sent through his hand
to people, whom the Baroness considered had offended
her—of anonymous letters also, which if traced would
have landed them both in the County Court. But Mr.
Milliken was out at elbows. He found it very convenient
to hang about the Red House for weeks together, to the
saving of his pocket—receiving douceurs sometimes in
actual coin of the realm at the hands of his benefactress,
and making himself useful to her in any way in return.
Lately, notwithstanding her grand promises to Harriet
Brandt of introductions to lords, and princes, the Baroness
had thought it would be a very good thing for her
favourite jackal if the young heiress took a fancy for

12*

him, and gave him full leave in consequence to go in
and conquer if he could. She would praise his appearance and his qualities to the girl, before his very face
—calling attention to the fact of what a clever creature
he was, and what a fine figure he possessed, and how
well he was connected, and advising her in her coarse
fashion to cultivate his acquaintance better. She even
descended to having visions in the broad daylight, and
prophesying the future, for them both.

"'Arriet!" she would suddenly exclaim, "I see a
man standing be'ind you!"

"O! gracious!" the girl would reply, jumping in her
seat, "I wish you would not say such things, Madame!"

"Rubbish! Why shouldn't I say 'em, if they're
there? Stop a bit! Let me see 'im plainly! 'E's got
dark 'air, slightly sprinkled with grey—a fine nose—
deep-set eyes, with bushy eyebrows—no 'air on 'is face
—a tall figure, and long 'ands and feet! 'E's living in
this world too! Do you know anybody that answers to
the description?"

"No!" replied the girl, though she recognised it at
once as being meant for Mr. Milliken.

"Well! if you don't know 'im now, you will before
long, but it's my belief you've met. And mark my words!
you and 'e will be closely connected in life! I shouldn't
wonder if 'e turns out to be your future 'usband!"

"O! nonsense!" exclaimed Harriet, trying to speak
lightly, "I'm not going to marry anybody, thank you,
Madame Gobelli, unless it's one of the princes you promised to introduce me to."

"O! princes are all rubbish!" replied the Baroness,
forgetting her former assertions, "they've none of them

got any money, and yours wouldn't go far enough for 'em. *They* want a gal with something like five thousand a year at 'er back. I'd rather 'ave an Englishman any day, than a dirty little German prince!"

But Harriet Brandt was not the sort of woman to be forced into an intimacy against her will. Born under an hereditary curse, as she undoubtedly had been, and gifted with the fatal propensity of injuring, rather than benefiting those whom she took a fancy for, she was an epicure in her taste for her fellow creatures, and would not have permitted Mr. Alexander Milliken to take a liberty with her, had he been the last man left upon the earth. She avoided his society as much as it was possible to do, without being rude to her hostess, but as the Baroness was continually calling her to her side, it was difficult to do so. Meanwhile the days went on very differently from what she had anticipated when coming to the Red House. Bobby was languid and indifferent to everything but hanging about the place where she might have located herself—sitting on the sofa beside her, with his heavy head on her shoulder, and his weak arm wound about her waist. Miss Wynward feared he must have contracted some species of malaria at the seaside, and Harriet could see for herself that the lad was much altered from the time when they first met—the Baroness alone, either from ignorance or obstinacy, declaring that nothing ailed him but laziness, and she would give him the stick if he didn't exert himself more. Sometimes Harriet took him out with her— for a drive into the country, or to a concert or *matinée* in London, but what was that compared to the entertainment of Royalty and Aristocracy, which she had been promised. And she had not heard a word from Captain Pullen, though her first letter of appeal had been succeeded by two or three more. Such a rebuff would have driven another girl to despondency or tears, but that was not the effect it had on Harriet Brandt. If you throw a bone to a tigress and then try to take it away, she does not weep—she fights for her prey. Harriet Brandt, deprived of the flatteries and attentions of Captain Pullen, did not weep either, but set her pretty teeth together, and determined in her own mind that if she were to give him up she would know the reason why. She was reckless—she did not care what she did to obtain it, but she would learn the truth of his defalcation if she travelled down to Aldershot for the purpose. She was in this mood one day, when the maidservant who answered the door came to tell her that a lady was in the drawing-room, and desired to see her. The Baroness had gone out that afternoon and taken Mr. Milliken with her, so that Harriet was alone. She eagerly demanded the name of her visitor.

"The lady didn't give me her name," replied the servant, "but she asked if Miss Brandt was at home, plain enough!"

"Go back and say that I will be with her in a minute!" said Harriet.

She had decided in her own mind that the stranger must be Margaret Pullen, bringing her, doubtless, some news of her brother-in-law. She only stayed to smoothe her hair, which was rather disordered from Bobby laying his head on her shoulder, before, with a heightened colour, she entered the drawing-room. What was her surprise to encounter, instead of Mrs. Pullen, Miss Leyton

—Miss Leyton, who had been so reserved and proud with her at Heyst, and who even though she had sought her out at the Red House, looked as reserved and proud as before. Harriet advanced with an extended hand, but Elinor Leyton did not appear to see the action, as she coldly bowed and sank into her chair again.

Harriet was rather taken aback, but managed to stammer out,

"I am very glad to see you, Miss Leyton! I thought you and Mrs. Pullen had forgotten all about me since leaving Heyst."

"We had not forgotten, Miss Brandt," replied Elinor, "but we had a great deal of trouble to encounter in the death of Mrs. Pullen's baby, and that put everything else for awhile out of our minds. But—but—lately, we have had reason to remember your existence more forcibly than before!"

She spoke slowly and with an evident effort. She was as agitated as it was in her nature to be the while, but she did not show it outwardly. Elinor Leyton had at all times the most perfect command over herself. She was dressed on the present occasion with the utmost neatness and propriety, though she had left her home labouring under a discovery which had pierced her to the very soul. She was a woman who would have died upon the scaffold, without evincing the least fear.

"Reason to remember my existence!" echoed Harriet, "I do not understand you."

"I think you soon will!" said Elinor, as she took three letters from her hand-bag and laid them on the table, "I do not think you can fail to recognise that handwriting, Miss Brandt!"

Harriet stooped down and read the address upon the envelopes. They were her own letters to Captain Pullen.

"How did you get these?" she demanded angrily, as she seized them in her hand. "Is thieving one of your proclivities, Miss Leyton?"

"No, Miss Brandt, thieving, as you elegantly put it, is not one of my proclivities! But Captain Pullen has been staying in the house of my father, Lord Walthamstowe, at Richmond, and left those letters behind him—thrown in the empty grate just as they are, a proof of how much he valued them! One of the housemaids, whilst setting his room in order after his departure, found them and brought them to me. So I determined that I would return them to your hands myself!"

"And have you read them?" demanded Harriet.

"I have read them! I considered it my duty!"

"Your duty!" replied the other, scornfully, "what duty is there in a mean, dishonourable action like that? What right had you to interfere with things that don't belong to you? These letters concern myself and Captain Pullen alone!"

"I deny that, Miss Brandt! They concern me quite as much, if not more—Captain Pullen is my affianced husband! We are to be married in the spring!"

"I don't believe it!" cried Harriet, starting to her feet. "A woman who would read letters not addressed to her, would say anything! You are *not* engaged to be married to Captain Pullen!"

"Indeed! And on what grounds do you refuse to believe my statement?"

"Because he made love to me all the time he was in Heyst! Because he used to kiss me and tell me again and again that I was the only woman who had ever touched his heart! Because he had arranged to follow the Baroness's party to Brussels, only to be near me, and he would have done so, had *you* not prevented him!"

Her great eyes were blazing with indignation and mortified vanity—her slender hands were clenched—she looked as if she were about to spring upon her rival and tear her to pieces—whilst Miss Leyton sat there, calm and collected—and smiled at her ravings.

"You are quite mistaken," she said after a pause, "I have never mentioned your name to Captain Pullen —I had no idea, until those letters fell into my hands, that he had so far forgotten what he owes to me, as to address you in any terms but those of mere acquaint-anceship. But now that I *do* know, it must of course be put a stop to at once and for ever! It was to tell you so, that I came here this afternoon."

"Put a stop to! Do you imagine that I am going to give up Captain Pullen at your request? You are vastly mistaken!"

"But you must—you *shall!*" exclaimed Elinor, getting (for her) quite excited. "He is engaged to marry me, and I will not allow him to keep up any communication with you! My decision is final, and you will be good enough to respect it!"

"Your decision is *final!*" cried Harriet in mocking tones. "Oh! indeed, is it? And what about Ralph's decision? Does that count for nothing? What if Ralph refuses to give me up?"

Elinor rose to her feet, trembling with indignation at the other's boldness.

"You shall not call him 'Ralph'," she exclaimed. "How dare you speak of a man who is nothing to you, in such familiar terms?"

"But *is* he nothing to me?" retorted Harriet, "and am I nothing to him? We must have that question answered first. Ralph told me to call him by his name, and he calls me Hally. How can you prevent our doing so? He loves me—he has told me so—and I shall write to him as often as I choose—yes! and I will take him from you, if I choose, and keep him into the bargain! What do you say to that?"

"I say that you are a bold, brazen girl, not fit for me to associate with, and that I refuse to be contaminated by your presence any longer! Let me go!"

She made an effort to gain the door, as she spoke, but Harriet barred her exit.

"No, no, Miss Leyton," she said, "you don't come here to insult me, and then leave before you have heard all I have to say to you! In the first place your assurance to-day is the first I ever heard of your being engaged to marry Captain Pullen. *He* didn't take the trouble to make it public. He never mentioned you except to say what a cold, reserved, unpleasant nature you had, and how impossible it would be for a man with any human feeling to get on with you! That is what *he* thought! And he said it too, when he had his arm round my waist, and his face close to mine. And now he has come to England, I suppose he is afraid to carry on with me any more, for fear that you should hear of it! But I don't mean to let him off so easily, I can tell you! He shall answer those letters, which you *say* he threw away in the grate, but which you are just as likely to have pilfered from his desk, before he is many days older!"

"You cannot *make* him answer them," said Elinor, proudly, "whatever you may affirm!"

"Not on paper perhaps, but by word of mouth! I will take them back to him at Aldershot, and see whether he can deny what I have told when he is face to face with me!"

"Surely!—surely!—you would never proceed to so unmaidenly an extremity," exclaimed Elinor, losing sight for a moment of her indignation in her horror at the idea. "You must not think of such a thing! You would create a scandal in the Camp! You would be despised for it ever after!"

"I can take care of myself!" replied Harriet, boldly, "you need not fear for me! And if even you *do* get your own way about this matter, you will have the satisfaction all your married life of knowing that your husband was a coward and a traitor to you, even during your engagement, and that you will never be able to trust him further than you can see him, to the end! If you can care for such a husband, take him, for I'm sure I wouldn't. But he shall answer to me for all that!"

"Oh! Miss Brandt, let me go, pray let me go!" said Elinor in a tone of such unmistakeable pain, that the other involuntarily drew back, and let her push her way past her to the door.

As Miss Leyton disappeared, Harriet Brandt commenced to pace up and down the length of the drawing-room. It was not the swaying walk of disappointment and despair; it was determined and masterful, born of anger and a longing for revenge. All the Creole in her, came to the surface—like her cruel mother, she would have given over Ralph Pullen to the vivisecting laboratory, if she could. Her dark eyes rolled in her passion; her slight hands were clenched upon each other; and her crimson lips quivered with the inability to express all she felt. Bobby, glancing in upon her from the French windows which opened on the garden, crept to her side and tried to capture her clenched hands, and to keep her restless body still. But she threw him off, almost brutally. At that moment she *was* brutal.

"Leave me alone," she exclaimed impatiently, "don't touch me! Go away!"

"O! Hally," the boy replied, sympathetically, "what is the matter? Has anyone offended you? Let me know? Let me try to comfort you! Or tell me what I shall do to help you."

"*Do!*" cried the girl, contemptuously, "what could *you* do?—a baby tied to your mother's apron-string! Leave me to myself, I say! I don't want you, or anyone! I want to be alone! Boys are of no use! It requires a *man* to revenge a woman's wrong!"

The lad, after one long look of bitter disappointment, walked quietly away from the spot, and hid his grief in some sequestered part of the garden. Hally despised him—she, who had kissed him and let him lay his head upon her shoulder and tell her all his little troubles—said he was of no use, when she stood in need of help and comfort! When, if she only knew it, he was ready to stand up in her defence against twenty men, if need be, and felt strong enough to defeat them all! But she had called him a baby, tied to his mother's apron-strings. The iron entered into his very soul.

Meanwhile, Elinor Leyton, having blindly found her way out of the Red House, hailed a passing hansom, and gave the driver directions to take her to a certain number in Harley Street, where Margaret Pullen was staying with her godfather, Doctor Phillips. She knew no one else to whom she could go in this great trouble, which made her feel as if her life had suddenly been cut in two. Yet she made no outward moan. Most young women having kept a bold front, as she had done, towards the enemy, would have broken down, as soon as they found themselves alone. But Elinor Leyton was not in the habit of breaking down. As soon as she had started for her destination, she leaned her head upon the back of the cab, closed her eyes and set her teeth fast together. Her face grew deadly pale, and an observer would have noted the trembling of her lips, and the ball which rose and fell in her throat. But she uttered no sound, not even a sigh—her misery was too deep for words.

Since she had returned to London, Margaret Pullen had stayed with Doctor Phillips, for he had insisted that it should be so. The telegram which had conveyed to Colonel Pullen the news of his little daughter's death, had been answered by one to say that he had applied for immediate leave, and should join his wife as soon as he received it. And Margaret was now expecting his arrival, every day—almost every hour. She looked very sad in her deep mourning dress, as she came forward to greet Elinor, but as soon as she caught sight of her visitor's face, she forgot her own trouble in her womanly sympathy for her friend.

"My dear Elinor!" she exclaimed, "what has brought you to town? You have bad news for me—I can read it in your eyes. Nothing wrong with Ralph, I hope!"

She kissed the girl affectionately, and held her hand, but Elinor did not answer. She turned her white face towards her friend, and bit her lips hard, but the words would not come.

"You are suffering, my poor dear," went on Margaret, tenderly, as she made her sit down, and removed her hat and cloak. "Can't you trust me with your trouble? Haven't I had enough of my own? Ah! cry, that's better. God sends us tears, in order that our hearts may not break! And now, what is it? Is anyone ill at home?"

Elinor shook her head. The tears were rolling slowly one by one, down her marble cheeks, but she jerked them away as they came, as though it were a shame to weep.

After a long pause, she swallowed something in her throat and commenced in a husky voice:

"It concerns Ralph, Margaret! He has been untrue to me! All is over between us!"

"Oh! surely not!" said Margaret, "have you had a full explanation with him? Who told you he had been untrue? Has Ralph asked for a release from his engagement?"

"No! but he shall have it!"

She then went on to tell the story of the finding of Harriet Brandt's letters in Captain Pullen's grate—and of the interview she had had with the girl that afternoon.

"She did not attempt to deny it," continued Elinor. "On the contrary she declared that he had made love to her all the time he was at Heyst—that he had said she was the only woman who had ever touched his heart, and that no man with human feelings could be happy with such a cold, reserved nature as mine! And if you could see her letters to him, Margaret—I wish I had not given them to her, but she snatched them from my hand—they were *too* dreadful! I never read such letters from a woman to a man. I did not know they could be written."

"But, Elinor, it strikes me that all this time, you have only heard one side of the question. What does it signify what Miss Brandt may say? The only thing of importance to you is, what Ralph will say."

"But there were her letters—they told their own story! They were full of nothing but 'dearests' and 'darlings', and reminders of how he had embraced her in one place, and what he had said to her in another—such letters as I could not write to a man, if it were to save my life!"

"I can quite understand that! Miss Brandt and you possess two totally different natures. And cannot you understand that a girl like that, half educated, wholly ignorant of the usages of society, with a passionate undeveloped nature and a bold spirit, might write as you have described her doing, against the wishes of the recipient of her letters? You say that Ralph threw her epistles in the grate just as they were. Does that look as if he valued them, or felt himself to be guilty concerning their reception?"

"But, Margaret, you know he *did* make himself con-

spicuous with the Gobellis and Miss Brandt at Heyst!
I think everyone noticed their intimacy!"

"I noticed it also, and I was very sorry for it, but,
Elinor, my dear, it was partly your own fault! You
were so much opposed to the idea of your engagement
to Ralph being made public, that I feared it might lead
to some *contretemps*. And then," she continued gently,
"don't be offended if I say that your reserve with him,
and your objection to anything like love-making on his
part is in itself calculated to drive a young man to
society he cares less for!"

"But—but—still—I love him!" said poor Elinor,
with a tremendous effort.

"I know you do," replied Margaret, kissing her
again, "and better and more faithfully, perhaps, than
half the women who show their love so openly—yet,
men are but men, Elinor, and as a rule they do not
believe in the affection which is never expressed by
caresses and fond words."

"Well! whether I have been right or wrong, it is
over now," said Miss Leyton, "and Ralph can go to
Miss Brandt or anyone else he chooses for amusement.
I shall never stand in his way, but I cannot brook an
affront, so I shall write and release him from his promise
to me at once!"

"No, no, Elinor, you must not do anything so rash!
I beg—I implore you, to do nothing, until Ralph has
had an opportunity of denying the charges brought
against him by this girl. They may be utterly untrue!
She may be simply persecuting him. Depend upon it,
you have only to ask him for an explanation of those
letters, and everything will be satisfactorily cleared up."

THE BLOOD OF THE VAMPIRE.

"You have more belief in him than I have, Margaret. Miss Brandt has great confidence in her cause. She told me that she had not only taken him from me, but she meant to keep him, and expressed her intention of going down to Aldershot and confronting Ralph with the letters she had written him!"

At this intelligence, Margaret grew alarmed for her friend's peace of mind.

"No! no! that must never be," she exclaimed, "that girl must not be permitted to make a scandal in the Camp, and get your name perhaps mixed up with it! It must be prevented."

"I fancy you will find that a difficult task," said Elinor; "she seems the most determined young woman I have ever come across. She became so vehement at last, that she frightened me, and I was only too glad to get out of the house."

"Elinor," said Mrs. Pullen suddenly, "will you leave this matter in my hands to settle in my own way?"

"What do you intend to do? See Miss Brandt yourself? I advise you not! She will only insult you, as she did me."

"No! I shall not see her myself, I promise you that, but I will send a proper ambassador to interview Miss Brandt and the Baroness. This sort of thing must not be allowed to go on, and unless Ralph comes forward to second the girl's assertions (which I am sure he will never do), she and her friend Madame Gobelli must be made to understand that if they don't behave themselves, the law will be called into requisition to enforce obedience. I should not be at all surprised if the Baroness were not at the bottom of all this."

"At anyrate, it has ruined my life!" said Elinor, mournfully.

"Nonsense! my dear girl, no such thing! It is only an unpleasant episode which will soon be forgotten. But let it make you a little more careful for the future, Elinor. Ralph is a very conceited man. He has been spoilt by the women all his life, '*pour l'amour de ses beaux yeux*.' He has been used to flattery and attention, and when he doesn't get it he misses it, and goes where it is to be found. It is rather a contemptible weakness, but he shares it in common with most of his sex, and you have promised, remember, to take him for better or worse!"

"Not yet, thank goodness!" retorted Elinor, with something of her usual spirit. "He and father got talking together about the marriage, the other day, when he was down at Richmond, and fixed it, I believe, for the spring, but they will have to unfix it again now, if I am not mistaken."

"No such thing," replied Margaret, "and now you have consented—have you not?—to leave the settlement of this other affair in my hands."

"If you wish it, Margaret! But, remember, no compromise! If Ralph has really promised this girl what she says, let him keep his promises, for I will have none of him. And now I must go home or they will wonder what has become of me!"   .

Margaret was not sorry to see her depart, for she was most anxious to summon Anthony Pennell, her husband's cousin, to her aid, and ask his advice as to what was best to be done in the circumstances.

She had great faith in Anthony Pennell, not only in

his genius, which was an accepted thing, but in his good sense, which is not usually found associated with the higher quality. He was a man of about thirty, with a grand intellect—a sound understanding—a liberal mind, and a sympathetic disposition. He had been originally intended for the Bar, but having "taken silk," and made a most promising debut, he had suddenly blossomed into an author, and his first novel had taken London by storm.

He had accomplished the rare feat of being lifted up at once on the waves of public opinion and carried over the heads of all his fellows.

Since his first success, he had continued writing— had given up the law in consequence—and was now making a large and steady income.

But Anthony Pennell's great charm lay in his unassuming manner and modest judgment of his own work. His triumphs were much more astonishing to him than to his friends. In person, he was less handsome than his cousin Ralph Pullen, but much more manly looking, having been a distinguished athlete in his College days, and still finding his best recreation on the cricket field and the golf ground. He was very fair, with a white skin, embrowned here and there by sun and outdoor exercise—short, curly hair—a fine figure, standing six foot high, and the bluest of blue eyes. He was smoking in his own chambers late that afternoon, when he received a telegram from Margaret Pullen, "Can you come over this evening?" and as soon as he had changed his lounging coat, he obeyed her summons.

CHAPTER XII.

ANTHONY PENNELL was a very fresh, pleasant, and good-looking presentment of a young English gentleman, as he entered the room where Margaret was sitting with Doctor Phillips that evening. It had been arranged between them beforehand, that as little as need be should be confided to him of Harriet Brandt's former history. All that was necessary for him to know, was the danger that threatened to blast the future happiness of Ralph Pullen and Elinor Leyton.

"Well! Mrs. Pullen," he said, as he shook hands cordially with Margaret and the doctor, "and what important business is it, that you want to consult me upon? I thought, at the very least, that I should meet my cousin Arthur here!"

"If I had had Arthur, perhaps I should not have needed you," replied Margaret, with a faint smile. "But really, Mr. Pennell, I am in want of advice sorely, and the Doctor agreed with me that you would be the best person to whom I could apply!"

"I am at your service, Madam!" said the young man, gaily, as he seated himself.

Then she told him the story of Harriet Brandt—how Ralph had met her at the Lion d'Or, and devoted his time to her—and how she was persecuting him with letters, and had threatened to follow him to the Camp and interview him there.

"And it must be put a stop to, you know, Mr. Pennell," she concluded, "not only for Ralph's sake and Elinor's, but for the sake of the Walthamstowes and my husband. I am sure that Arthur would be exceedingly annoyed at any scandal of that sort, and especially as Lord Walthamstowe is so old a friend of his family!"

Anthony Pennell had looked very grave during her recital. After a pause he said,

"Are you sure that Ralph has not given this young lady good cause to run after him?"

"I think not—I hope not! There was very little amusement in Heyst, and this girl, and the people with whom she is now staying—a Baron and Baroness Gobelli, they call themselves—were amongst the visitors to the Lion d'Or. Miss Leyton is rather a stickler for the proprieties, and used to refuse to walk out with Ralph alone in the evenings, and I was too much occupied with my poor darling baby to accompany them," said Margaret, in a faltering voice, "so Ralph took to going to the Baroness's private rooms instead, and became intimate with Miss Brandt!"

"You acknowledge then, that he *was* intimate with her!"

"I think he must have been—because it appears that he had agreed to join their party at Brussels, when—when—my great trouble obliged him to return to England with us instead."

"Did you know this young lady, Mrs. Pullen?"

"I did, and at one time I was rather intimate with her, that is, before the Baroness took her up, when she passed almost all her time with them."

"She is, I suppose, very attractive in person?"

"O! dear no, not at all!" cried Margaret, with a woman's dull appreciation of the charms of one of her own sex, "she has fine eyes, and what men would, I suppose, call a good figure, but no complexion and an enormous mouth. Not at all pretty, but nice-looking at times,—that is all!"

"Clever?" said Pennell, interrogatively.

"I do not think so! She had just come out of a Convent school and was utterly unused to society. But she has a very good voice and plays well on the mandoline!"

"Ladies are not always the best judges of their own sex," remarked Anthony, turning to Doctor Phillips, "what do *you* say, Doctor? Had you an opportunity of appraising Miss Brandt's beauties and accomplishments for yourself?"

"I would rather say nothing, Mr. Pennell," replied the Doctor. "The fact is, I knew her parents in the West Indies, and could never believe in anything good coming from such a stock. Whatever the girl may be, she inherits terrible proclivities, added to black blood. She is in point of fact a quadroon, and not fit to marry into any decent English family!"

"O! dear!" exclaimed Mr. Pennell laconically,

"And how do you expect me to help you?" he enquired, after a pause.

"I want you to see the Baroness, or Miss Brandt, and tell them that this girl must cease all communication with Captain Pullen," said Margaret, "tell them that he is engaged to marry Miss Leyton—that the marriage is fixed to take place next spring, and that the Walthamstowe family will be excessively annoyed if any scandal of this sort occurs to break it off."

"Do they not know that such an engagement exists?"

"No! that is the unfortunate part of it! Elinor Leyton is so absurdly scrupulous that she will not have the fact made public, and forbade me to tell Miss Brandt about it! Elinor went to the Red House where Miss Brandt is staying this morning and had a most stormy interview with her. She came here afterwards in a most distressed state of mind. Harriet Brandt had told her that she had secured Ralph Pullen and meant to keep him—that he had told her he loved her—and that Miss Leyton was too cold and prudish a nature for any man to be happy with! Of course Elinor was terribly upset. She seldom shows her feelings, but it was quite impossible for her to disguise them to-day. I begged her to leave the matter in my hands, and she consented to do so. That is why I telegraphed for you."

"It is rather an awkward predicament!" said Anthony Pennell, thoughtfully, "you will forgive me for saying, Mrs. Pullen, that Ralph is so very likely to have done this sort of thing, that I feel one might be treading on very delicate ground—in fact, putting one's foot in it— by interfering. You know what Ralph is—selfish and indolent and full of vanity. He considers it far too much trouble to make love (as it is called) to a woman, but he will accept any amount of love that is offered him, so long as it gives him no trouble. If this Miss Brandt is all that you and the doctor here say of her, she may possibly have drawn Ralph on, and taken his languid satisfaction as proof that he agreed to all she said and did. But it will make the *dénouement* just as unpleasant. Besides, how will Ralph himself take my interference in the matter? He may have some designs on this girl—some ideas in the future connected with her— and will ask what business I had to come between them."

"O! no! Did I not tell you that he had left her letters in his grate!"

"That might be part of his indolent carelessness, or they may have been left there by design, as a means of breaking the ice between himself and Miss Leyton. Is not he, after all, the most proper person to appeal to? Why not wait till your husband returns, and let him speak to his brother?"

"I am so afraid in that case, that Ralph might consider that he had gone too far with Miss Brandt, and honour demanded that he should marry her! And, Mr. Pennell, Doctor Phillips could tell you things, if he chose, to prove to you that Harriet Brandt is not a fit wife for any decent man."

Anthony Pennell thought again for a few minutes—sitting silent with his hand caressing his smooth chin. Then he said:

"If you are very much bent on my doing what I can in this matter, I see only one way to accomplish it. I must enter the Red House under a flag of truce. Did you know this Baroness Gobelli? Can you tell me what sort of woman she is? I never heard the name before!"

"She is quite a character," replied Margaret; "I believe her husband *is* a German Baron, but she was a Mrs. Bates, and is an extraordinary Baroness. A strange mixture also, of vulgarity and refined tastes. She drops all her aspirates, yet talks familiarly of aristocratic and royal titles, she dresses like a cook out on Sundays, and yet has a passion for good paintings and old china."

At the last words, Anthony Pennell pricked up his ears.

"A passion for old china!" he exclaimed, "then there must be some good in her!   Cannot you give me an introduction to the Red House on the plea that I am a connoisseur and am desirous of seeing her collection?"

"Of course I can, but how can you approach these people in amity, with a censure of Miss Brandt's conduct in your hand?   Madame Gobelli is infatuated with Harriet Brandt!   I was telling poor Elinor only this afternoon, that I should not be at all surprised if she were at the bottom of all this unpleasantness."

"She could not be at the bottom of anything unless Ralph had given her cause," replied Mr. Pennell, who had never had a good opinion of his cousin's straightforward dealing, "and however it may turn out, I should think he would have a heavy reckoning to settle with Miss Leyton!   This is not the first time, remember! You have not forgotten the trouble Arthur had to get him out of that scrape with the laundress's girl at Aldershot, the year before last!"

"Yes!   Arthur told me about it," replied Margaret. "But you are going to help us, this time, Mr. Pennell, are you not?"

"In so far as procuring an introduction to the Baroness, and taking my opportunity to let her know the true state of affairs with Miss Leyton, yes," said Mr. Pennell, "but there, my responsibility must cease.   Should Ralph have committed himself in writing, or anything of that sort, you must promise to let them fight it out their own way.   I daresay there will be no trouble about the matter.   I can see how it has occurred at a glance.   Ralph has been merely amusing himself with the girl, and she has taken his philandering in earnest.   But I wish he would leave that sort of thing off. It will ruin his married life if he does not!"

"Yes! indeed, and Elinor Leyton really loves him, more, I am sure, than he imagines. She declared this afternoon, that if it were not put a complete stop to, she should break off her engagement. And I think she would be right!"

"So do I," acquiesced Anthony Pennell. "Well! if these people are ordinarily decent, they will, as soon as they hear the truth, prevent their young friend interfering with another woman's rights. Write me the introduction, Mrs. Pullen, and I will pay the Red House a visit as soon as its owner gives me leave. And now let us talk of something pleasanter. How soon do you expect Arthur to arrive?"

"Any day," replied Margaret, "and I am longing so for him to come!"

"Of course you are! Will he remain long in England?"

"Only a few weeks! He has taken three months' leave. Then, I shall return with him to Hoosur."

"And you like the idea of India?"

"O! anything—anything—to find myself with him again," she answered feverishly.

The conversation turned upon more indifferent subjects, and armed with the note of introduction to the Baroness, Anthony Pennell presently took his leave. He did not like the task imposed upon him, and he hardly knew how he should set about it, but on consideration he thought he could do no harm by having a look at the young lady, who had taken the fancy of his fickle-minded cousin Ralph, and leaving his future action to be decided by the interview. He sat down therefore before turning into bed, and wrote a note to the Baroness, enclosing the introduction from Mrs. Pullen, and asking permission to call and inspect her rare collection of china, of which he had heard so much.

His letter reached the Red House on the following morning, at an unfortunate moment, when Madame Gobelli was giving full display to the worst side of her eccentric character.

The Baroness was not a lover of animals, either dogs or horses. She was merciless to the latter and the former she kicked whenever they came in her way. It was considered necessary, however, for the safety of the Red House, that it should be guarded by a watch-dog, and a miserable retriever, which answered to that name, lived in a rotten cask in the stable yard. This unhappy animal, which had neither sufficient food, exercise, nor straw to lie on, was in the habit of keeping up a continuous baying at night, in remonstrance at the cruelty of its treatment, which was a cause of annoyance to the neighbours, who had often written to the Baroness about it in vain.

On the morning in question, a Captain Hill, who lived on one side of the Red House, with his parents, sent in his card to Madame Gobelli and asked for an interview. She admitted him at once. She liked men of all sorts, and particularly if they were young and she could kiss them with impunity, under the pretence that she was old enough to be their mother.

She therefore welcomed Captain Hill quite amiably. She came in from the garden to receive him, attired in a Genoa velvet dress that trailed half a yard on the damp ground behind, and a coarse Zulu hat perched on her large bullet head. She was attended by Harriet Brandt, who had been making a tour of the premises with her, and was always eager to see anybody who might call at the Red House. Miss Wynward also, who was dusting the china with a feather brush as the visitor was announced, continued her occupation, and without apologising for doing so, or asking leave.

Harriet had not yet been able to determine the exact place which this lady held in the Baroness's household, for she was treated as one of the family, and yet degraded at times to the position of a servant.

The Baroness expected her to cook, or dust rooms, or darn stockings, or do anything required of her, whilst she introduced her to all her friends as if on a perfect equality with themselves. As she entered the drawing-room through one of the French windows, she shook hands familiarly with Captain Hill, and introduced him to both her companions.

"Well!" she went on, "and so you've come to see us at last! I thought you were going to live and die in that tumble-down old place of yours, without so much as a shake of the 'and! I 'ope you're all well at 'ome!"

The stranger did not seem to know how to receive these civilities. He had not seated himself, but stood in the centre of the room with his hat in his hand, as though he found a difficulty in stating his errand at the Red House.

"Take a chair," said Madame Gobelli in her rough way, "there's enough and to spare, and my young friend 'ere won't eat you!"

Still Captain Hill deliberated about accepting her offer.

"Thank you," he commenced, "but I shall not detain you above a few moments. I came to speak to you about your dog, Madame Gobelli. My parents are both very old, and my mother especially delicate—indeed, I fear that she may never rise from her bed again!"

Here his voice faltered a little, but quickly recovering himself he went on,

"She sleeps very little, and that little has now become impossible to her on account of the incessant barking of your yard dog. I am here to-day by the wish of my mother's medical attendant, Doctor Parker, to tell you that the noise is seriously affecting her health, and to beg that you will adopt some measures to have the annoyance stopped."

As the Baroness understood the reason for which her neighbour had called upon her, her countenance palpably changed. The broad smile faded from her face and was replaced by an ominous frown. If there was one thing which she resented above another, it was being called to task for any disturbance in her household. Without taking any notice apparently of Captain Hill's complaint, she turned to Miss Wynward and said,

"Miss Wynward, come 'ere! Does that dog bark at night?"

"Sometimes, my lady," replied the governess dubiously.

"I don't believe it! You're lying! 'Arriet, does Nelson ever bark so as to disturb anyone?"

"He barks whenever there is a ring at the bell, or a stranger enters the grounds, Madame," said Harriet, with politic evasion.

"Oh! I assure you he does more than that!" inter-

posed the visitor, "the poor animal howls without ceas-
ing. Either he is ill, or the servants do not give him
sufficient food!"

But at this censure cast upon her domestics whom
she bullied from morning till night, the Baroness's un-
controlled temper burst forth.

"'Ow dare you come 'ere," she exclaimed loudly,
"and bring false accusations against my servants? No
one in this 'ouse is kept short of food. What do you
mean—a rubbishing fellow like you—by coming 'ere,
and accusing the Baron of starving 'is animals? There's
more money spent upon our animals, I bet, than goes
in your poverty-stricken 'ouse-'old in a year!"

Captain Hill was now offended, as he well might be.

"I do not know what knowledge you may possess
of the exigencies of my parents' household, Madam," he
replied, "but what I came here to tell you is this—that
from whatever cause it may arise, the howling and whin-
ing of your dog is a public nuisance and it must be
stopped!"

"Must, must!" exclaimed Madame Gobelli, shaking
her stick at him, "and pray 'oo's to make me stop it?"

"_I_ will," said Captain Hill, "the noise is endanger-
ing the life of my mother, and I shall insist upon the
animal being destroyed, or taken elsewhere. If you cannot take a friendly hint—if you have so callous a nature
that the sufferings of an aged and invalid lady cannot
excite your sympathy, the law shall teach you that, whatever you may fail to feel, you cannot annoy your neighbours with impunity!"

"Fine neighbours indeed!" cried the Baroness, her
whole face trembling and contorted with passion. "A

beggarly lot of half-pay officers and retired parsons! I'll soon see if you'll be allowed to come riding the 'igh 'orse over me! Confound your impudence! Do you know 'oo I am?"

"A Billingsgate fishwoman, I should imagine, from your language! Certainly not a gentlewoman!" said Captain Hill, his eyes blazing with his wrath.

"'Ang you! I'll soon teach you 'ow to insult a lady that's connected with Royalty!"

At that, the stranger burst into a derisive laugh.

"Down the back stairs!" he muttered to himself, but Madame Gobelli caught the words.

"Get out of my 'ouse," she cried. "'Ere, Miss Wynward, see this fellow out at the front door, and never you let 'im in again, or I'll give you a month's warning! Down the back stairs indeed! Confound you! If you don't clear out this very minute, I'll lay my stick across your back! You'll make me destroy my dog, will you, and just because your trumpery mother don't like 'is barking! Go 'ome and tell 'er to 'old 'er own row! And you accuse my servants of not giving 'im enough to eat. You'd be glad enough to see 'is dinner on your own table once or twice a week. Out with you, I say— out with you at once, and don't let me see your ugly mug and your carroty 'ead in 'ere again, or I'll set the dog you don't like upon you."

Captain Hill had turned white as a sheet with anger.

"You'll hear more of this, Madam, and from my solicitor next time," he said. "Heartless, unfeeling woman! How can you call yourself a mother, when you have no pity for a son's grief at his mother's illness? Pray God you may not have occasion to remember this

morning, when you have to part from your own
son!"

He rushed from the room as he spoke, and they
heard the hall door slam after him. For a minute after
he left, there was a dead pause between the three women.
His last words seemed to have struck the Baroness as
with a two-edged sword. She stood silent, staring into
vacancy, and breathing hard, whilst Harriet Brandt and
Miss Wynward regarded each other with furtive dismay.
The silence was broken by Madame Gobelli bursting
into a harsh laugh.

"I don't fancy 'e will show 'is face in my 'ouse again,
in an 'urry," she exclaimed. "It was as good as a play
to watch 'im, trying to brave it out! Confound 'is old
mother! Why don't she die and 'ave done with it! I've
no patience with old people 'anging on in that way, and
worrying the 'ole world with their fads! Well! what is
it?" she continued to a maid who brought her a
letter.

"By the post, my lady!"

The Baroness broke the seal. There was such a
look of scare upon her features, that some people might
have thought she was glad to have anything to do that
should hide it from her companions. The letter was
from Anthony Pennell, whose name was familiar to her,
as to all the world.

As she finished its perusal, her manner entirely
altered. The broad smile broke out on her countenance
—her eyes sparkled—one would have thought she could
never be in anything but a beaming good temper.

"'Olloa! 'Arriet!" she exclaimed, "'ere's news for
you! 'Oo do you think this letter's from?"

"How can I guess?" replied the girl, though her thoughts had flown at once to Ralph Pullen.

"From Mr. Anthony Pennell, the great author, you know, and own cousin to that rapscallion, Captain Pullen! Now we shall 'ear all about the 'andsome Captain! Mr. Pennell says 'e wants to come 'ere and see my china, but I know better! 'E's bringing you a message from 'is cousin, mark my words! I can see it written up be'ind you!"

Harriet's delicate face flushed with pleasure at the news.

"But why shouldn't Captain Pullen have come himself?" she asked, anxiously.

"I can't tell you that! Perhaps 'e is coming, be'ind the other, and this is only a feeler! There's wheels within wheels in these big families, sometimes, you know, and the Pullens are connected with a lot of big-wigs! But we'll 'ave some news, anyway! You just sit down, my dear, and write Mr. Pennell a pretty note in my name— you write a prettier 'and than I do—and say we shall be very pleased to see 'im to-morrow afternoon, if convenient, and I 'ope 'e will stay to dinner afterwards and be introduced to the Baron—will you?"

"O! yes, of course, Madame, if you wish it!" replied the girl, smiles dimpling her face at the thought of her triumph over Elinor Leyton.

"Now, Miss Wynward, we must 'ave a first-rate dinner to-morrow for Mr. Pennell, and you and Bobby 'ad better dine at one o'clock, or you'll spoil the table. Let me see! We'll 'ave——"

But turning to enforce her orders, the Baroness discovered that Miss Wynward had quitted the room.

"Why! where 'as the woman gone? Did you see 'er leave the room, 'Arriet?"

"I did not! I was too much occupied listening to you," replied the girl from the table, where she was inditing the answer to Anthony Pennell's note.

"'Ere, Miss Wynward! Miss Wynward!" screamed the Baroness from the open door, but no reply came to her call.

"I must go and see after 'er!" she said, as she stumped from the room, as intent upon procuring a good dinner for one young man, as she had been in insulting the other, and turning him from her doors.

Meanwhile Captain Hill, hot and angry, was striding away in the direction of his own home, when he heard a soft voice calling his name in the rear. He turned to encounter the spare, humiliated form of Miss Wynward.

"Captain Hill," she ejaculated, "I beg your pardon, but may I speak to you for a moment?"

Recognising her as having been in the room, when the Baroness had so grossly insulted him, he waited rather coldly for her to come up with him.

"Don't think me impertinent or interfering," faltered Miss Wynward, "but I was so shocked—so distressed— I could not let you go without saying how grieved and sorry I am!"

"I do not quite understand you," replied Captain Hill.

"O! yes, surely, did you not see me in the room just now! I felt as if I should die of shame! But if you knew what it is to be dependent—to be unable to speak or to expostulate—you would guess perhaps——"

"Yes! Yes! I think I can understand. But pray don't

distress yourself about it! It was my own fault! I should have addressed her first through my solicitor. But I thought she was a gentlewoman!"

"It is her temper that gets the better of her," said Miss Wynward in an apologetic tone, "she is not always so bad as she was this morning!"

"That is fortunate for the world at large," replied Captain Hill, gravely. "I could have forgiven her vulgarity, but not her heartlessness. I can only think that she is a most terrible woman."

"That is what everybody says," answered his companion, "but she will admit of no remonstrance. She *will* have her own way, and the Baron is as powerless to refrain her, as you, or I. But that she should so insult a gentleman like yourself, even descending to oaths and personalities—O! I cannot tell you how much I felt it—how ashamed I was, and how anxious that you should not confound me with anything the Baroness said, or did!"

"Indeed," said Captain Hill, holding out his hand, "you need have no fear on that score. I hope I know a gentlewoman when I see her! But tell me, since your eyes are open to all this, how is it that a lady like yourself can stay under the roof of so terrible a person? There are plenty of other situations to be had! Why do you not leave her, and go elsewhere?"

He was struck by the look of mingled anxiety and fear with which she regarded him.

"O! Captain Hill, there are reasons that are difficult to explain—that I could not tell to anyone on so short an acquaintance. But the Baroness possesses great power—she could ruin me, I believe she could *kill* if she chose!"

14*

"She threatens you then!"

"Yes!" came from Miss Wynward's lips, but in almost a whisper.

"Well! this is hardly the time and place to discuss such a question," said Captain Hill, "but I should much like to see more of you, Miss Wynward! If you have any time at your disposal, will you come over and see my old mother? She is quite confined to her room, but I know it would please her to have a quiet talk with you!"

A light glistened in Miss Wynward's washed-out eyes, and a smile stole over her countenance.

"Do you really mean it, Captain Hill?"

"I never say anything that I do not mean," he answered, "I am sure both my parents would be glad to give you their advice, and my dear father, who is a clergyman, though past an active ministry, may be able to be of use to you in a more practical way. At any-rate, you will come and see us. That is a bargain!" and he held out his hand to her again in farewell.

"O! I will—I will, indeed," exclaimed Miss Wynward, gratefully, "and thank you so very much for the per-mission. You have put a little hope into my life!"

She seized the hand he proffered her, and kissed it, as an inferior might have done, and then hurried back to the Red House, before he had had time to remonstrate with her on the proceeding.

CHAPTER XIII.

WHEN Anthony Pennell received the Baroness's in-vitation, penned in the delicate foreign handwriting of Harriet Brandt, he accepted it at once. Being out of the season, he had no engagement for that evening, but he would have broken twenty engagements, sooner than miss the chance, so unexpectedly offered him, of meeting in an intimate family circle, the girl who appeared to have led his cousin Ralph's fancy astray. He pictured her to himself as a whitey-brown young woman with thick lips and rolling eyes, and how Ralph, who was so daintily particular where the *beau sexe* was concerned, could have been attracted by such a specimen, puzzled Anthony altogether. The knowledge that she had money struck him unpleasantly, for he could think of no other motive for Captain Pullen having philandered with her, as he evidently had done. At anyrate, the idea that there was the least chance of allying herself with their family, must be put out of her head, at once and for ever.

Mr. Pennell amused himself with thinking of the scare he should create at the dinner table, by "springing" the news of Ralph's intended marriage upon them, all at once. Would the young lady have hysterics, he wondered, or faint away, or burst into a passion of tears? He laughed inwardly at the probability! He felt very cruel over it! He had no pity for the poor quadroon, as Doctor Phillips had called her. It was better that she should suffer, than that Elinor Leyton should have to break off her engagement. And, by Margaret Pullen's account, Miss Brandt had been both defiant and insulting to Miss Leyton. She must be a brazen, unfeeling sort of girl—it was meet that she paid the penalty of her foolhardiness.

It was in such a mood that Anthony Pennell arrived at the Red House at five o'clock in the afternoon, that he might have the opportunity to inspect the collection of china that had gained him an entrance there.

The Baroness had promised to be home in time to receive· him, but he was punctual and she was not. Harriet Brandt was loitering about the garden, which was still pleasant enough on fine days in the middle of September, when the news that Mr. Pennell was in the drawing-room was brought to her by Miss Wynward. Harriet had been very eager to meet Anthony Pennell— not because she was pining after his cousin, but because her feminine curiosity was strong to discover *why* Ralph had deserted her, and if he had been subjected to undue influence to force him to do so. But now that the time had come, she felt shy and nervous. Suppose he, Mr. Pennell, had seen Miss Leyton meanwhile, and heard all that had taken place between them, when she visited the Red House. And suppose he should take Miss Leyton's part! Harriet's mind was full of "supposes" as she turned to Miss Wynward and said,

"O! I can't go and receive him, Miss Wynward! Mr. Pennell has come to see the Baroness, not me! Cannot you entertain him until she comes home? She will not be long now!"

"Her ladyship's last words to me, Miss Brandt, were, that if she had not returned from the factory by the time Mr. Pennell arrived, you were to receive him and give him afternoon tea in her stead! I hope you will do as her ladyship desired!"

"Well! I suppose I must then," replied Harriet, screwing up her mouth, with a gesture of dissatisfaction, "but do send in the tea, quickly, please!"

"It shall be up, Miss Brandt, as soon as I can get

back to make it! Mr. Pennell seems a very pleasant gentleman! I wouldn't mind if I were you!"

Miss Wynward hurried back to the house, as she spoke, and Harriet walked slowly over the lawn towards the drawing-room windows.

Anthony Pennell, who had been bending over some rare specimens of old Chelsea, looked up suddenly as she approached, and was struck dumb with admiration. She had improved wonderfully in looks since she had been in Europe, though the women who lived with her continually, were slow to perceive it. Her delicate complexion had acquired a colour like that of a blush rose, which was heightened by contrast with her dark, glowing eyes, whilst her hair, by exposure to the rays of the sun, had caught some of its fire and showed ruddily, here and there, in streaks of auburn. Her figure, without having lost its lissom grace, was somewhat fuller, and her manner was altogether more intelligent, and less *gauche* than it had been. But the dark eyes were still looking for their prey, and the restless lips were incessantly twitching and moving one over the other. She was beautifully dressed that evening—she had not been in London for a month, without finding a way to spend her money—and Anthony Pennell, like most artistic natures, was very open to the influence of dress upon a woman. Harriet wore a frock of the palest lemon colour, cut quite plain, but perfect in every line and pleat and fold, and finished off at the throat with some rare lace, caught up here and there with tiny diamond pins.

"By Jove! what a beautiful girl!" was Mr. Pennell's inward ejaculation as he saw her drawing nearer the spot where he stood. It was strange that his first

judgment of Harriet Brandt should have been the same
as that of his cousin, Ralph Pullen, but it only proves
from what a different standpoint men and women judge
of beauty.   As Harriet walked over the grass, Anthony
Pennell noted each line of her swaying figure—each tint
of her refined face—with the pretty little hands hanging
by her side, and the slumbrous depths of her magnificent
eyes.   He did not, for one moment, associate her with
the idea which he had formed of the West Indian heiress
who was bent on capturing his cousin Ralph.   He concluded she was another young friend who might be
partaking of the Baroness's hospitality.   He bowed low
as she entered through the open French window looking
as a Georgian or Cashmerian houri might have looked,
he thought, if clad in the robes of civilisation.   Harriet
bowed in return, and said timidly,

"I am so sorry that Madame Gobelli is not here to
receive you, but she will not keep you waiting more than
a few minutes, I am sure.   She particularly said that
she would not be later than five o'clock."

"She has left a very charming substitute in her
place," replied Pennell, with another bow.

"I believe you have come to see the china," continued Harriet, "I do not know much about it myself,
but Miss Wynward will be here in a minute, and she
knows the name of every piece, and where it came
from!"

"That will be eminently satisfactory," rejoined Anthony Pennell, "but I happen to be a connoisseur in
such things myself.   I have one or two charming bits
of old Sèvres and Majolica in my chambers, which I
think the Baroness would like to see if she will honour

me with a visit to my little place. A lonely bachelor like myself must take up some hobby, you know, to fill his life, and mine happens to be china. Madame Gobelli appears to have some lovely Chelsea there. I would like to steal one or two of those groups on the cabinet. Will you hold the door open for me, whilst I run away with them?"

At this sally, Harriet laughed, and Mr. Pennell thought she looked even handsomer when she laughed than when she was pensive.

"Here is the tea!" she cried nervously, as Miss Wynward appeared with the tray. "O! Miss Wynward, surely Madame cannot be much longer now! Have you looked down the road to see if she is coming?"

"The carriage has just turned into the stable yard," replied Miss Wynward, and in another minute, the doorway was filled with the ample proportions of the Baroness.

"'Olloa! Mr. Pennell, and so you've stolen a march upon me!" was her first greeting, "'ow are you?" extending her enormous hand, "'ave you been looking at the china? Wait till I've 'ad my tea; I'll show you one or two bits that'll make your mouth water! It's my 'obby! I used to save my pocket money when I was a little gal to buy china. I remember my grandfather, the Dook of—but there, I 'aven't known you long enough to let you into family secrets. Let's 'ave our tea and talk afterwards! I 'ope 'Arriet 'as entertained you well!"

"This young lady—" commenced Anthony Pennell, interrogatively.

"To be sure, Miss 'Arriet Brandt! 'Asn't she introduced 'erself to you? She's like a daughter of the 'ouse to us! We look upon 'er as one of our own, Gustave

and me! Miss Brandt from Jamaica! And she knew
your cousin, Captain Pullen, too, at Heyst, we all did,
and we're dying to 'ear what 'as become of 'im, for 'e's
never shown 'is face at the Red 'Ouse!"

The murder was out now, and Harriet waited trem-
blingly for the result! What did Mr. Pennell know?
What would he say?

But Mr. Pennell said nothing—he was too much
startled to speak. *This,* Harriet Brandt—this lovely girl,
the quadroon of whom both Doctor Phillips and Mrs.
Pullen had spoken so disparagingly?—of whom they had
said that she was not fit to be the wife of any decent
man? Oh! they must be fools and blind—or he was
dreaming! The Baroness was not slow to see the look
upon his face and to interpret it rightly.

"Are you surprised? You needn't look so incredulous!
I give you my word that this is 'Arriet Brandt—the
same young lady that knew Mrs. Pullen and her brother-
in-law and Miss Leyton over at Heyst. What sort of a
character 'ave they been giving 'er be'ind 'er back?"

"Indeed, I assure you, Madame—" commenced Mr.
Pennell, deprecatingly.

"You needn't take the trouble to tell any tarradiddles
about it! I can see it in your face! I didn't think
much of that cousin of yours from the beginning; 'e's
got a shifty sort of look, and as for that cold bit of
goods, Miss Leyton, well, all I say is, God 'elp the man
that marries 'er, for she's enough to freeze the sun himself! But I liked Mrs. Pullen well enough, and I was
sorry to 'ear that she 'ad lost 'er baby, for she was
quite wrapt up in it! But I daresay she'll soon 'ave
another!"

Without feeling it incumbent on him to enter into an argument as to the probability of the Baroness's last suggestion, Anthony Pennell was glad of the digression, as it gave him an opportunity of slurring over the dangerous subject of Ralph Pullen's character.

"The loss of her child was a very great blow to my poor cousin," he replied, "and she is still suffering from it, bitterly. Else, I have no doubt that you would have seen something of her—and the others," he added in a lower tone. After a slight interval, he ventured to raise his eyes and see how the girl opposite to him had taken what was said, but it did not appear to have made much impression on her—she was, on the contrary, gazing at him with that magnetic glánce of hers as though she wanted to read into his very soul.

"Don't go and say that I want to see 'em," said the Baroness as, having devoured enough cake and bread and butter to feed an ordinary person for a day, she rose and led the way into another room. "I don't want to see anybody at the Red 'Ouse that doesn't want to come, and I 'aven't expected the ladies. But as for Captain Pullen, 'oo made an engagement to follow our party to Brussels, and then never took the trouble to write a line to excuse 'imself for breaking 'is word, why, I say 'e's a jerry sneak, and you may tell 'im so if you like! *We* didn't want 'im. 'E proposed to come 'imself, and I engaged 'is room and everything, and then 'e skedaddled without a word, and I call it beastly be- 'aviour. You mustn't mind my plain speaking, Mr. Pennell. I always say what I think! And I would like to break my stick over Captain Pullen's back and that's the truth."

They were walking along the passage now, on their way to the Baron's library—the Baroness in front with her hand leaning heavily on Pennell's shoulder, and Harriet lingering a little behind. Anthony Pennell pondered awhile before he replied. Was this the time to announce Ralph's intended marriage. How would the girl behind them take it?

He turned slightly and looked at her face as the thought passed through his mind. Somehow the eyes that met his reassured him. He began to think it must be a mistake—that she did not care for Ralph as much as Mrs. Pullen had supposed—that she was only offended perhaps (as her hostess evidently was) by the curt and uncivil manner in which he had treated them both. So he replied,

"I have not the slightest excuse to make for my cousin's conduct, Madame Gobelli. It appears to me that he has treated you with very scant civility, and he ought to be ashamed of himself. But as you know, his little niece's death was very sudden and unexpected, and the least he could do was to escort his sister-in-law and Miss Leyton back to England, and since then——"

"Well! and what since then?" demanded the Baroness, sharply.

"Lord Walthamstowe and he have come to an arrangement," said Pennell, speaking very slowly, "that his marriage with Miss Elinor Leyton shall take place sooner than was at first intended. The Limerick Rangers are under orders for foreign service, and Captain Pullen naturally wishes to take his wife out with him, and though, of course, all this is no excuse for his omitting to write you a letter, the necessary preparations and the consequent excitement *may* have put his duty out of his head. Of course," he continued, "you know that Ralph is engaged to marry Miss Leyton?"

"I 'eard something of it," replied the Baroness reluctantly, "but one never knows what is true and what is not. Anyway, Captain Pullen didn't give out the news 'imself! 'E seemed 'appy enough without Miss Leyton, didn't 'e, 'Arriet?"

But turning round to emphasise her words, she found that Harriet had not followed them into the library. Whereupon she became confidential.

"To tell you the truth, Mr. Pennell," she continued, "'e just be'aved like a scoundrel to our little 'Arriet there. 'E ran after the gal all day, and spent all 'is evenings in our private sitting-room, gazing at 'er as if 'e would eat 'er, whilst she sang and played to 'im. 'E never said a word about marrying Miss Leyton. It was all ''Ally, 'Ally, 'Ally' with 'im. And if the gal 'adn't been a deal too clever for 'im, and wise enough to see what a vain zany 'e is, she might 'ave broken 'er 'eart over it. The conceited jackanapes!"

"But she has not fretted," said Anthony Pennell eagerly.

"Not she! I wouldn't let 'er! She's meat for Captain Pullen's master! A gal with fifteen 'undred a year in 'er own 'ands, and with a pair of eyes like that! Oh! no! 'Arriet can pick up a 'usband worth two of your cousin any day!"

"I should think so indeed," replied Mr. Pennell fervently, "I have heard Mrs. Pullen mention Miss Brandt, but she did not prepare me for meeting so beautiful a girl. But I can hardly wonder at my cousin running away from her, Madame Gobelli. Knowing himself to be already engaged, Miss Brandt must have proved a most dangerous companion. Perhaps he found his heart was no longer under his own control, and thought discretion the better part of valour. You must try and look upon his conduct in the best light you can!"

"Oh! well! it don't signify much anyway, for 'e's no miss at the Red 'Ouse, I can tell you, and 'Arriet could marry to-morrow if she chose, and to a man worthy of 'er. But now you must look at my Spode."

She walked up to a tall cabinet at one end of the room, which was piled with china, and took up a fragile piece in her hands.

"Do you see that?" she said, turning up the plate and showing the mark upon the bottom, "there it is, you see! There's the M. These five pieces are said to be the oldest in existence. And here's a cup of Limoges. And that's Majolica. Do you know the marks of Majolica. They're some of the rarest known! A cross on a shield. The first real bit of china I ever possessed was a Strasbourg. Have you ever seen any Dutch Pottery—marked with an A.P.? I picked that up at an old Jew's shop in the market in Naples. And this Capo di Monte, strange to say, in a back alley in Brighton. There's nothing I like better than to grub about back slums and look for something good. Some of my best pieces 'ave come out of pawnbrokers' shops. That plate you're looking at is old Flemish—more than two 'undred years, I believe! It came out of the rag market at Bruges. There used to be first-rate pickings to be 'ad at Bruges and Ghent and in Antwerp some years ago, but the English 'ave pretty well cleared 'em out."

"I never saw a better private collection, Madame Gobelli," said Anthony Pennell, as he gloated over the delicate morsels of Sèvres and Limoges and Strasbourg. "The Baron should have had an old curiosity and bric-a-brac establishment, instead of anything so prosaic as boots and shoes."

"O! I couldn't 'ave 'ad it!" exclaimed the Baroness, "it would 'ave gone to my 'eart to sell a good bargain when I 'ad made it! My cups and saucers and plates and teapots are like children to me, and if I thought my Bobby would sell 'em when I was gone, I believe I should rise from my grave and whack 'im."

The woman became almost womanly as her eyes rested lovingly on her art treasures. It seemed incongruous to Pennell, to watch her huge coarse hands, with their thick stumpy fingers and broad chestnut nails, fingering the delicate fabric with apparent carelessness. Cup after cup and vase and plate she almost tossed over each other, as she pushed some away to make room for others, and piled them up on the top of one another, until he trembled lest they should all come toppling down together.

"You are more used to handle these treasures than I am," he remarked presently, "I should be too much afraid of smashing something, to move them so quickly as you do."

"I never broke a bit of china in my life," returned the Baroness energetically. "I've broken a stick over a man's back, more than once, but never 'ad an accident with my plates and dishes. 'Ow do you account for that?"

"You must have a flow of good luck!" said Mr.

Pennell, "I am so fearful for mine that I keep all the best under glass!"

"I 'ave more friends to 'elp me than perhaps you know of," said the Baroness, mysteriously, "but it ain't only that! I never let a servant dust it! Miss Wynward does it, but she's too much afraid to do more than touch 'em with the tip of her feather brush. They come to me sometimes and complain that the china is dirty. 'Let it be dirty,' I say, '*that* won't break it, but if you clean it, you will!' Ha! ha! ha!"

At that moment Harriet Brandt entered the room, moving sinuously across the carpet as a snake might glide to its lair. Anthony Pennell could not take his eyes off that gliding walk of hers. It seemed to him the very essence of grace. It distracted all his attention from the china.

"The Baron has just come in," observed Harriet to her hostess.

"Oh! well! come along and leave the rest of the china till after dinner," said Madame Gobelli. "Gustave likes to 'ave 'is dinner as soon as 'e comes 'ome."

She thrust her arm through that of Anthony Pennell, and conducted him to the dining-room, where the Baron (without having observed the ceremony of changing his coat or boots) was already seated just as he had come in, at the table. He gave a curt nod to the visitor as Mr. Pennell's name was mentioned to him, and followed it up immediately by a query whether he would take fish. Mr. Pennell sat out the meal with increasing amazement at every course. He, who was accustomed, in consequence of his popularity, to sit at the tables of some of the highest in the land, could liken this one to nothing but a farmhouse dinner. Course succeeded course, in rapid succession, and there was no particular fault to find with anything, but the utter want of ceremony—the mingling of well-known and aristocratic names with the boot and shoe trade—and the way in which the Baron and Baroness ate and drank, filled him with surprise. The climax was reached when Mr. Milliken, who was late for dinner, entered the room, and his hostess, before introducing him to the stranger, saluted him with a resounding smack on either cheek.

Pennell thought it might be his turn next, and shuddered. But the wine flowed freely, and the Baroness, being in an undoubted good humour, the hospitality was unlimited. After dinner, the Baron having settled to sleep in an armchair, Madame Gobelli proposed that the party should amuse themselves with a game of "Hunt the slippers."

She was robed in an expensive satin dress, but she threw herself down on the ground with a resounding thump, and thrusting two enormous feet into view, offered her slipper as an inducement to commence the game.

Pennell stood aloof, battling to restrain his laughter at the comical sight before him. The Baroness's foot, from which she had taken the shoe, was garbed in a black woollen stocking full of holes, which displayed a set of bare toes. But, apparently quite unaware of the ludicrous object she presented, she kept on calling out for Harriet Brandt and Miss Wynward to come and complete the circle at which only Mr. Milliken and herself were seated. But Harriet shrank backwards and refused to play.

"No! indeed, Madame, I cannot. I do not know your English games!" she pleaded.

"Come on, we'll teach you!" screamed Madame Gobelli, "'ere's Milliken, 'e knows all about it, don't you, Milliken? 'E knows 'ow to look for the slipper under the gal's petticoats. You come 'ere, 'Arriet, and sit next me, and Mr. Pennell shall be the first to 'unt. Come on!"

But Miss Brandt would not "come on". She remained seated, and declared that she was too tired to play and did not care for *les jeux innocents,* and she had a headache, and anything and everything, before she would comply with the outrageous request preferred to her.

Madame Gobelli grumbled at her idleness and called her disobliging, but Anthony admired the girl for her steadfast refusal. He did not like to see her in the familiar society of such a woman as the Baroness—he would have liked still less to see her engaged in such a boisterous and unseemly game as "Hunt the slipper."

He took the opportunity of saying,

"Since you are disinclined for such an energetic game, Miss Brandt, perhaps you would oblige me by singing a song! I should so much like to hear the mandoline. Mrs. Pullen has spoken to me of your efficiency on it."

"If Madame Gobelli wishes it, I have no objection," replied Harriet.

"Oh! well! if you are all going to be so disagreeable as not to play a good game," said the Baroness, as Mr. Milliken pulled her on her feet again, "'Arriet may as well sing to us! But a good romp first wouldn't 'ave done us any 'arm!"

She adjourned rather sulkily to a distant sofa with Mr. Milliken, where they entertained each other whilst Harriet tuned her mandoline and presently let her rich voice burst forth in the strains of "Oh! ma Charmante." Anthony Pennell was enchanted. He had a passion for music, and it appealed more powerfully to him than anything else. He sat in rapt attention until Harriet's voice had died away, and then he implored her to sing another song.

"You cannot tell what it is for me, who care more for music than for anything else in this world, to hear a voice like yours. Why! you will create a perfect *furore* when you go into society. You could make your fortune on the stage, but I know you have no need of that!"

"Oh! one never knows what one may have need of," said Harriet gaily, as she commenced "Dormez, ma belle", and sang it to perfection.

"You must have had a very talented singing-master," observed Pennell when the second song was finished.

"Indeed no! My only instructress was a nun in the Ursuline Convent in Jamaica. But I always loved it," said the girl, as she ran over the strings of her mandoline in a merry little tarantelle, which made everyone in the room feel as if they had been bitten by the spider from which it took its name, and wanted above all other things to dance.

How Pennell revelled in the music and the performer! How he longed to hear from her own lips that Ralph's treatment had left no ill effects behind it.

When she had ceased playing, he drew nearer to

15*

her, and under the cover of the Baroness's conversation
with Mr. Milliken and the Baron's snores, they managed
to exchange a few words.

"How can I ever thank you enough for the treat
you have given me!" he began.

"I am very glad that you liked it!"

"I was not prepared to hear such rare talent! My
experience of young ladies' playing and singing has not
hitherto been happy. But you have great genius. Did
you ever sing to Mrs. Pullen whilst in Heyst?"

"Once or twice."

"And to my cousin, Ralph Pullen?"

"Yes!"

"I cannot understand his having treated the Baroness
with such scant courtesy. And you also, who had been
kind enough to allow him to enjoy your society. You
would not have found me so ungrateful. But you have
heard doubtless that he is going to be married shortly!"

"Yes! I have heard it!"

"And that has, I suppose, put everything else out
of his head! Perhaps it may be as well, especially for
his future wife. There are some things which are
dangerous for men to remember—such as your lovely
voice, for example!"

"Do you think so?" Harriet fixed her dark eyes
on him, as she put the question.

"I am sure it will be dangerous for me, unless you
will give me leave to come and hear it again. I shall
not be able to sleep for thinking of it. Do you think
the Baroness will be so good as to enrol me as a visitor
to the house?"

"You had better ask her!"

"And if she consents, will you sing to me some-times?"

"I am always singing or playing! There is nothing else to do here. The Baron and Baroness are almost always out, and I have no company but that of Bobby and Miss Wynward. It is terribly dull, I can tell you. I am longing to get away, but I do not know where to go."

"Have you no friends in England?"

"Not one, except Mr. Tarver, who is my solicitor!"

"That sounds very grim. If you will let me count myself amongst your friends, I shall be so grateful."

"I should like it very much! I am not so ignorant as not to have heard your name and to know that you are a celebrated man. But I am afraid I shall prove a very stupid friend for you."

"I have no such fear, and if I may come and see you sometimes, I shall count myself a very happy man."

"I am generally alone in the afternoon," replied Miss Brandt, sophistically.

In another minute Mr. Pennell was saying good-night to his hostess and asking her permission to repeat his visit at some future time.

"And if you and Miss Brandt would so far honour me, Madame Gobelli, as to come and have a little lunch at my chambers in Piccadilly, I shall feel myself only too much indebted to you. Perhaps we might arrange a *matinée* or a concert for the same afternoon, if it would please you? Will you let me know? And pray fix as early a date as possible. And I may really avail myself of your kind permission to come and see you again. You may be sure that I shall not forget to do

so. Good-night! Good-night, Baron! Good-night, Miss
Brandt!" and with a nod to Mr. Milliken he was gone.

"Ain't 'e a nice fellow? Worth two of that conceited jackanapes, 'is cousin," remarked the Baroness as
he disappeared, "what do you think of 'im, 'Arriet?"

"Oh! he is well enough," replied Miss Brandt with a
yawn, as she prepared also to take her departure, "he
is taller and broader and stronger looking than Captain
Pullen—and he must be very clever into the bargain."

"And 'e never said a word about 'is books," exclaimed Madame Gobelli, "only fancy!"

"No! he never said a word about his books," echoed
Harriet.

CHAPTER XIV.

ANTHONY PENNELL had promised to let Margaret
Pullen hear the result of his visit to the Red House, and
as he entered her presence on the following evening, she
saluted him with the queries,

"Well! have you been there? Have you seen her?"

To which he answered soberly,

"Yes! I have been there and I have seen her!"

"And what do you think of her? What did she
say? I hope she was not rude to you!"

"My dear Mrs. Pullen," said Pennell, as he seated
himself, and prepared for a long talk, "you must let me
say in the first place, that I should never have recognised
Miss Brandt from your description of her! You led me
to expect a *gauche* schoolgirl, a half-tamed savage, or a
juvenile virago. And I am bound to say that she struck
me as belonging to none of the species. I sent your

note of introduction to Madame Gobelli, and received a very polite invitation in return, in accordance with which I dined at the Red House yesterday."

"You *dined* there!" exclaimed Margaret with renewed interest. "Oh! do tell me all about it, from the very beginning. What do you think of that dreadful woman, the Baroness, and her little humpty Baron, and did you tell Miss Brandt of Ralph's impending marriage?"

"My dear lady, one question at a time, if you please. In the first place I arrived there rather sooner than I was expected, and Madame Gobelli had not returned from her afternoon drive, but Miss Harriet Brandt did the honours of the tea-table in a very efficient manner, and with as much composure and dignity as if she had been a duchess. We had a very pleasant time together until the Baroness burst in upon us!"

"Are you chaffing me?" asked Margaret, incredulously. "What do you really think of her?"

"I think she is, without exception, the most perfectly beautiful woman I have ever seen!"

"*What!*" exclaimed his companion.

She had thrown herself back in her armchair, and was regarding him as if he were perpetrating some mysterious joke, which she did not understand.

"How extraordinary; how very extraordinary!" she exclaimed at length, "that is the very thing that Ralph said of her when they first met."

"But why extraordinary? There are few men who would not endorse the opinion. Miss Brandt possesses the kind of beauty that appeals to the senses of animal creatures like ourselves. She has a far more dangerous quality than that of mere regularity of feature. She attracts without knowing it. She is a mass of magnetism."

"O! do go on, Mr. Pennell! Tell me how she received the news you went to break to her!"

"I never broke it at all. There was no need to do so. Miss Brandt alluded to the magnificent Captain Pullen's marriage with the greatest nonchalance. She evidently estimates him at his true value, and does not consider him worth troubling her head about!"

"You astonish me! But how are we to account then for the attitude she assumed towards Miss Leyton, and the boast she made of Ralph's attentions to her?"

"Bravado, most likely! Miss Leyton goes to the Red House all aflame, like an angry turkey cock, and accuses Miss Brandt of having robbed her of her lover, and what would you have the girl do? Not cry Peccavi, surely, and lower her womanhood? She had but one course—to brave it out. Besides, you have heard only one side of the question, remember! I can imagine Miss Leyton being very 'nasty' if she liked!"

"You forget the letters which Miss Brandt wrote to Ralph and which were found in his empty grate at Richmond!"

"I do not! I remember them as only another proof of how unworthy he is of the confidence of any woman."

"Really, Mr. Pennell, you seem to be all on Miss Brandt's side!"

"I am, and for this reason. If your ideas concerning her are correct, she displayed a large amount of fortitude whilst speaking of your brother-in-law yesterday. But my own belief is, that you are mistaken—that Miss Brandt is too clever for Ralph, or any of you

—and that she cares no more for him in that way than you do. She considers doubtless that he has behaved in a most ungentlemanly manner towards them all, and so do I. I did not know what excuse to make for Ralph! I was ashamed to own him as a relation."

"Harriet Brandt *did* then confide her supposed wrongs to you!"

"Not at all! When she mentioned Ralph's name, it was like that of any other acquaintance. But when she was out of the room, the Baroness told me that he had behaved like a scoundrel to the girl—that he had never confided the fact of his engagement to her, but run after her on every occasion, and then after having promised to join their party in Brussels, and asked Madame Gobelli to engage his room for him, he left for England without even sending her a line of apology, nor has he taken the least notice of them since!"

"Ah! but you know the reason of his sudden departure!" cried Margaret, her soft eyes welling over with tears.

"My dear Mrs. Pullen," said Anthony Pennell, sympathetically, "even at that sad moment, Ralph might have sent a telegram, or scratched a line of apology. We have to attend to such little courtesies, you know, even if our hearts are breaking! And how can you excuse his not having called on them, or written since? No wonder the Baroness is angry. She did not restrain her tongue in speaking of him yesterday. She said she never wished to see his face again."

"Does she know that Elinor went to the Red House?"

"I think not! There was no mention of her name!"

"Then I suppose we may at all events consider the affair *une chose finie?*"

"I hope so, sincerely! I should not advise Master Ralph to show his face at the Red House again. The Baroness said she longed to lay her stick across his back, and I believe she is quite capable of doing so!"

"Oh! indeed she is," replied Margaret, smiling, "we heard a great many stories of her valour in that respect from Madame Lamont, the landlady of the Lion d'Or. Has Miss Brandt taken up her residence altogether with Madame Gobelli?"

"I think not! She told me her life there was very dull, and she should like to change it."

"She is in a most unfortunate position for a young girl," remarked Margaret, "left parentless, with money at her command, and in a strange country! And with the strange stigma attached to her birth—"

"I don't believe in stigmas being attached to one's birth," returned Pennell hastily, "the only stigmas worth thinking about, are those we bring upon ourselves by our misconduct—such a one, for instance, as my cousin Ralph has done with regard to Miss Brandt! I would rather be in her shoes than his. Ralph thinks, perhaps, that being a stranger and friendless she is fair game—"

"Who is that, taking my name in vain?" interrupted a languid voice at the open door, as Captain Pullen advanced into the room.

Margaret Pullen started and grew very red at being detected in discussing her brother-in-law's actions, but Anthony Pennell, who was always ruffled by his cousin's affected walk and drawl, blurted the truth right out.

"*I* was," he replied, hardly touching the hand which

Captain Pullen extended to him, "I was just telling Mrs. Pullen of the high estimation in which your name is held at the Red House!"

It was now Ralph's turn to grow red. His fair face flushed from chin to brow, as he repeated,

"The Red House! what Red House?"

"Did they not mention the name to you? I mean the residence of Madame Gobelli. I was dining there yesterday."

"Dining there, were you? By Jove! I didn't know you were acquainted with the woman. Isn't she a queer old party? Baroness Boots, eh? Fancy your knowing them! I thought you were a cut above that, Anthony!"

"If the Gobellis were good enough for you to be intimate with in Heyst, I suppose they are good enough for me to dine with in London, Ralph! I did not know until last evening, however, that you had left them to pay for your rooms in Brussels, or I would have taken the money over with me to defray the debt."

Ralph had seated himself by this time, but he looked very uneasy and as if he wished he had not come.

"Did the old girl engage rooms for me?" he stammered. "Well! you know the reason I could not go to Brussels, but of course if I had known that she had gone to any expense for me, I would have repaid her. Did she tell you of it herself?" he added, rather anxiously.

"Yes! and a good many more things besides. As you have happened to come in whilst we are on the question, I had better make a clean breast of it. Perhaps you have heard that Miss Leyton has been to the Red House and had an interview with Miss Brandt!"

"Yes! I've just come from Richmond, where we've had a jolly row over it," grumbled Ralph, pulling his moustaches.

"Your family all felt that sort of thing could not go on—that it must end one way or the other—and therefore I went to the Red House, ostensibly to view Madame Gobelli's collection of china, but in reality to ascertain what view of the matter she and Miss Brandt took—and to undeceive them as to your being in a position to pursue your intimacy with the young lady any further."

"And what the devil business have you to meddle in my private affairs?" demanded Captain Pullen rousing himself.

"Because, unfortunately, your mother happened to be my father's sister," replied Pennell sternly, "and the scrapes you get in harm me more than they do yourself! One officer more or less, who gets into a scrape with women, goes pretty well unnoticed, but I have attained a position in which I cannot afford to have my relations' names bandied about as having behaved in a manner unbecoming gentlemen."

"Who dares to say that of me?" cried Ralph angrily.

"Everybody who knows of the attention you paid Miss Brandt in Heyst," replied Anthony Pennell, boldly, "and without telling her that you were already engaged to be married. I do not wonder at Miss Leyton being angry about it! I only wonder she consents to have any more to do with you in the circumstances."

"O! we've settled all that!" said Ralph, testily, "we had the whole matter out at Richmond this afternoon, and I've promised to be a good boy for the future, and never speak to a pretty woman again! You need not wonder any more about Elinor! She is only glad enough to get me back at any price!"

"Yes? And what about Miss Brandt?" enquired Pennell.

"Is she worrying about this affair?" asked Captain Pullen, quickly.

"Not a bit! I think she estimates your attentions at their true value. I was alluding to the opinion she and her friends must have formed of your character as an officer and a gentleman."

"O! I'll soon set all that right! I'll run over to the Red House and see the old girl, if you two will promise not to tell Elinor!"

"I should not advise you to do that! I am afraid you might get a warm reception. I think Madame Gobelli is quite capable of having you soused in the horse-pond. You would think the same if you had heard the names she called you yesterday."

"What did she call me?"

"Everything she could think of. She considers you have behaved not only in a most ungentlemanly manner towards her, but in a most dishonourable one to Miss Brandt. She particularly told me to tell you that she never wished to see your face again."

"Damn her!" exclaimed Captain Pullen, wrathfully, "and all her boots and shoes into the bargain. A vulgar, coarse old tradesman's wife! How dare she——"

"Stop a minute, Ralph! The Baroness's status in society makes no difference in this matter. You know perfectly well that you did wrong. Let us have no more discussion of the subject."

Captain Pullen leaned back sulkily in his chair.

"Well! if I *did* flirt a little bit more than was prudent with an uncommonly distracting little girl," he muttered presently, "I am sure I have had to pay for it! Lord Walthamstowe insists that if I do not marry Elinor before the Rangers start for Malta the engagement shall be broken off, so I suppose I must do it! But it is a doosid nuisance to be tied up at five-and-twenty, before one has half seen life! What the dickens I am to do with her when I've got her, I'm sure I don't know!"

"O! you will find married life very charming when you're used to it!" said Pennell consolingly, "and Miss Leyton is everything a fellow could wish for in a wife! Only you must give up flirting, my boy, or if I mistake not, you'll find you've caught a tartar!"

"I expect to have to give up everything," said the other with a sour mouth.

As soon as he perceived a favourable opportunity, Anthony Pennell rose to take his leave. He did not wish to quarrel with Ralph Pullen about a girl whom he had only seen once, at the same time he feared for his own self-control, if his cousin continued to mention the matter in so nonchalant a manner. Pennell had always despised Captain Pullen for his easy conceit with regard to women, and it seemed to him to have grown more detestably contemptible than before. He was anxious therefore to quit the scene of action. But, to his annoyance, when he bade Margaret good-evening, Ralph also rose and expressed his wish to walk with him in the direction of his chambers.

"I suppose you couldn't put me up for the night, old chappie!" he said with his most languid air.

"Decidedly not!" replied Pennell. "I have only my own bedroom, and I've no intention of your sharing it. Why do you not go back to Richmond, or put up at an hotel?"

"Doosid inhospitable!" remarked Captain Pullen, with a faded smile.

"Sorry you think so, but a man cannot give what he does not possess. You had better stay and keep your sister-in-law company for a little while. I have work to do and am going straight home!"

"All right! I'll walk with you a little way," persisted Ralph, and the two young men left the house together.

As soon as they found themselves in the street, Captain Pullen attacked his cousin, eagerly.

"I say, Pennell, what is the exact direction of the Red House?"

"Why do you want to know?" enquired his companion.

"Because I feel that I owe the Baroness a visit. I acknowledge that I was wrong not to write and make my apologies, but you must know what it is—with a deuce of a lot of women to look after, and the whole gang crying their eyes out, and everything thrown on my shoulders, coffin, funeral, taking them over from Heyst to England, and all—it was enough to drive everything else out of a man's head. You must acknowledge that."

"You owe no excuses to me, Pullen, neither do I quite believe in them. You have had plenty of time

since to remedy your negligence, even if you did forget
to be courteous at the moment!"

"I know that, and you're quite right about the other
thing. I had more reasons than one for letting the
matter drop. You are a man and I can tell you with
impunity what would set the women tearing my eyes
out. I *did* flirt a bit with Harriet Brandt, perhaps more
than was quite prudent in the circumstances—"

"You mean the circumstance of your engagement to
Miss Leyton?"

"Yes and No! If I had been free, it would have
been all the same—perhaps worse, for I should not have
had a loophole of escape. For you see Miss Brandt is
not the sort of girl that any man could marry."

"Why not?" demanded Pennell with some asperity.

"Oh! because—well! you should hear old Phillips
talk of her and her parents. They were the most awful
people, and she has black blood in her, her mother was
a half-caste, so you see it would be impossible for any
man in my position to think of marrying her! One
might get a piebald son and heir! Ha! ha! ha! But
putting all that aside, she is one of the demndest
fascinating little women I ever came across—you would
say so too, if you had seen as much of her as I did—I
can't tell you what it is exactly, but she has a drawing
way about her, that pulls a fellow into the net before
he knows what he is about. And her voice, by Jove!—
have you heard her sing?"

"I have, but that has nothing to do that I can see
with the subject under discussion. You, an engaged
man, who had no more right to philander with a girl,
than if you had been married, appear to me to have

followed this young lady about and paid her attentions, which were, to say the least of them, compromising, never announcing the fact, meanwhile, that you were bound to Miss Leyton. After which, you left her, without a word of explanation, to think what she chose of your conduct. And now you wish to see her again, in order to apologise. Am I right?"

"Pretty well, only you make such a serious matter out of a little fun!"

"Well, then, I repeat that if you are wise, you will save yourself the trouble, Ralph! Miss Brandt is happily too sensible to have been taken in by your pretence of making love to her. She estimates you at your true value. She knows that you are engaged to Elinor Leyton —that you were engaged all the time she knew you— and, I think, she rather pities Miss Leyton for being engaged to you!"

But this point of view had never presented itself before to the inflated vanity of Ralph Pullen.

"*Pities* her!" he exclaimed, "the devil!"

"I daresay it seems incomprehensible to you that any woman should not be thankful to accept at your hands the crumbs that may fall from another's table, but with regard to Miss Brandt, I assure you it is true! And even were it otherwise, I am certain Madame Gobelli would not admit you to her house. You know the sort of person she is! She can be very violent if she chooses, and the names she called you yesterday, were not pretty ones. I had much trouble, as your relative, to stand by and listen to them quietly. Yet I could not say that they were undeserved!"

"O well! I daresay!" returned Ralph, impatiently.

"Let us allow, for the sake of argument, that you are right, and that I behaved like a brute! The matter lies only between Hally Brandt and myself. The old woman has nothing to do with it! She never met the girl till she went to Heyst. What I want to do is to see Hally again and make my peace with her! You know how easily women are won over. A pretty present—a few kisses and excuses,—a few tears—and the thing is done. I shouldn't like to leave England without making my peace with the little girl. Couldn't you get her to come to your chambers, and let me meet her there? Then the Baroness need know nothing about it!"

"I thought you told us just now, that you had had a reconciliation with Miss Leyton on condition that you were to be a good boy for the future. Does that not include a surreptitious meeting with Miss Brandt?"

"I suppose it does, but we have to make all sorts of promises where women are concerned. A nice kind of life a man would lead, if he consented to be tied to his wife's apron-strings, and never go anywhere, nor see anyone, of whom she did not approve. I swore to everything she and old Walthamstowe asked me, just for peace's sake,—but if they imagine I'm going to be hampered like that, they must be greater fools than I take them for!"

"You must do as you think right, Pullen, but I am not going to help you to break your word!"

"Tell me where the Red House is! Tell me whereabouts Hally takes her daily walks!" urged Captain Pullen.

"I shall tell you nothing—you must find out for yourself!"

"Well! you are damned particular!" exclaimed his cousin, "one would think this little half-caste was a princess of the Blood Royal. What is she, when all's said and done? The daughter of a mulatto and a man who made himself so detested that he was murdered by his own servants—the bastard of a——"

"Stop!" cried Pennell, so vehemently that the passers-by turned their heads to look at him, "I don't believe it, and if it is true, I do not wish to hear it! Miss Brandt may be all that you say—I am not in a position to contradict your assertions—but to me she represents only a friendless and unprotected woman, who has a right to our sympathy and respect."

"A friendless woman!" sneered Captain Pullen, "yes! and a doosid good-looking one into the bargain, eh, my dear fellow, and much of your sympathy and respect she would command if she were ugly and humpbacked. O! I know you, Pennell! It's no use your coming the benevolent Samaritan over me! You have an eye for a jimper waist and a trim ancle as well as most men. But I fancy your interest is rather thrown away in this quarter. Miss Brandt has a thorny path before her. She is a young lady who will have her own way, and with the glorious example of the Baroness the way is not likely to be too carefully chosen. To tell the truth, old boy, I ran away because I was afraid of falling into the trap. The girl wishes intensely to be married, and she is not a girl whom men will marry, and so—we need go no further. Only, I should not be surprised if, notwithstanding her fortune and her beauty, we should find Miss Harriet Brandt figuring before long, amongst the free lances of London."

"And you would have done your best to send her there!" replied Anthony Pennell indignantly, as he stopped on the doorstep of his Piccadilly chambers. "But I am glad to say that your folly has been frustrated this time, and Miss Brandt sees you as you are! Good-night!" and without further discussion, he turned on his heel and walked upstairs.

"By Jove!" thought Ralph, as he too went on his way, "I believe old Anthony is smitten with the girl himself, though he has only seen her once! That was the most remarkable thing about her—the ease with which she seemed to attract, looking so innocent all the while, and the deadly strength with which she resisted one's efforts to get free again. Perhaps it is as well after all that I should not meet her. I don't believe I could trust myself, only speaking of her seems to have revived the old sensation of being drawn against my will— hypnotised, I suppose the scientists would call it—to be near her, to touch her, to embrace her, until all power of resistance is gone. But I do hope old Anthony is not going to be hypnotised. He's too good for that."

Meanwhile Pennell, having reached his rooms, lighted the gas, threw himself into an armchair, and rested his head upon his hands.

"Poor little girl!" he murmured to himself. "Poor little girl!"

Anthony Pennell was a Socialist in the best and truest sense of the world. He loved his fellow creatures, both high and low, better than he loved himself. He wanted all to share alike—to be equally happy, equally comfortable—to help and be helped, to rest and depend upon one another. He knew that the dream was only a dream

—that it would never be fulfilled in his time, nor any other; that some men would be rich and some poor as long as the world lasts, and that what one man can do to alleviate the misery and privation and suffering with which we are surrounded, is very little. What little Pennell could do, however, to prove that his theories were not mere talk, he did. He made a large income by his popular writings and the greater part of it went to relieve the want of his humbler friends, not through governors and secretaries and the heads of charitable Societies, but from his own hand to theirs. But his Socialism went further and higher than this. Money was not the only thing which his fellow creatures required— they wanted love, sympathy, kindness, and consideration —and these he gave also, wherever he found that there was need. He set his face pertinaciously against all scandal and back-biting, and waged a perpetual warfare against the tyranny of men over women; the ill-treatment of children; and the barbarities practised upon dumb animals and all living things. He was a liberal-minded man, with a heart large enough and tender enough to belong to a woman—with a horror of cruelty and a great compassion for everything that was incapable of defend- ing itself. He was always writing in defence of the People, calling the attention of those in authority to their misfortunes; their evil chances; their lack of opportunity; and their patience under tribulation. For this purpose and in order to know them thoroughly, he had gone and lived amongst them; shared their filthy dens in White- chapel, partaken of their unappetising food in Stratford; and watched them at their labour in Homerton. His figure and his kindly face were well-known in some of the worst and most degraded parts of London, and he could pass anywhere, without fear of a hand being lifted up against him, or an oath called after him in salutation. Anthony Pennell was, in fact, a general lover—a lover of Mankind.

And that is why he leant his head upon his hand as he ejaculated with reference to Harriet Brandt, "Poor little girl."

It seemed so terrible in his eyes that just because she was friendless, and an orphan, just because her parents had been, perhaps, unworthy, just because she had a dark stream mingling with her blood, just because she needed the more sympathy and kindness, the more protection and courtesy, she should be considered fit prey for the sensualist—a fit subject to wipe men's feet upon!

What difference did it make to Harriet Brandt herself, that she was marked with an hereditary taint? Did it render her less beautiful, less attractive, less graceful and accomplished? Were the sins of the fathers ever to be visited upon the children?—was no sympathetic fellow-creature to be found to say, "If it is so, let us forget it! It is not your fault nor mine! Our duty is to make each other's lives as happy as possible and trust the rest to God."

He hoped as he sat there, that before long, Harriet Brandt would find a friend for life, who would never remind her of anything outside her own loveliness and loveable qualities.

Presently he rose, with a sigh, and going to his bookcase drew thence an uncut copy of his last work, "God and the People." It had been a tremendous success, having already reached the tenth edition. It dealt largely, as its title indicated, with his favourite theory, but it was light and amusing also, full of strong nervous language, and bristling every here and there, with wit— not strained epigrams, such as no Society conversation-alists ever tossed backward and forward to each other —but honest, mirth-provoking humour, arising from the humorous side of Pennell's own character, which ever had a good-humoured jest for the oddities and comicali-ties of everyday life.

He regarded the volume for a moment as though he were considering if it were an offering worthy of its des-tination, and then he took up a pen and transcribed upon the fly leaf the name of Harriet Brandt—only her name, nothing more.

"She seems intelligent," he thought, "and she may like to read it. Who knows, if there is any fear of the sad destiny which Ralph prophesies for her, whether I may not be happy enough to turn her ideas into a worthier and more wholesome direction. With an independent fortune, how much good might she not accomplish, amongst those less happily situated than herself! But the other idea—No, I will not entertain it for a moment! She is too good, too pure, too beautiful, for so horrible a fate! Poor little girl! Poor, poor little girl!"

CHAPTER XV.

THE holiday season being now over, and the less fashionable people returned to town, Harriet Brandt's curiosity was much excited by the number of visitors who called at the Red House, but were never shewn into the drawing-room. As many as a dozen might arrive in the course of an afternoon and were taken by Miss Wynward straight upstairs to the room where Madame Gobelli and Mr. Milliken so often shut themselves up together. These mysterious visitors were not objects of charity either, but well-dressed men and women, some of whom came in their own carriages, and all of whom appeared to be of the higher class of society. The Baroness had left off going to the factory, also, and stayed at home every day, apparently with the sole reason of being at hand to receive her visitors.

Harriet could not understand it at all, and after having watched two fashionably attired ladies accompanied by a gentleman, ascend the staircase, to Madame Gobelli's room, one afternoon, she ventured to sound Miss Wynward on the subject.

"Who were the ladies who went upstairs just now?" she asked. •

"Friends of the Baroness, Miss Brandt!" was the curt reply.

"But why do they not come down to the drawing-room then? What does Madame Gobelli do with them in that little room upstairs? I was passing one day just after someone had entered, and I heard the key turned in the lock. What is all the secrecy about?"

"There is no secrecy on my part, Miss Brandt. You know the position I hold here. When I have shewn the visitors upstairs, according to my Lady's directions, my duty is done!"

"But you must know why they come to see her!"

"I know nothing. If you are curious on the subject, you must ask the Baroness."

But Harriet did not like to do that. The Baroness had become less affectionate to her of late—her fancy was already on the wane—she no longer called the attention of strangers to her young friend as the "daughter of the house"—and Harriet felt the change, though she could scarcely have defined where it exactly lay. She had begun to feel less at home in her hostess's presence, and her high spirit chafed at the alteration in her manner. She realised, as many had done before her, that she had out-stayed her welcome. But her curiosity respecting the people who visited Madame Gobelli upstairs was none the less. She confided it to Bobby—poor Bobby who grew whiter and more languid ever day—but her playful threat to invade the sacred precincts and find out what the Baroness and her friends were engaged upon, was received by the youth with horror. He trembled as he begged her not to think of such a thing.

"Hally, you mustn't, indeed you mustn't! You don't know—you have no idea—what might not happen to you, if you offended Mamma by breaking in upon her

privacy. O! don't, pray don't! She can be so terrible
at times—I do not know what she might not do or
say!"

"My dear Bobby, I was only in fun! I have not
the least idea of doing anything so rude. Only, if you
think that I am frightened of your Mamma or any other
woman, you are very much mistaken. It's all nonsense!
No one person can harm another in this world!"

"O! yes, they can—if they have *help*," replied the
boy, shaking his head.

"Help! what help? The help of Mr. Milliken, I
suppose! I would rather fight him than the Baroness
any day—but I fear neither of them."

"O! Hally, you are wrong," said the lad, "you
must be careful, indeed you must—for my sake!"

"Why! you silly Bobby, you are actually trembling!
However, I promise you I will do nothing rash! And I
shall not be here much longer now! Your Mamma is
getting tired of me, I can see that plainly enough! She
has hardly spoken a word to me for the last two days.
I am going to ask Mr. Pennell, to advise me where to
find another home!"

"No! no!" cried the lad, clinging to her, "you shall
not leave us! Mr. Pennell shall not take you away! I
will kill him first!"

He was getting terribly jealous of Anthony Pennell,
but Harriet laughed at his complaints and reproaches
as the emanations of a love-sick schoolboy. She was
flattered by his feverish longing for her society, and his
outspoken admiration of her beauty, but she did not
suppose for one moment that Bobby was capable of a
lasting, or dangerous, sentiment.

Mr. Pennell had become a familiar figure at the Red House by this time. His first visit had been speedily succeeded by another, at which he had presented Harriet Brandt with the copy of his book—an attention, which had he known it, flattered her vanity more than any praises of her beauty could have done. A plain woman likes to be told that she is good-looking, a handsome one that she is clever. Harriet Brandt was not unintelligent, on the contrary she had inherited a very fair amount of brains from her scientific father—but no one ever seemed to have found it out, until Anthony Pennell came her way. She was a little tired of being told that she had lovely eyes, and the most fascinating smile, she knew all that by heart, and craved for something new. Mr. Pennell had supplied the novelty by talking to her as if her intellect were on a level with his own—as if she were perfectly able to understand and sympathise with his quixotic plans for the alleviation of the woes of all mankind—with his Arcadian dreams of Liberty, Equality and Fraternity,—and might help them also, if she chose, not with money only, but by raising her own voice in the Cause of the People. Harriet had never been treated so by anyone before, and her ardent, impetuous, passionate nature, which had a large amount of gratitude in its composition, fixed itself upon her new friend with a vehemence which neither of them would find it easy to overcome—or to disentangle themselves from. Her love (eager to repair the void left by the desertion of Captain Pullen) had poured itself, by means of looks and sighs and little timid, tender touches upon Anthony Pennell like a mountain torrent that had burst its bounds, and he had been responsive—he had opened his arms to receive the flood, actuated not only by the admiration which he had conceived for her from the first, but by the intense, yearning pity which her loneliness and friendlessness had evoked in his generous, compassionate nature. In fact they were desperately in love with each other, and Harriet was expecting each time he came, to hear Anthony Pennell say that he could no longer live without her. And Bobby looked on from a little distance—and suffered. The next time that Mr. Pennell came to see her, Harriet confided to him the mystery of the upstairs room, and asked his opinion as to what it could possibly mean.

"Perhaps they are people connected with the boot trade," suggested Anthony jestingly, "does Madame keep a stock of boots and shoes up there, do you think?"

"O! no! Mr. Pennell, you must not joke about it! This is something serious! Poor Bobby grew as white as a sheet when I proposed to make a raid upon the room some day and discover the mystery, and said that his mother was a terrible woman, and able to do me great harm if I offended her!"

"I quite agree with Bobby in his estimate of his Mamma being a terrible woman," replied Mr. Pennell, "but it is all nonsense about her being able to harm you! *I* should soon see about that!"

"What would you do?" asked Harriet, with downcast eyes.

"What would I *not* do to save you from anything disagreeable, let alone anything dangerous. But the Baroness is too fond of you, surely, to do you any harm!"

Harriet pursed up her lips.

"I am not so sure about her being fond of me, Mr. Pennell! She used to profess to be, I know, but lately her manner has very much altered. She will pass half a day without speaking a word to me, and they have cut off wine and champagne and everything nice from the dinner table. I declare the meals here are sometimes not fit to eat. And I believe they grudge me the little I consider worthy my attention."

"But why do you stay here, if you fancy you are not welcome?" asked Pennell, earnestly, "you are not dependent on these people or their hospitality."

"But where am I to go?" said the girl, "I know no one in London, and Miss Wynward says that I am too young to live at an hotel by myself!"

"Miss Wynward is quite right! You are far too young and too beautiful. You don't know what wicked men and women there are in the world, who would delight in fleecing an innocent lamb like you. But I can soon find you a home where you could stay in respectability and comfort, until—until——"

"Until *what*," asked Harriet, with apparent ingenuousness, for she knew well enough what was coming.

They were seated on one of those little couches made expressly for conversation, where a couple can sit back to back, with their faces turned to one another. Harriet half raised her slumbrous black eyes as she put the question, and met the fire in his own. He stretched out his arms and caught her round the waist.

"Hally! Hally! you know—there is no need for me to tell you! Will you come home to me, dearest? Don't ever say that you are friendless again! Here is

your friend and your lover and your devoted slave for
ever! My darling—my beautiful Hally, say you will be
my wife—and make me the very happiest man in all
the world!"

She did not shrink from his warm wooing—that
was not her nature! Her eyes waked up and flashed
fire, responsive to his own; she let her head rest on his
shoulder, and turned her lips upwards eagerly to meet
his kiss, she cooed her love into his ear, and clasped
him tightly round the neck as if she would never let
him go.

"I love you—I love you," she kept on murmuring,
"I have loved you from the very first!"

"O! Hally, how happy it makes me to hear you say
so," he replied, "how few women have the honesty
and courage to avow their love as you do. My sweet
child of the sun! The women in this cold country have
no idea of the joy that a mutual love like ours has the
power to bestow. We will love each other for ever and
ever, my Hally, and when our bodies are withered by
age, our spirits shall still go loving on."

He—the man whose whole thoughts hitherto had
been so devoted to the task of ameliorating the condition of his fellow-creatures, that he had had no time
to think of dalliance, succumbed as fully to its pleasures
now, as the girl whose life had simply been a ripening
process for the seed which had burst forth into flower.
They were equally passionate—equally loving—equally
unreserved—and they were soon absorbed in their own
feelings, and noticed nothing that was taking place
around them.

But they were not as entirely alone as they imagined.

A pale face full of misery was watching them through one of the panes in the French windows, gazing at what seemed like his death doom, too horribly fascinated to tear himself away. Bobby stood there and saw Hally —*his* Hally, as he had often fondly called her, without knowing the meaning of the word—clasped in the arms of this stranger, pressing her lips to his, and being released with tumbled hair and a flushed face, only to seek the source of her delight again. At last Bobby could stand the bitter sight no longer, and with a low moan, he fled to his own apartment and flung himself, face downward on the bed. And Anthony Pennell and Harriet Brandt continued to make love to each other, until the shadows lengthened, and six o'clock was near at hand.

"I must go now, my darling," he said at last, "though it is hard to tear myself away. But I am so happy, Hally, so very, very happy, that I dare not complain."

"Why cannot you stay the evening?" she urged.

"I had better not! I have not been asked in the first instance, and if what you say about the Baroness's altered demeanour towards yourself be true, I am afraid I should find it difficult to keep my temper. But we part for a very short time, my darling! The first thing to-morrow, I shall see about another home for you, where I can visit you as freely as I like! And as soon as it can ever be, Hally, we will be married—is that a promise?"

"A promise, yes! a thousand times over, Anthony! I long for the time when I shall be your wife!"

"God bless you, my sweet! You have made my future life look all sunshine! I will write to you as soon as ever I have news and then you will lose no time in leaving your present home, will you?"

"Not an instant that I can help," replied Harriet, eagerly; "I am longing to get away. I feel that I have lost my footing here!"

And with another long embrace, the lovers parted. As soon as Anthony had left her, Harriet ran up to her room, to cool her feverish face and change her dress for dinner. She was really and truly fond of the man she had just promised to marry, and if anything could have the power to transform her into a thinking and responsible woman, it would be marriage with Anthony Pennell. She was immensely proud that so clever and popular a writer should have chosen her from out the world of women to be his wife, and she loved him for the excellent qualities he had displayed towards his fellow men, as well as for the passionate warmth he had shewn for herself. She was a happier girl than she had ever been in all her life before, as she stood, flushed and triumphant, in front of her mirror and saw the beautiful light in her dark eyes, and the luxuriant growth of her dusky hair, and the carmine of her lips, and loved every charm she possessed for Anthony's sake. She felt less vexed even with the Baroness than she had done, and determined that she would not break the news of her intended departure from the Red House, that evening, but try to leave as pleasant an impression behind her as she could! And she put on the lemon-coloured frock, though Anthony was not there to see it, from a feeling that since he approved of her, she must be careful of her appearance for the future, to do justice to his opinion.

Madame Gobelli appeared to be in a worse temper than usual that evening. She stumped in to the dining-room and took her seat at table without vouchsafing a word to Harriet, although she had not seen her since luncheon time. She found fault with everything that Miss Wynward did, and telling her that she grew stupider and stupider each day, ordered her to attend her upstairs after dinner, as she had some friends coming and needed her assistance. The ex-governess did not answer at first, and the Baroness sharply demanded if she had heard her speak.

"Yes! my lady," she replied, slowly, "but I trust that you will excuse my attendance, as I have made an engagement for this evening!"

Madame Gobelli boiled over with rage.

"Engagement! What do you mean by making an engagement without asking my leave first? You can't keep it! I want you to 'elp me in something and you'll 'ave to come!"

"You must forgive me," repeated Miss Wynward, firmly, "but I cannot do as you wish!"

Harriet opened her eyes in amazement. Miss Wynward refusing a request from Madame Gobelli. What would happen next?

The Baroness grew scarlet in the face. She positively trembled with rage.

"'Old your tongue!" she screamed. "You'll do as I say, or you leave my 'ouse."

"Then I will leave your house!" replied Miss Wynward.

Madame Gobelli was thunderstruck! Where was this insolent menial, who had actually dared to defy her,

going?   What friends had she?   What home to go to?
She had received no salary from her for years past, but
had accepted board and lodging and cast-off clothes in
return for her services.   How could she face the world
without money?

"You go at your peril," she exclaimed, hoarse with
rage, "you know what will 'appen to you if you try to
resist me!   I 'ave those that will 'elp me to be revenged
on my enemies!   You know that those I 'ate, *die!*
And when I 'ave my knife in a body, I turn it!   You
'ad better be careful, and think twice about what you're
going to do."

"Your ladyship cannot frighten me any longer," replied Miss Wynward, calmly, "I thank God and my
friends that I have got over that!   Nor do I believe any
more in your boasted powers of revenge!   If they are
really yours, you should be ashamed to use them."

"Gustave!" shrieked the Baroness, "get up and put
this woman from the door.   She don't stop in the Red
'Ouse another hour!   Let 'er pack up.'er trumpery and
go!   Do you 'ear me, Gustave?   Turn 'er out of the room!"

"Mein tear! mein tear! a little patience!   Miss Wynward will go quietly!   But the law, mein tear, the law!
We must be careful!"

"Damn the law!" exclaimed the Baroness.   "'Ere,
where's that devil Bobby?   Why ain't 'e at dinner?
What's the good of my 'aving a 'usband and a son if
neither of 'em will do my bidding!"

Then everyone looked round and discovered that
Bobby was not at the table.

"Where's Bobby?" demanded the Baroness of the
servant in waiting.

"Don't know, I'm sure," replied the domestic, who like most of Madame Gobelli's dependents, talked as familiarly with her as though they had been on an equality. "The last time I saw 'im was at luncheon."

"I will go and look for him," said Miss Wynward quietly, as she rose from table.

"No! you don't!" exclaimed the Baroness insolently, "you don't touch my child nor my 'usband again whilst you remain under this roof. I won't 'ave them polluted by your fingers. 'Ere, Sarah, you go upstairs and see if Bobby's in 'is room. It'll be the worse for 'im if 'e isn't."

Sarah took her way upstairs, in obedience to her employer's behest, and the next minute a couple of shrieks, loud and terrified, proceeded from the upper story. They were in Sarah's voice, and they startled everyone at the dinner table.

"Oh! what is that?" exclaimed Harriet, as her face grew white with fear.

"Something is wrong!" said Miss Wynward, as she hastily left the room. .

The Baroness said nothing, until Miss Wynward's voice was heard calling out over the banisters,

"Baron! will you come here, please, at once!"

Then she said,

"Gustave! 'elp me up," and steadying herself by means of her stick, she proceeded to the upper story, accompanied by her husband and Harriet Brandt. They were met on the landing by Miss Wynward, who addressed herself exclusively to the Baron.

"Will you send for a doctor at once," she said eagerly, "Bobby is very ill, very ill indeed!"

"What is the matter?" enquired the stolid German.

"It's all rubbish!" exclaimed Madame Gobelli, forcing her way past the ex-governess, "'ow can 'e be ill when 'e was running about all the morning? 'Ere, Bobby," she continued, addressing the prostrate figure of her son which was lying face downward on the bed, "get up at once and don't let's 'ave any of your nonsense, or I'll give you such a taste of my stick as you've never 'ad before! Get up, I say, at once now!"

She had laid hold of her son's arm, and was about to drag him down upon the floor, when Miss Wynward interposed with a face of horror.

"Leave him alone!" she cried, indignantly. "Woman! cannot you see what is the matter? Your son has left you! He is *dead!*"

The Baroness was about to retort that it was a lie and she didn't believe it, when a sudden trembling overtook her, which she was powerless to resist. Her whole face shook as if every muscle had lost control, and her cumbersome frame followed suit. She did not cry, nor call out, but stood where the news had reached her, immovable, except for that awful shaking, which made her sway from head to foot. The Baron on hearing the intelligence turned round to go downstairs and dispatch William, who was employed in the stables, in search of a medical man. Miss Wynward took the lifeless body in her arms and tenderly turned it over, kissing the pallid face as she did so—when Harriet Brandt, full of mournful curiosity, advanced to have a look at her dead playmate. Her appearance, till then unnoticed, seemed to wake the paralysed energies of the Baroness into life.

She pushed the girl from the bed with a violence that sent her reeling against the mantelshelf, whilst she exclaimed furiously,

"Out of my sight! Don't you dare to touch 'im! This is all *your* doing, you poisonous, wicked creature!"

Harriet stared at her hostess in amazement! Had she suddenly gone mad with grief?

"What do you mean, Madame?" she cried.

"What I say! I ought to 'ave known better than to let you enter an 'ouse of mine! I was a fool not to 'ave left you be'ind me at Heyst, to practise your devilish arts on your army captains and foreign grocers, instead of letting you come within touch of my innocent child!"

"You are mad!" cried Harriet. "What have I done? Do you mean to insinuate that Bobby's death has anything to do with me?"

"It is *you* 'oo 'ave killed 'im," screamed the Baroness, shaking her stick, "it's your poisonous breath that 'as sapped 'is! I should 'ave seen it from the beginning. Do you suppose I don't know your 'istory? Do you think I 'aven't 'eard all about your parents and their vile doings—that I don't know that you're a common bastard, and that your mother was a devilish negress, and your father a murderer? Why didn't I listen to my friends and forbid you the 'ouse?"

"Miss Wynward!" said Harriet, who had turned deadly white at this unexpected attack, "what can I say? What can I do?"

"Leave the room, my dear, leave the room! Her ladyship is not herself! She does not know what she is saying!"

"Don't I?" screamed Madame Gobelli, barring the

way to the door, "I am telling 'er nothing but the truth, and she doesn't go till she 'as 'eard it! She has the vampire's blood in 'er and she poisons everybody with whom she comes in contact. Wasn't Mrs. Pullen and Mademoiselle Brimont both taken ill from being too intimate with 'er, and didn't the baby die because she carried it about and breathed upon it? And now she 'as killed my Bobby in the same way—curse 'er!"

Even when reiterating the terrible truth in which she evidently believed, Madame Gobelli showed no signs of breaking down, but stood firm, leaning heavily on her stick and trembling in every limb.

Harriet Brandt's features had assumed a scared expression.

"Miss Wynward!" she stammered piteously, "Oh! Miss Wynward! this cannot be true!"

"Of course not! Of course not!" replied the other, soothingly, "her ladyship will regret that she has spoken so hastily to you to-morrow."

"I shan't regret it!" said the Baroness sturdily, "for it is the truth! Her father and her mother were murderers who were killed by their own servants in revenge for their atrocities, and they left their curse upon this girl—the curse of black blood and of the vampire's blood which kills everything which it caresses. Look back over your past life," she continued to Harriet, "and you'll see that it's the case! And if you don't believe me, go and ask your friend Dr. Phillips, for 'e knew your infamous parents and the curse that lies upon you!"

"Madame! Madame!" cried Miss Wynward, "is this a moment for such recrimination? If all this were true, it is no fault of Miss Brandt's! Think of what lies here, and that he loved her, and the thought will soften your feelings!"

"But it don't!" exclaimed the Baroness, "when I look at my dead son, I could kill 'er, because she has killed 'im."

And in effect, she advanced upon Harriet with so vengeful a look that the girl with a slight cry, darted from the room, and rushed into her own.

"For shame!" said Miss Wynward, whose previous fear of the Baroness seemed to have entirely evaporated, "how dare you intimidate an innocent woman in the very presence of Death?"

"Don't you try to browbeat me!" replied the Baroness.

"I will tell you what I think," said Miss Wynward boldly, "and that is, that you should blush to give way to your evil temper in the face of God's warning to yourself! You accuse that poor girl of unholy dealings —what can you say of your own? You, who for years past have made money by deceiving your fellow creatures in the grossest manner—who have professed to hold communication with the spiritual world for their satisfaction when, if any spirits have come to you, they must have been those of devils akin to your own! And because I refused to help you to deceive—to take the place of that miserable cur Milliken and play cheating tricks with cards, and dress up stuffed figures to further your money-getting ends, you threatened me with loss of home and character and friends, until, God forgive me, I consented to further the fraud, from fear of starving. But now, thank Heaven, I have no more fear of you!

Yes! you may shake your stick at me, and threaten to take my life, but it is useless! *This,"* pointing to the dead boy upon the bed, "was the only tie I had to the Red House, and as soon as he is dressed for his grave, I shall leave you for ever!"

"And where would you go?" enquired the Baroness. The voice did not sound like her own; it was the cracked dry voice of a very old woman.

"That is no concern of yours, my lady," replied Miss Wynward, as she prepared to quit the room. "Be good enough to let me pass! The inexcusable manner in which you have insulted that poor young lady, Miss Brandt, makes me feel that my first duty is to her!"

"I forbid you—" commenced Madame Gobelli in her old tone, but the ex-governess simply looked her in the face and passed on. She made the woman feel that her power was gone.

Miss Wynward found Harriet in her own room, toss-. ing all her possessions into her travelling trunks. There was no doubt of her intention. She was going to leave the Red House.

"Not at this time of night, my dear," said Miss Wynward, kindly, "it is nearly nine o'clock."

"I would go if I had to walk the street all night!" replied Harriet, feverishly.

Her eyes were inflamed with crying, and she shook like an aspen leaf.

"Oh! Miss Wynward, such awful things to say! What could she mean? What have I done to be so cruelly insulted? And when I am so sorry for poor Bobby too!"

She began to cry afresh as she threw dresses, mantles, stockings, and shoes one on the top of the other, in her endeavour to pack as quickly as possible.

"Let me help you, dear Miss Brandt! It is cruel that you should be driven from the house in this way! But I am going too, as soon as the doctor has been and dear Bobby's body may be prepared for burial. It is a great grief to me, Miss Brandt; I have had the care of him since he was five years old, and I loved him like my own. But I am glad he is dead! I am glad he has escaped from it all, for this is a wicked house, a godless, deceiving and slanderous house, and this trouble has fallen on it as a Nemesis. I will not stay here a moment longer now he has gone! I shall join my friends to-morrow."

"I am glad you have friends," said Harriet, "for I can see you are not happy here! Do they live far off? Have you sufficient money for your journey? Forgive my asking!"

Miss Wynward stooped down and kissed the girl's brow.

"Thank you so much for your kind thought, but it is unnecessary. You will be surprised perhaps," continued Miss Wynward, blushing, "but I am going to be married."

"And so am I," was on Harriet's lips, when she laid her head down on the lid of her trunk and began to cry anew. "Oh! Miss Wynward, what did she mean? Can there be any truth in it? Is there something poisonous in my nature that harms those with whom I come in contact? How can it be? *How* can it be?"

"No! no! of course not!" replied her friend, "Cannot you see that it was the Baroness's temper that made her speak so cruelly to you? But you are right to go! Only, where are you going?"

"I do not know! I am so ignorant of London. Can you advise me?"

"You will communicate with your friends to-morrow?" asked Miss Wynward anxiously.

"Oh! yes! as soon as I can!"

"Then I should go to the Langham Hotel in Portland Place for to-night at all events! There you will be safe till your friends advise you further. What can I do to help you?"

"Ask Sarah or William to fetch a cab! And to have my boxes placed on it! There is a *douceur* for them," said Harriet, placing a handsome sum in Miss Wynward's hand.

"And you will not see the Baroness again?" asked her companion.

"No! no! for God's sake, no. I could not trust myself! I can never look upon her face again!"

In a few minutes the hired vehicle rolled away from the door, bearing Harriet Brandt and her possessions to the Langham Hotel, and Miss Wynward returned to the room where Bobby lay. Madame Gobelli stood exactly where she had left her, gazing at the corpse. There were no tears in her eyes—only the continuous shaking of her huge limbs.

"Come!" said Miss Wynward, not unkindly, "you had better sit down, and let me bring you a glass of wine! This terrible shock has been too much for you."

But the Baroness only pushed her hand away, impatiently.

"Who was that driving away just now?" she enquired.

"Miss Brandt! You have driven her from the house with your cruel and unnecessary accusations. No one liked Bobby better than she did!"

"Has the doctor arrived?"

"I expect so! I hear the Baron's voice in the hall now!"

Almost as she spoke, the Baron and the doctor entered the room. The medical man did what was required of him. He felt the heart and pulse of the corpse—turned back the eyelids—sighed professionally, and asked how long it was since it had happened.

He was told that it was about an hour since they had found him.

"Ah! he has been dead longer than that! Three hours at the least, maybe four! I am afraid there must be an inquest, and it would be advisable in the interests of science to have a post mortem. A great pity, a fine grown lad—nineteen years old, you say—shall probably detect hidden mischief in the heart and lungs. I will make all the necessary arrangements with the Baron. Good evening!"

And the doctor bowed himself out of sight again.

"It is quite true then," articulated the Baroness thickly. "He is gone!"

"Oh! yes, my lady, he is gone, poor dear boy! I felt sure of that!"

"It is quite certain?"

"Quite certain! The body is already stiffening!"

The Baroness did not utter a sound, but Miss Wynward glancing at her, saw her body sway slowly backwards and forwards once or twice, before it fell heavily to the ground, stricken with paralysis.

CHAPTER XVI.

DOCTOR PHILLIPS was a great favourite with the *beau sexe.* He was so mild and courteous, so benevolent and sympathetic, that they felt sure he might be trusted with their little secrets. Women, both old and young, invaded his premises daily, and therefore it was no matter of surprise to him, when, whilst he was still occupied with his breakfast on the morning following Harriet Brandt's flight from the Red House, his confidential servant Charles announced that a young lady was waiting to see him in his consulting room.

"No name, Charles?" demanded the doctor.

"No name, Sir!" replied the discreet Charles without the ghost of a smile.

"Say that I will be with her in a minute!"

Doctor Phillips finished his cutlet and his coffee before he rose from table. He knew what ladies' confidences were like and that he should not have much chance of returning to finish an interrupted meal.

But as he entered his consulting room, his air of indifference changed to one of surprise. Pacing restlessly up and down the carpet, was Harriet Brandt, but so altered that he should hardly have recognised her. Her face was puffy and swollen, as though she had wept all night, her eyelids red and inflamed, her whole demeanour wild and anxious.

"My dear young lady—is it possible that I see Miss Brandt?" the doctor began.

She turned towards him and coming up close to his side, grasped his arm. "I must speak to you!" she exclaimed, without further preliminary, "you are the only person who can set my doubts at rest."

"Well! well! well!" he said, soothingly, for the girl looked and spoke as though her mind were disordered. "You may rely that I will do all I can for you! But let us sit down first!"

"No! no!" cried Harriet, "there is no time, I cannot rest; you must satisfy my mind at once, or I shall go mad! I have not closed my eyes all night—the time was interminable, but how could I sleep! I seemed to be torn in pieces by ten thousand devils!"

"My dear child," said Doctor Phillips, as he laid his hand on hers and looked her steadily in the face, "you are over-excited. You must try to restrain yourself."

He went up to a side table and, pouring out some cordial, made her drink it. Harriet gulped it down, and sank back exhausted in a chair. She was weak and worn-out with the excitement she had passed through.

"Come! that is better," said the docter, as he saw the tears stealing from beneath her closed eyelids, "now, don't hurry yourself! Keep quiet till you feel strong enough to speak, and then tell me what it is that brings you here!"

The allusion appeared to stir up all her misery again. She sat upright and grasped the doctor by the arm as she had done at first.

"You must tell me," she said breathlessly, "you must tell me all I want to know. They say you knew my father and mother in Jamaica! Is that true!"

The old doctor began to feel uncomfortable. It is

one thing to warn those in whom you are interested against a certain person, or persons, and another to be confronted with the individual you have spoken of, and forced to repeat your words. Yet Doctor Phillips was innocent of having misjudged, or slandered anyone.

"I *did* know your father and mother—for a short time!" he answered cautiously.

"And were they married to each other?"

"My dear young lady, what is the use of dragging up such questions now? Your parents are both gone to their account—why not let all that concerned them rest also?"

"No! no! you forget that I live—to suffer the effects of their wrong-doing! I *must* know the truth—I will not leave the house until you tell me! Were they married? Am I a—a—bastard?"

"If you insist upon knowing, I believe they were not married—at least it was the general opinion in the Island. But would not Mr. Tarver be the proper person to inform you of anything which you may wish to know?"

Harriet seized his hand and carried it to her forehead—it was burning hot.

"Feel that!" she exclaimed, "and you would have me wait for weeks before I could get any satisfaction from Mr. Tarver, and not then perhaps! Do you think I could live through the agony of suspense. I should kill myself before the answer to my letter came. No! you are the only person that can give me any satisfaction. Madame Gobelli told me to ask you for the truth, if I did not believe her!"

"Madame Gobelli," reiterated the doctor in surprise.

"Yes! I was staying with her at the Red House

until last night, and then she was so cruel to me that
I left. Her son Bobby is dead, and she accused me of
having killed him. She said that my father was a
murderer and my mother a negress—that they were
both so wicked that their own servants killed them, and
that I have inherited all their vices. She said that it
was *I* who killed Mrs. Pullen's baby and that I had
vampire blood in me, and should poison everyone I
came in contact with. What does she mean? Tell me
the truth, for God's sake, for more depends upon it
than you have any idea of."

"Madame Gobelli was extremely wrong to speak in
such a manner, and I do not know on what authority
she did so. What can she know of your parents or
their antecedents?"

"But you—you—" cried Harriet feverishly, "what
do *you* say?"

Doctor Phillips was silent. He did not know what
to say. He was not a man who could tell a lie glibly
and appear as if he were speaking the truth. Patients
always guessed when he had no hope to give them, however soothing and carefully chosen his words might be.
He regarded the distracted girl before him for some moments in compassionate silence, and then he answered:

"I have said already that if a daughter cannot hear
any good of her parents, she had better hear nothing
at all!"

"Then it is true—my father and mother were people
so wicked and so cruel that their names are only fit for
execration. If you could have said a good word for
them, you would! I can read that in your eyes!"

"The purity and charity of your own life can do much to wipe out the stain upon theirs," said the doctor. "You have youth and money, and the opportunity of doing good. You may be as beloved, as they were——"

"Hated," interposed the girl, "I understand you perfectly! But what about my possessing the fatal power of injuring those I come in contact with! What truth is there in that? Answer me, for God's sake! Have I inherited the vampire's blood? Who bequeathed to me that fatal heritage?"

"My dear Miss Brandt, you must not talk of such a thing! You are alluding only to a superstition!"

"But have I got it, whatever it may be?" persisted Harriet. "Had I anything to do with the baby's death, or with that of Bobby Bates? I loved them both! Was it my love that killed them? Shall I always kill everybody I love? I *must* know—I *will!*"

"Miss Brandt, you have now touched upon a subject that is little thought of or discussed amongst medical men, but that is undoubtedly true. The natures of persons differ very widely. There are some born into this world who nourish those with whom they are associated; they *give out* their magnetic power, and their families, their husbands or wives, children and friends, feel the better for it. There are those, on the other hand, who *draw* from their neighbours, sometimes making large demands upon their vitality—sapping their physical strength, and feeding upon them, as it were, until they are perfectly exhausted and unable to resist disease. This proclivity has been likened to that of the vampire bat who is said to suck the breath of its victims. And

it was doubtless to this fable that Madame Gobelli
alluded when speaking to you."

"But have I got it?   Have I got it?" the girl demanded, eagerly.

The doctor looked at her lustrous glowing eyes, at
her parted feverish lips; at the working hands clasped
together; the general appearance of excited sensuality,
and thought it was his duty to warn her, at least a little,
against the dangers of indulging such a temperament as
she unfortunately possessed.   But like all medical men,
he temporised.

"I should certainly say that your temperament was
more of the *drawing* than the *yielding* order, Miss
Brandt, but that is not your fault, you know.   It is a
natural organism.   But I think it is my duty to warn
you that you are not likely to make those with whom
you intimately associate, stronger either in mind or body.
You will always exert a weakening and debilitating effect
upon them, so that after awhile, having sapped their
brains, and lowered the tone of their bodies, you will
find their affection, or friendship for you visibly decrease.
You will have, in fact, *sucked them dry*.   So, if I may
venture to advise you I would say, if there is any one
person in the world whom you most desire to benefit
and retain the affection of, let that be the very person
from whom you separate, as often as possible.   You
must never hope to keep anyone near you for long,
without injuring them.   Make it your rule through life
never to cleave to any one person altogether, or you will
see that person's interest in you wax and wane, until it
is destroyed!"

"And what if I—marry?" asked Harriet, in a strained voice.

"If you insist upon my answering that question, I should advise you seriously *not* to marry! I do not think yours is a temperament fitted for married life, nor likely to be happy in it! You will not be offended by my plain speaking, I hope. Remember, you have forced it from me!"

"And that is the truth, medically and scientifically —that I must not marry?" she repeated, dully.

"I think it would be unadvisable, but everyone must judge for himself in such matters. But marriage is not, after all, the ultimatum of earthly bliss, Miss Brandt! Many married couples would tell you it is just the reverse. And with a fortune at your command, you have many pleasures and interests quite apart from that very over-rated institution of matrimony. But don't think I am presuming to do more than advise you. There is no real reason—medical or legal—why you should not choose for yourself in the matter!"

"Only—only—that those I cling to most nearly, will suffer from the contact," said Harriet in the same strained tones.

"Just so!" responded the doctor, gaily, "and an old man's advice to you is, to keep out of it as he has done! And now—if there is anything more—" he continued, "that I can do for you——"

"Nothing more, thank you," replied the girl rising, "I understand it all now!"

"Will you not see your old friend, Mrs. Pullen, before you go?" asked the doctor. "She and her husband are staying with me!"

"Oh! no, no," cried Harriet, shrinking from the idea, "I *could* not see her, I would rather go back at once!"

And she hurried from the consulting-room as she spoke.

Doctor Phillips stood for awhile musing, after her departure. Had he done right, he thought, in telling her, yet how in the face of persistent questioning, could he have done otherwise? His thoughts were all fixed upon Ralph Pullen and the scenes that had taken place lately with him, respecting this girl. He did not dream she had an interest in Anthony Pennell. He did not know that they had met more than once. He thought she might still be pursuing Ralph; still expecting that he might break his engagement with Miss Leyton in order to marry herself; and he believed he had done the wisest thing in trying to crush any hopes she might have left concerning him.

"A most dangerous temperament," he said to himself, as he prepared to receive another patient, "one that is sufficient to mar a man's life, if not to kill him entirely. I trust that she and Captain Pullen may never meet again. It was evident that my remarks on marriage disappointed the poor child! Ah! well, she will be much better without it!"

And here the discreet Charles softly opened the door and ushered in another lady.

An hour later, Anthony Pennell, who had projected a visit to the Red House that afternoon, received a note by a commissionaire instead, containing a few, hurried lines. "Come to me as soon as you can," it said, "I have left Madame Gobelli. I am at the Langham Hotel, and very unhappy!" Needless to say that ten minutes after the reception of this news, her lover was rushing to her presence, as fast as hansom wheels could take him. He was very desperately and truly in love with Harriet Brandt. Like most men who use their brains in fiction, his work, whilst in course of progression, occupied his energies to such an extent that he had no time or thought for anything else. But the burden once lifted, the romance written, the strain and anxiety removed, the pendulum swung in the other direction, and Anthony Pennell devoted all his attention to pleasure and amusement. He had been set down by his colleagues as a reserved and cold-blooded man with regard to the other sex, but he was only self-contained and thoughtful. He was as warm by nature, as Harriet herself, and once sure of a response, could make love with the best, and as he flew to her assistance now. He resolved that if anything unpleasant had occurred to drive her from the Red House, and launch her friendless on the world, he would persuade her to marry him at once, and elect him her protector and defence.

His fair face flushed with anticipation as he thought of the joy it would be to make her his wife, and take her far away from everything that could annoy or harass her.

Having arrived at the Langham and flung a double fare to the cab-driver, he ran up the high staircase with the light step of a boy, and dashed into Harriet's private room. The girl was sitting, much as she had done since returning from her interview with the doctor —silent, sullen, and alone, at war with Heaven and Destiny and all that had conduced to blight the brightest hopes she had ever had.

"Hally, my darling, why is this?" exclaimed Pennell,

as he essayed to fold her in his arms.   But she pushed
him off, not unkindly but with considerable determination.
"Don't touch me, Tony!—don't come near me.   You
had better not!   I might harm you!"

"What is the matter?   Are you ill?   If so, you know
me too well to imagine that I should fear infection."

"No! no! you do not understand!" replied Harriet,
as she rose from her seat and edged further away from
him, "but I am going to tell you all!   It is for that I
sent for you!"

Then, waving him from her with her hand, she
related the whole story to him—what the Baroness had
accused her of, and what Doctor Phillips had said in
confirmation of it, only that morning.   Pennell had heard
something of it before, through Margaret Pullen, but he
had paid no attention to it, and now, when Harriet repeated it in detail, with swollen eyes and quivering lips,
he laughed the idea to scorn.

"Pooh! Nonsense!   I don't believe a word of it,"
he exclaimed, "it is a parcel of old woman's tales.
Phillips should be ashamed of himself to place any
credence in it, far more to repeat it to you!   Hally,
my darling! you are surely not going to make yourself
unhappy because of such nonsense.   If so, you are not
the sensible girl I have taken you for!"

"But, Tony," said the girl, still backing from his
advances, "listen to me!   It is not all nonsense, indeed.
I know for myself that it is true!   Having been shut up
for so many years in the Convent dulled my memory
for what went before it, but it has all come back to me
now!   It seems as if what Madame Gobelli and Doctor
Phillips have said, had lifted a veil from my eyes, and I

can recall things that had quite escaped my memory before. I can remember now hearing old Pete say, that
when I was born, I was given to a black wet nurse, and
after a little while she was taken so ill, they had to send
her away, and get me another, and the next one—*died!*
Pete used to laugh and call me the puma's cub, but I
didn't know the meaning of it, then. And—Oh! stop a
moment, Tony, till I have done—there was a little white
child, I can see her so plainly now. They called her
little Caroline, I think she must have belonged to the
planter who lived next to us, and I was very fond of
her. I was quite unhappy when we did not meet, and
I used to creep into her nursery door and lie down in
the cot beside her. Poor little Caroline! I can see her
now! So pale and thin and wan she was! And one
night, I remember her mother came in and found me
there and called to her husband to send the 'Brandt
bastard' back to Helvetia. I had no idea what she
meant, but I cried because she sent me home, and I
asked Pete what a bastard was, but he would not tell
me. And," went on Harriet in a scared tone, "little
Caroline *died!* Pete carried me on his shoulder to see
the funeral, and I would not believe that Caroline could
be in the narrow box, and I struck Pete on the face for
saying so!"

"Well! my darling! and if you did, are these childish
reminiscences to come between our happiness? Why
should they distress you, Hally? Madame Gobelli's in-
solence must have been very hard to bear—I acknowledge that, and I wish I had been by to prevent it, but
you must make excuses for her. I suppose the poor
creature was so mad with grief that she did not know

what she was saying! But you need never see her again,
so you must try to forgive her!"

"But, Anthony, you do not understand me! What
the Baroness said was *true!* I see it now! *I killed
Bobby!*"

"My dearest, you are raving! *You killed Bobby!*
What utter, utter folly! How could you have killed Bobby?"

Harriet passed her hand wearily across her brow, as
if she found it too hard to make her meaning plain.

"Oh! yes, I did! We were always together, in the
garden or the house! And he used to sit with his head
on my shoulder and his arm round my waist, I should
not have allowed it! I should have driven him away!
But he loved me, poor Bobby, and it will be the same,
Doctor Phillips says, with everybody I love! I shall only
do them harm!"

"Hally! I shall begin to think in another moment
that you are ill yourself—that you have a fever or something, and that it is affecting your brain!"

"There was a sister at the Convent, Sister Theodosia, who was very good to me when I first went
there," continued the girl in a dreamy voice, as if she
had not heard his words; "and she used to sit with me
upon her lap for hours together, because I was sad.
But she grew ill and they had to send her away up to
the hill, where they had their sanatorium. That made
the fourth in Jamaica!"

"Now! I will not have you talk any more of this
nonsense," said Pennell, half annoyed by her persever-
ance, "and to prove to you what a little silly you are to
imagine that everyone who falls ill, or dies, or who comes
within the range of your acquaintance, owes it to your

influence, tell me how it is that your father and mother, who must have lived nearer to you than anybody else, did not fall sick and die also."

"My parents saw less of me than anybody," replied Harriet, sadly, "they were ashamed of their 'bastard', I suppose! But old Pete loved me, and took me with him everywhere, and he didn't get sick," she concluded, with a faint smile.

"Of course not! See! what rubbish you have been talking—making yourself and me unhappy for nothing at all! So now let me take you in my arms and kiss the remembrance of it away!"

He was about to put his suggestion into execution, but she still shrank from him.

"No! no! indeed you must not! It is all true! I cannot forget Olga Brimont, and Mrs. Pullen, and the baby, and poor Bobby! It is true, indeed it is, and I have been accursed from my birth."

And she burst into a torrent of passionate tears.

Pennell let her expend some of her emotion, before he continued,

"Well! and what is to be the upshot of it all!"

"I must part from you," replied the girl, "Indeed, indeed I must! I cannot injure you as I have done others! Doctor Phillips said I was not fit for marriage —that I should always 'weaken and hurt those whom I loved most—and that I should draw from them, physically and mentally, until I had sapped all their strength —that I have the blood of the vampire in me, the vampire that sucks its victims' breaths until they die!"

"Doctor Phillips be damned!" exclaimed Pennell, "what right has he to promulgate his absurd and untenable theories, and to poison the happiness of a girl's life, with his folly? He is an old fool, a dotard, a senseless ass, and I shall tell him so! Vampire be hanged! And if it were the truth, I for one could not wish for a sweeter death! Come along, Hally, and try your venom upon me! I am quite ready to run the risk!"

He held out his arms to her again, as he spoke, and she sank on her knees beside him.

"Oh! Tony! Tony! cannot you read the truth? I love you, dear, I love you! I never loved any creature in this world before I loved you. I did not know that it was given to mortals to love so much! And my love has opened my eyes! Sooner than injure you, whom I would die to save from harm, I will separate myself from you! I will give you up! I will live my lonely life without you, I *could* do that, but I can never, never consent to sap your manhood and your brains, which do not belong to me but to the world, and see you wither, like a poisoned plant, the leaves of which lie discoloured and dead upon the garden path."

Never in the course of their acquaintanceship had Harriet Brandt seemed so sweet, so pathetic, so unselfish to Anthony Pennell as then. If he had resolved not to resign her from the first, he did so a thousand times more now. He threw his arms around her kneeling figure and lowered his head until it lay upon the crown of her dusky hair.

"My darling! my darling! my own sweet girl!" he murmured, "our destinies are interwoven for ever! No one and nothing shall come between us! You cannot give me up unless you have my consent to doing so. I hold your sacred promise to become my wife, and I shall not release you from it!"

"But if I harmed you?" she said fearfully.

"I do not believe in the possibility of your harming me," he replied, "but if I am to die, which is what I suppose you mean, I claim my right to die in your arms. But whenever it happens, you will have neither hastened, nor retarded it!"

"Oh! if I could only think so!" she murmured.

"You must! Why cannot you trust my judgment as much as that of Madame Gobelli or old Phillips— a couple of mischief-makers. And now, Hally, when shall it be?"

"When shall 'what' be?" she whispered.

"You know what I mean as well as I do! When shall we be married? We have no one to consult but ourselves! I am my own master and you are alone in the world! These things are very easily managed, you know. I have but to go to Doctors' Commons for a special license to enable us to be married at a registrar's office to-morrow. Shall it be to-morrow, love?"

"Oh! no! no! I could not make up my mind so soon!"

"But why not? Would you live in this dull hotel all by yourself, Hally?"

"I do not know! I am so very unhappy! Leave me, Anthony, for God's sake, leave me, whilst there is time! You do not know the risk you may be running by remaining by my side! How can I consent to let you, whom I love like my very life, run any risk for my sake! Oh! I love you—I love you!" cried the impassioned girl, as she clung tightly to him. "You are my lord and master and my king, and I will never, *never* be so selfish as to harm you for the sake of my own gratification. You must go away—put the seas between us—never see me, never write or speak to me more —only save yourself, my beloved, save yourself!"

He smiled compassionately, as he would have smiled at the ravings of a child, as he raised her from her lowly position and placed her in a chair.

"Do you know what I am going to do, little woman?" he said cheerfully. "I am going to leave you all alone to think this matter over until to-morrow. By that time you will have been able to compare the opinions of two people who do not care a jot about you, with those of mine who love you so dearly. Think well over what they have said to you, and I have said to you, and you have said to me! Remember, that if you adhere to your present determination, you will make both yourself and me most unhappy, and do no one any good. As for myself, I venture to say that if I lose you my grief and disappointment will be so great, that, in all probability, I shall never do any good work again. But be a sensible girl—make up your mind to marry me, and give the lie to all this nonsense, and I'll write a book that will astonish the world! Come, Hally, is it to be ruin or success for me?—Ruin to spend my life without the only woman I have ever cared for, or success to win my wife and a companion who will help me in my work and make my happiness complete?"

He kissed her tear-stained face several times, and left her with a bright smile.

"This time to-morrow, remember, and I shall come with the licence in my pocket."

CHAPTER XVI.

DOCTOR PHILLIPS did not meet Margaret and her husband until luncheon time and then they were full of an encounter which they had had during their morning walk.

"Only fancy, Doctor!" exclaimed Margaret, with more animation than she had displayed of late, "Arthur and I have been shopping in Regent Street, and whom do you think we met?"

"I give it up, my dear," replied the doctor, helping himself to cold beef. "I am not good at guessing riddles."

"Ralph and Elinor! They had just come from some exhibition of pictures in New Bond Street, and I never saw them so pleased with each other before. Ralph was looking actually 'spooney', and Elinor was positively radiant."

"*Souvent femme varie,*" quoted Doctor Phillips, shrugging his shoulders.

"Oh! but, Doctor, it made Arthur and me so glad to see them. Elinor is very fond of Ralph, you know, although she has shewn it so little. And so I have no doubt is he of her, and there would never have been any unpleasantness between them, it it had not been for that horrid girl, Harriet Brandt."

"It is not like you, my dear Margaret, to condemn

anyone without a hearing. Perhaps you have not heard the true case of Miss Harriet Brandt. Although I am glad that Ralph has disentangled himself from her, I still believe that he behaved very badly to both the young ladies, and whilst I am glad to hear that Miss Leyton smiles upon him again, I think it is more than he deserves!"

"And I agree with you, Doctor," interposed Colonel Pullen, "I have never seen this Miss Brandt, but I know what a fool my brother is with women, and can quite understand that he may have raised her hopes just to gratify his own vanity. I have no patience with him."

"Well! for Miss Leyton's sake let us hope that this will be his last experience of dallying with forbidden pleasures. But what will you say when I tell you that one of my visitors this morning has been the young lady in question—Miss Brandt!"

"Harriet Brandt!" exclaimed Margaret, "but why—is she ill?"

"Oh! no! Her trouble is mental—not physical."

"She is not still hankering after Ralph, I hope."

"You are afraid he might not be able to resist the bait! So should I be. But she did not mention Captain Pullen. Her distress was all about herself!"

"Oh! do tell me about it, Doctor, if it is not a secret! You know I have a kind of interest in Harriet Brandt!"

"When she does not interfere with the prospects of your family," observed the doctor, drily, "exactly so! Well, then, the poor girl is in great trouble, and I had very little consolation to give her! She has left Madame Gobelli's house. It seems that the old woman insulted her terribly and almost turned her out."

"Oh! that awful Baroness!" cried Margaret; "it is only what might have been expected! We heard dread'ful stories about her at Heyst. She has an uncontrollable temper and, when offended, a most vituperative tongue. Her ill-breeding is apparent at all times, but it must be overwhelming when she is angry. But how did she insult Miss Brandt?"

"You remember what I told you of the girl's antecedents! It appears that the Baroness must have got hold of the same story, for she cast it in her teeth, accusing her moreover of having caused the death of her son."

"Madame Gobelli's son? What! Bobby—Oh! you do not mean to say that Bobby—is *dead?*"

"Yes! There was but one son, I think! He died yesterday, as I understood Miss Brandt. And the mother in her rage and grief turned upon the poor girl and told her such bitter truths, that she rushed from the house at once. Her visit to me this morning was paid in order to ascertain if such things were true, as the Baroness, very unjustifiably I think, had referred her to me for confirmation."

"And what did you tell her?"

"What could I tell her? At first I declined to give an opinion, but she put such pertinent questions to me, that unless I had lied, I saw no way of getting out of it. I glossed over matters as well as I could, but even so, they were bad enough. But I impressed it upon her that she must not think of marrying. I thought it the best way to put all idea of catching Captain Pullen out of her mind. Let him once get safely married, and she can decide for herself with regard to the next. But at all hazards, we must keep Ralph out of her way, for between you and me and the post, she is a young woman whom most men would find it difficult to resist."

"Oh! yes! she and Ralph must not meet again," said Margaret, dreamingly. Her thoughts had wandered back to Bobby and Heyst, and all the trouble she had encountered whilst there. What despair had attacked her when she lost her only child, and now Madame Gobelli —the woman she so much disliked—had lost her only child also.

"Poor Madame Gobelli!" she ejaculated, "I cannot help thinking of her! Fancy Bobby being—*dead!* And she used to make him so unhappy, and humiliate him before strangers! How she must be suffering for it now! How it must all come back upon her! Poor Bobby! Elinor will be sorry to hear that he is gone! She used to pity him so, and often gave him fruit and cakes. Fancy his being dead! I cannot believe it."

"It is true, nevertheless! But it is the common lot, Margaret! Perhaps, as his mother used to treat him so roughly, the poor lad is better off where he is."

"Oh! of course, I have no doubt of that! But he was all she had—like me!" said Margaret, with her eyes over-brimming. Her husband put his arms round her, and let her have her cry out on his shoulder.

Then, as he wiped her tears away she whispered,

"Arthur, I should like to go and see her—the Baroness, I mean! I can sympathise so truly with her, I might be able to say a few words of comfort!"

"Do as you like, my darling," replied Colonel Pullen, "that is, if you are sure that the woman won't insult you, as she did Miss Brandt!"

"Oh! no! no! I am not in the least afraid! Why should she? I shall only tell her how much I feel for her own our common loss——"

She could not proceed, and the doctor whispered to the Colonel.

"Let her do as she wishes! The best salve for our own wounds is to try and heal those of others."

Margaret rose and prepared to leave the room.

"I shall go at once," she said, "I suppose there is no chance of my meeting Harriet Brandt there!"

"I think not! She told me she had left the Red House for good and all, but she did not say where she was staying! Though, after all, I think she is in most want of comfort of the two."

"Oh! no!" replied Margaret, faintly, "there is no grief like that of—of—" She did not finish her sentence, but left the room hastily in order to assume her walking things.

"Will she ever get over the loss of her child?" demanded Colonel Pullen, gloomily. The doctor regarded him with a half-amused surprise.

"My dear fellow, though it is useless to preach the doctrine to a bereaved mother, the loss of an innocent baby is perhaps the least trying in the category of human ills. To rear the child, as thousands do, to be unloving, or unsympathetic, or ungrateful, is a thousand times worse. But it is too soon for your dear wife to acknowledge it. Let her go to this other mother and let them cry together. It will do her all the good in the world!"

And the doctor, having finished his luncheon, put on his top-coat and prepared to make a round of professional calls.

Margaret came back ready for her visit.

"I shall not offer to go with you, darling," said the Colonel, "because my presence would only be inconvenient. But mind you keep the cab waiting, or you may find some difficulty in getting another in that district. What address shall I give the driver?"

"First to our florist in Regent Street that I may get some white flowers."

In another minute she was off, and in about an hour afterwards, she found herself outside the Red House, which looked gloomier than ever, with all the blinds drawn down. Margaret rang the front door bell, which was answered by Miss Wynward.

"Can I see Madame Gobelli?" commenced Margaret, "I have just heard the sad news, and came to condole with her!"

Miss Wynward let her into the hall and ushered her into a side room.

"You will excuse my asking if you are a friend of her ladyship's," she said.

"I can hardly call myself a friend," replied Margaret, "but I stayed with her in the same hotel at Heyst last summer, and I knew the dear boy who is dead. I was most grieved to hear of his death, and naturally anxious to enquire after the Baroness. But if she is too upset to see me, of course I would not think of forcing my presence upon her!"

"I don't think her ladyship would object to receiving any friend, but I am not sure if she would recognise you!"

"Not recognise me? It is not three months since we parted."

"You do not understand me! Our dear boy's death was so sudden—I have been with him since he was five years old, so you will forgive my mentioning him in such a fashion—that it has had a terrible effect upon his poor mother. In fact she is paralysed! The medical men think the paralysis is confined to the lower limbs, but at present they are unable to decide definitely, as the Baroness has not opened her lips since the event occurred."

"Oh! poor Madame Gobelli!" cried Margaret, tearfully, "I felt sure she loved him under all her apparent roughness and indifference!"

"Yes! I have been with them so long, that I know her manner amounted at times to cruelty, but she did not mean it to be so! She thought to make him hardy and independent, instead of which it had just the opposite effect! But she is paying bitterly for it now! I really think his death will kill her, though the doctors laugh at my fears!"

"I—I—too have lost my only child, my precious little baby," replied Margaret, encouraged by the sympathetic tenderness in the other woman's eyes, "and I thought also at first that I must die—that I could not live without her—but God is so good, and there is such comfort in the thought that whatever we may suffer, our darlings have missed all the bitterness and sin and disappointments of this world, that at last—that is, sometimes—one feels *almost* thankful that they are safe with Him!"

"Ah! Madame Gobelli has not your hope and trust, Madam!" said Miss Wynward, "if she had, she would be a better and happier woman. But I must tell you

19*

that she is in the same room as Bobby! She will not
be moved from there, but lies on the couch where we
placed her when she fell, stricken with the paralysis,
gazing at the corpse!"

"Poor dear woman!" exclaimed Margaret.

"Perhaps you would hardly care to go into that
room!"

"Oh! I should like it! I want to see the dear boy
again! I have brought some flowers to put over him!"

"Then, what name shall I tell her ladyship?"

"Mrs. Pullen, say Margaret Pullen whose little baby
died at Heyst—then I think she will remember!"

"Will you take a seat, Mrs. Pullen, whilst I go upstairs and see if I can persuade her to receive you?"

Margaret sat down, and Miss Wynward went up to
the chamber which had once been Bobby's. On the bed
was stretched the body of the dead boy, whilst opposite
to it lay on a couch a woman with dry eyes, but palsied
limbs, staring, staring without intermission at the silent
figure which had once contained the spirit of her son.
She did not turn her head as Miss Wynward entered
the room.

"My lady," she said, going up to her, "Mrs. Pullen
is downstairs and would like to see you! She told me
to say that she is Margaret Pullen whose baby died in
Heyst last summer, and she knew Bobby and has brought
some flowers to strew over his bed. May she came up?"

But she received no answer. Madame Gobelli's features
were working, but that was the only sign of life which
she gave.

"Mrs. Pullen is so very sorry for your loss," Miss
Wynward went on, "she cried when she spoke of it,

and as she has suffered the same, I am sure she will sympathise with you. May I say that you will see her?"

Still there was no response, and Miss Wynward went down again to Margaret.

"I think you had better come up without waiting for her consent," she said, "if seeing you roused her, even to anger, it would do her good. Do you mind making the attempt?"

"No," replied Margaret, "but if the Baroness gets very angry, you must let me run away again. I am quite unequal to standing anything like a scene!"

"You will have but to quit the room. Whatever her ladyship may say she cannot move from her couch. She attacked poor Miss Brandt most unwarrantably last evening, but that was in the first frenzy of her grief. She is quite different now!"

"Poor woman!" again ejaculated Margaret, as she followed Miss Wynward, not without some inward qualms, to the presence of Madame Gobelli. But when she caught sight of the immovable figure on the couch, all her fear and resentment left her, overcome by a mighty compassion. She went straight up to the Baroness and bending down tenderly kissed her twitching face.

"Dear Madame," she said, "I am—we all are—so truly sorry for your grievous loss. It reminds me of the bitter time, not so long ago, you may remember, when I lost my darling little Ethel, and thought for the while that my life was over! It is so hard, so unnatural, to us poor mothers, to see our children go before ourselves! I can weep with you tear for tear! But do remember—try to remember—that he is safe—that though you remain here with empty arms for awhile, death can no more take your boy from you, than a veil over your face can take God's light from. you. He is there, dear Madame Gobelli—just in the next room with the door closed between you, and though I know full well how bitter it is to see the door closed, think of the time when it will open again—when you and I will spring through ít and find, not only our dear Bobby and Ethel, but Christ our Lord, ready to give them back into our arms again!"

The Baroness said nothing, but two tears gathered in her eyes and rolled down her flabby cheeks. Margaret turned from her for a minute and walking up to the bed, knelt down beside it in prayer.

"Dear Christ!" she said, "Thou Who knowest what our mothers' hearts are called upon to bear, have pity on us and give us Thy Peace! And open our eyes that we may gather strength to realise what our dear children have escaped by being taken home to Thee—the sin, the trouble, the anxiety, the disappointment—and make us thankful to bear them in their stead, and give us grace to look forward to our happy meeting and reunion in the Better Land."

Then she rose and bent over the dead boy.

"Dear Bobby!" she murmured, as she kissed the cold brow, and placed the white blossoms in his hands and round his head. "Good-bye! I know how happy you must be now, in company with the spirits of all those whom we have loved and who have gone home before us—how grateful you must feel to the dear Redeemer Who has called you so early—but don't forget your poor mother upon earth! Pray for her, Bobby,— never cease to ask our dear Lord to send her comfort

and peace and joy in believing. For His own dear sake.
Amen!"

When she turned again, the Baroness's cheeks were
wet with tears and she was stretching forth her arms
towards her.

"Oh!" she gasped, as Margaret reached her side, "I
am a godless woman—I am a godless woman!"

"No! no! my dear friend, we are none of us godless," replied Margaret, "we may think we are, but God
knows better! We may forsake Him, but He never for-
sakes us! We should never be saved if we waited till
we wanted to be so. It is *He* Who wants *us*—that is
our great safeguard! He wanted our two dear children
—not to spite us, but to draw us after them. Try to
look at it in that light, and then Bobby's death will
prove your greatest gain."

"I am a godless woman," repeated the Baroness,
"and this is my punishment!" pointing to the bed. "I
loved him best of all! My 'eart is broken!"

"So much the better, if it was a hard heart," rejoined Margaret, smiling. "Who was it that said, 'If
your heart is broken, give the pieces to Christ and He
will mend it again'? Never think of Bobby, dear Madame Gobelli, except as with Christ—walking with Him,
talking with Him, learning of Him and growing in grace
and the love of God daily! Never disassociate the two
memories, and in a little while you would hate yourself
if you could separate them again. God bless you! I
must go back to my husband now!"

"You will come again?" said the Baroness.

"I am afraid I shall have no time! We sail for
India on Saturday, but I shall not forget you. Good-bye,

Bobby," she repeated, with a last look at the corpse,
"remember your mother and me in your prayers."

As Miss Wynward let her out of the Red House,
she remarked,

"I could never have believed that anyone could
have had so much influence over her ladyship as you
have, Mrs. Pullen.   I hope you will come again."

"I shall not be able to do so.   But Madame Gobelli
will have you to talk to her!   You live here altogether,
do you not?"

"I have lived here for many years, but I am on the
point of leaving.   Bobby was my only tie to the Red
House, or I should have gone long ago."

"But now that the Baroness is so helpless surely you
will delay your departure until she no longer needs you."

"I shall not leave her until she has secured a better
woman in my stead.   But to tell you the truth, I am
going to be married, Mrs. Pullen, and I consider my first
duty is towards my future husband and his parents who
are very old!"

"Oh! doubtless!   May I ask his name?"

"Captain Hill!   He lives in the next house to this
—Stevenage!   You are surprised, perhaps, that a man
who has been in the army should marry a poor governess
like myself.   That is his goodness.   I know that I am
worn and faded and no longer young—thirty-three on
my last birthday—but he is good enough to care for me
all the more for the troubles I have passed through.
Mine has been a chequered life, Mrs. Pullen, but I have
told Captain Hill everything, and he still wishes to make
me his wife!   I ought to be a happy woman for the
future, ought I not?"

"Indeed yes," said Margaret, heartily, "and I sincerely hope that you may be so! But I can't help thinking of poor Madame Gobelli! Is the Baron good to her?"

"Pretty well!" answered Miss Wynward, "but he is very stolid and unsympathetic! It is strange to think that her heart must have been bound up in that boy, and yet at times she was positively cruel to him!"

"It has all been permitted for some good purpose," said Margaret, as she bade her farewell, "perhaps her remorse and self-accusation are the only things which would have brought her down upon her knees."

She returned home considerably saddened by what she had seen, but in three days she was to accompany her husband to India, and in the bustle of preparation, and the joy of knowing that she was not to be separated from him again, her heart was comforted and at peace. Never once during that time did she give one thought to Harriet Brandt. Miss Wynward had hardly mentioned her name, and no one seemed to know where she had gone. The girl had passed out of their lives altogether.

Margaret only regretted one thing in leaving England—that she had not seen Anthony Pennell again. Colonel Pullen had called twice at his chambers, but had each time found him from home. Margaret wanted to put in a good word for the Baroness with him. She thought perhaps that he might see her, after awhile, and speak a few words of comfort to her. But she was obliged to be content with writing her wishes in a farewell letter. She little knew how hardened Anthony Pennell felt, at that moment, against anyone who had treated the woman he loved in so harsh a manner.

Harriet Brandt spent the time, after her lover had left her to think over and decide upon their mutual fate, in walking up and down the room. She was like a restless animal; she could not stay two moments in the same place. Even when night fell, and the inhabitants of the Langham Hotel had retired to rest, she still kept pacing up and down the room, without thinking of undressing herself or seeking repose, whilst her conscience wrestled in warfare with her inclinations. Her thoughts took her far, far back to the earliest remembrance of which her mind was capable. She thought of her hard, unfeeling, indifferent father—of her gross, flabby, sensual mother—and shuddered at the remembrance! What had *she* done?—she said to herself—wherein had *she* sinned, that she should have been cursed with such progenitors? How had they *dared* to bring her into the world, an innocent yet hapless child of sin—the inheritor of their evil propensities—of their lust, their cruelty, their sensuality, their gluttony—and worst of all, the fatal heritage that made her a terror and a curse to her fellow-creatures? How dared they? *How dared they?* Why had God's vengeance not fallen upon them before they had completed their cruel work, or having accomplished it, why did He not let her perish with them—so that the awful power with which they had imbued her, might have been prevented from harming others?

Harriet thought of little Caroline; of her two nurses; of Sister Theodosia—of Mrs. Pullen's baby; of Bobby Bates; until she felt as though she should go mad. No! no! she would never bring that curse upon her Beloved; he must go far away, he must never see her again, or else she would destroy herself in order that he might escape!

But if she persuaded Anthony to consent to her wishes—if she insisted upon a total separation between them, what would become of her? What should she do? She had no friends in England; Madame Gobelli had turned against her—she was all alone! She would live and die alone. How should she ever get to know people, or to obtain an entrance to Society. She would be a pariah to the end of her life! And if she did surmount all these obstacles, what would be the result, except a repetition of what had gone before? Strangers would come to know her—to like her—would grow more intimate, and she would respond to their kindness—with the same result. They would droop and fail, die perhaps, like Bobby and the baby—find out that she was the cause, and shun her ever after.

"Oh! God!" cried Harriet in her perplexity and anguish, "I am accursed! My parents have made me not fit to live!"

She passed that night through the agonies of Death —not the death that overtakes the believer in a God and a Future—but the darkness and uncertainty that enwraps the man who knows he is full of sin and yet has no knowledge that His Lord has paid his debt to the uttermost farthing—the doubt and anxiety that beset the unbeliever when he is called upon to enter the dark Valley. The poor child saw her destiny entangling her as in a net—she longed to break through it, but saw no means of escape—and she rebelled against the cruel lot that heredity had marked out for her.

"Why am *I* to suffer?" she exclaimed aloud; "I
have youth and health and good looks, and money—
everything, the world would say, calculated to make my
life a pleasant one, and yet, I am tortured by this awful
thought—that I must keep aloof from everybody, that I
am a social leper, full of contagion and death! Doctor
Phillips said that the more I loved a person, the more I
must keep away from him! It is incredible! unheard-of!
Could he have had any motive in saying such a thing?"

The remembrance of her flirtation with Ralph Pullen
recurred to her mind, and she seized it, as a drowning
man clutches at a straw.

"Was it a plant, after all? Did the old man want to
put me off the track of Captain Pullen? Margaret Pullen
is staying in the house—he said so—had she asked him
to get rid of me if possible? After all, am I torturing
myself by believing the story of my fatal power to be
true, when it was only a ruse to get rid of me? The
Baroness said the same thing, but she was mad about
poor Bobby and would have said anything to annoy me
—and, after all, what does it amount to? The baby
died in teething—heaps of babies do—and Bobby was
consumptive from the first—I have heard Miss Wynward
say so, and would have died anyway, as he grew to be
a man and had larger demands made upon his physical
strength. And for the others—what happened to them,
happens to all the world. It is *fortune de guerre;*
people drop every day like rotten sheep;—everyone
might accuse himself of causing the death of his neighbour. I have been frightening myself with a chimera.
Anthony said so, and he must know better than I! And

I can't give up Tony—*I can't, I can't, I can't!* It is of
no use thinking of it! Besides, he wouldn't let me! He
would never leave me alone, until I had consented to
marry him, so I may as well do it at the first as at the
last."

But the tide of triumphant feeling would be succeeded by a wave of despondency, which threatened to
upset all her casuistry.

"But if—*if*—it should be true, and Anthony should
—should—Oh! God! Oh! God! I dare not think of it!
I will kill myself before it shall occur."

When the morning dawned it found her quite unde-
cided—lamenting her unfortunate fate one instant, and
declaring that she could never give up her lover the
next. She tore off her clothes and took a cold bath,
and re-robed herself, but she was looking utterly ill and
exhausted when Pennell burst in upon her at eleven
o'clock.

"Well, darling," he exclaimed, "and have you made
up your mind by this time? Which death am I to die?
—suffocated in your dear embrace, or left to perish of
cold and hunger outside?"

"O! Tony," she cried, throwing herself into his
arms, "I don't know what to say! I have not closed my
eyes all night, trying to decide what will be for the best.
And I am as far off as ever—only I can never, *never*
consent to do anything that shall work you harm!"

"Then I shall decide for you," exclaimed her lover,
"and that is that you make me and yourself happy, and
forget all the rubbish these people have been telling you!
Depend upon it, whatever they may have said was for

their own gratification, and not yours, and that they would be quick enough to accept the lot that lies before you, were it in their power!"

"I have been so lonely and friendless all my life," said Harriet, sobbing in his arms, "and I have longed for love and sympathy so much, and now that they have come to me, it is hard, Oh! *so* hard, to have to give them up."

"So hard, Hally, for *me*, remember, as well as yourself, that we will not make the attempt. Now, I want you to place yourself in my hands, and start for Paris to-night!"

"To-night?" she cried, lifting such a flushed, startled, happy face from his breast, that he had no alternative but to kiss it again.

"Yes! to-night! What did I tell you yesterday—that I should come with the ring and the license in my pocket! I am as good as my word, and better—for I have given notice to the registrar of marriages in my district, that he is to be ready for us at twelve o'clock to-day. Am I not a good manager?"

"Tony! Tony! but I have not made up my mind!"

"I have made it up for you, and I will take no refusal! I have calculated it all to a nicety! Married at twelve—back here at one for lunch—a couple of hours to pack up, and off by the four o'clock train for Dover —sleep at the Castle Warden, and cross to-morrow to Paris! How will that do, Mrs. Pennell, eh?"

"Oh! ought I to do it, ought I to do it?" exclaimed Harriet, with a look of despair.

"If you don't I'll shoot myself. I swear it!"

"No! no! darling, don't say that! It is of you alone that I am thinking! God forgive me if I am doing wrong, but I feel that I cannot refuse you! Take me and do with me as you think best."

After which it came to pass, that Mr. and Mrs. Anthony Pennell started in very high spirits for Dover, by the four o'clock train that afternoon.

CHAPTER XVIII.

A FORTNIGHT afterwards, the married couple found themselves at Nice. Much as has been said and sung of the *lune de miel,* none ever surpassed, if it ever reached, this one in happiness. Harriet passed the time in a silent ecstasy of delight. Her cup of bliss was filled to overflowing; her satisfaction was too deep for words. To this girl, for whom the world had been seen as yet only through the barred windows of a convent—who had never enjoyed the society of an intellectual companion before; who had viewed no scenery but that of the Island; seen no records of the past; and visited no foreign capital—the first weeks of her married life were a panorama of novelties, her days one long astonishment and delight.

She could not adore Anthony Pennell sufficiently for having afforded her the opportunity of seeing all this, and more especially of feeling it. The presents he lavished upon her were as nothing in her eyes, compared to the lover-like attentions he paid her; the bouquets of flowers he brought her every morning; the glass of lemonade or milk he had ready to supply her need when they were taking their excursions; the warm shawl or mantle he carried on his arm in the evenings, lest the air should become too chilly for her delicate frame after sunset. Money Harriet had no need of, but love—love she had thirsted for, as the hart thirsts for the water-streams, yet had never imagined it could be poured out at her feet, as her husband poured it now.

And Pennell, on the other hand, though he had been much sought after and flattered by the fair sex for the sake of the fame he had acquired and the money he made, had never lost his heart to any woman as he had done to his little unknown wife. He had never met any-one like Hally before. She combined the intelligence of the Englishwoman with the *espièglerie* of the French—the devotion of the Creole with the fiery passion of the Spanish or Italian. He could conceive her quite capable of dying silently and uncomplainingly for him, or anyone she loved; or on the other hand stabbing her lover with-out remorse if roused by jealousy or insult.

He was hourly discovering new traits in her character which delighted him, because they were so utterly unlike any possessed by the women of the world, with whom he had hitherto associated. He felt as though he had captured some beautiful wild creature and was taming it for his own pleasure.

Harriet would sit for hours at a time in profound silence, contemplating his features or watching his actions —crouched on the floor at his feet, until he was fain to lay down his book or writing, and take to fondling her instead. She was an ever-constant joy to him; he felt it would be impossible to do anything to displease her so long as he loved her—that like the patient Griselda she would submit to any injustice and meekly call it justice if from *his* hand. And yet he knew all the while that the savage in her was *not* tamed—that at any moment, like the domesticated lion or tiger, her nature

might assert itself and become furious, wild and intract-
able. It was the very uncertainty that pleased him;
men love the women of whom they are not quite certain,
all the more. From Nice they wandered to Mentone,
but the proximity of the Monte Carlo tables had no
charm for Anthony Pennell. He was not a speculative
man: his brain was filled with better things, and he only
visited such places for the sake of reproduction. Although
the autumn was now far advanced, the air of Mentone
was too enervating to suit either of them, and Pennell
proposed that they should move on to Italy.

"I must show you Venice and Rome before we return
home, Hally," he said, "and when I come to think of it,
why should we return to England at all just yet? Why
not winter in Rome? Richards is always advising me to
take a good, long holiday. He says I overwork my brain
and it reacts upon my body—what better opportunity
could we find to adopt his advice? Hitherto I have
pooh-poohed the idea! Wandering over a foreign country
in solitary grandeur held no charms for me, but with
you, my darling, to double the pleasure of everything,
any place assumes the appearance of Paradise! What
do you say, little wife? Shall we set up our tent South
until the spring?"

"Don't you feel well, Tony?" asked Harriet, anxiously.

"Never better in my life, dear! I am afraid you will
not make an interesting invalid out of me. I am as fit
as a fiddle. But I fancy my next novel will deal with
Italy, and I should like to make a few notes of the spots
I may require to introduce. It is nothing to take me
away from you, darling. We will inspect the old places

together, and your quick eye and clear brain shall help
me in my researches.   Is it a settled thing, Hally?"

"O! yes, darling!" she replied, "anywhere with you!
The only place I shall ever object to, will be the one
where I cannot go with you."

"That place does not exist on this earth, Hally,"
said Pennell, "but if you are willing, we may as well
start to-morrow, for if we leave it till too late, we shall
find all the best winter quarters pre-engaged."

He left the room, as she thought rather hurriedly,
but as he gained the hotel corridor he slightly staggered
and leaned against the wall.   He had told his wife that
he was quite well, but he knew it was not the truth.
He had felt weak and enervated ever since coming to
Mentone, but he ascribed it to the soft mild atmosphere.

"Confound this dizziness!" he said inwardly, as the
corridor swam before his eyes, "I think my liver must be
out of order, and yet I have been taking plenty of
exercise.   It must be this mild moist air.   Heat never
did agree with me.   I shall be glad to get on.   We
shall find Florence cold by comparison."

He descended to the bureau and announced his intention of giving up his rooms on the morrow, and then
ordered a carriage and returned to take Hally out for a
drive.

In Florence they procured rooms in a grand old
palazzo, furnished with rococo chairs and tables, placed
upon marble floors.   Harriet was charmed and astonished
by the ease with which they got everything *en route,* as
though they possessed Aladin's lamp, she told Pennell,
and had but to wish to obtain.

"Ah! Hally!" said her husband, "we have something

better than the genie's lamp—we have money! *That* is
the true magician in this century. I am very thankful
that you have a fortune of your own, my dearest, because I know that whatever happens, my girl will be
able to hold her own with the world!"

Harriet grew pale.

"What *could* happen?" she stammered.

"My silly little goose, are we immortal?" he replied,
"I make a first-rate income, my dear, but have not laid
by enough as yet to leave you more than comfortably
off, but with your own money——"

"Don't speak of it, pray don't speak of it!" she exclaimed, with ashen lips, and noting her distress, Pennell
changed the subject.

"You are a lucky little woman," he continued, "I
wonder what some people would give to possess your
income—poor Margaret Pullen for instance."

"Why Mrs. Pullen in particular, Tony? Are they
poor?"

"Not whilst Colonel Pullen is on active service, but
he has nothing but his pay to depend upon, and whilst
he can work, he must. Which means a residence in
India, and perhaps separation from his wife and children
—if he should lose his health, a compulsory retirement;
and if he keeps it, toiling out there till old age, and
then coming home to spin out the remainder of his life
on an inadequate pension. A man who accepts service
in India should make up his mind to live and die in
the country, but so many accidents may prevent it.
And at the best, it means banishment from England and
all one's friends and relations. Poor Margaret feels that
severely, I am sure!"

"Has Mrs. Pullen many relations then?"

"She has a mother still living, and several brothers and sisters, besides her husband's family. What a sweet, gentle woman she is! She was kind to you, Hally, was she not, whilst you were abroad?"

By mutual agreement they never spoke of Heyst, or the Red House, or anything which was associated with what Pennell called his wife's infatuation regarding herself.

"Yes! she was very kind—at first," replied Harriet, "until—until—it all happened, and they went to England. Oh! do not let us talk of it!" she broke off suddenly.

"No! we will not! Have you unpacked your mandoline yet, Hally? Fetch it, dear, and let me hear your lovely voice again! I shall get you to sing to me when I am in the vein for composing! You would bring me all sorts of beautiful ideas and phantasies!"

"Should I? should I?" exclaimed the girl joyfully. "Oh! how lovely! I should do a part of your work then, shouldn't I, Tony?—I should inspire you! Why, I would sing day and night for that!"

"No! no! my bird, I would not let you tire yourself! A few notes now and then—they will help me more than enough. I must draw from you for my next heroine, Hally! I could not have a fairer model!"

"Oh! Tony!"

She rushed to him in the extremity of her delight and hid her face upon his breast.

"I am not good enough, not pretty enough! Your heroines should be perfect!"

"I don't think so! I prefer them to be of flesh and blood, like you!"

He stooped his head and kissed her passionately.

"Hally! Hally!" he whispered, "you draw my very life away!"

The girl got up suddenly, almost roughly, and walked into the next room to fetch her mandoline.

"No! no!" she cried to herself with a cold fear, "not that, my God, not that!"

But when she returned with the instrument, she did not revert to the subject, but played and sang as usual to her husband's admiration and delight.

They "did" Florence very thoroughly during the first week of their stay there, and were both completely tired.

"I must really stay at home to-morrow," cried Hally one afternoon on returning to dinner, "Tony, I am regularly fagged out! I feel as if I had a corn upon every toe!"

"So do I," replied her husband, "and I cannot have my darling knocked up by fatigue! We will be lazy to-morrow, Hally, and lie on two sofas and read our books all day! I have been thinking for the last few days that we have been going a little too fast! Let me see, child!—how long have we been married?"

"Six weeks to-morrow," she answered glibly.

"Bless my soul! we are quite an old married couple, a species of Darby and Joan! And have you been happy, Hally?"

The tears of excitement rushed into her dark eyes.

"*Happy!* That is no word for what I have been, Tony; I have been in Heaven—in Heaven all the while!"

"And so have I," rejoined her husband.

"I met some nuns whilst I was out this morning," continued Hally, "the sisters of the Annunciation, and they stopped and spoke to me, and were so pleased to hear that I had been brought up in a convent. 'And have you no vocation, my child?' asked one of them. 'Yes! Sister,' I replied, 'I have—a big, strong, handsome vocation called my husband.' They looked quite shocked, poor dears, at first, but I gave them a subscription for their orphan schools—one hundred francs —and they were so pleased. They said if I was sick whilst in Florence, I must send for one of them, and she would come and nurse me! I gave it as a thanksgiving, Tony—a thanksgiving offering because I am so very happy. I am not a good woman like Margaret Pullen, I know that, but I love you—*I love you!*"

"Who said that you were not a good woman?" asked Pennell, as he drew her fondly to his side, and kissed away the tears that hung on her dark lashes.

"Oh! I know I am not. Besides, you once said that Margaret Pullen was the best woman you had ever known."

"I think she is very sweet and unselfish," replied Pennell musingly, "she felt the loss of her infant terribly, Doctor Phillips told me, but the way in which she struggled to subdue her grief, in order not to distress others, was wonderful! Poor Margaret! how she mourns little Ethel to this day."

"Don't! *don't!*" cried Harriet in a stifled voice, "I cannot bear to think of it!"

"My darling, it had nothing to do with you! I have told you so a thousand times!"

"Yes! yes! I know you have—but I loved the little darling! It is dreadful to me to think that she is mouldering in the grave!"

"Come, child, you will be hysterical if you indulge in any more reminiscences! Suppose we go for a stroll through the Ghetto or some other antiquated part of Florence. Or shall we take a drive into the country? I am at your commands, Madam!"

"A drive, darling, then—a drive!" whispered his wife, as she left him to get ready for the excursion.

It was three hours before they returned to their rooms in the old palazzo. Harriet was dull and somewhat silent, and Anthony confessed to a headache.

"I am not quite sure now," he said, as they were dining, "whether a trip to Australia or America would not do us both more good than lingering about these mild, warm places. I think our constitutions both require bracing rather than coddling. Australia is a grand young country! I have often contemplated paying her a visit. What would you say to it, Hally?"

"I should enjoy it as much as yourself, Tony! You so often have a headache now! I think the drainage of these southern towns must be defective!"

"Oh! shocking! They are famous for typhoid and malarial fevers. They are not drained at all!"

"Don't let us stay here long then! What should I do if you were to fall ill?"

"You are far more liable to fall sick of the two, my darling," returned her husband, "I do not think your beautiful little body has much strength to sustain it. And then what should *I* do?"

"Ah! neither of us could do without the other, Tony!"

"Of course we couldn't, and so we will provide against such a contingency by moving on before our systems get saturated with miasma and mistral. Will you sing to me to-night, Hally?"

"Not unless you very much wish it! I am a little tired. I feel as if I couldn't throw any expression into my songs to-night!"

"Then come here and sit down on the sofa beside me, and let us talk!"

She did as he desired, but Pennell was too sleepy to talk. In five minutes he had fallen fast asleep, and it was with difficulty she could persuade him to abandon the couch and drag his weary limbs up to bed, where he threw himself down in a profound slumber. Harriet was also tired. Her husband was breathing heavily as she slipped into her place beside him. His arm was thrown out over her pillow, as though he feared she might go to sleep without remembering to wish him good-night! She bent over him and kissed him passionately on the lips.

"Good-night, my beloved," she whispered, "sleep well, and wake in happiness!"

She kissed the big hand too that lay upon her pillow and composed herself to sleep while it still encircled her.

The dawn is early in Florence, but it had broken for some time before she roused herself again. The

sun was streaming brightly into the long, narrow, un-
curtained windows, and everything it lighted on was
touched with a molten glory. Harriet started up in bed.
Her husband's arm was still beneath her body.

"Oh! my poor darling!" she exclaimed, as though the
fault were her own, "how cramped he must be! How
soundly we must have slept not to have once moved
through the night!"

She raised Tony's arm and commenced to chafe it.
How strangely heavy and cold it felt. Why! he was
cold all over! She drew up the bedclothes and tucked
them in around his chin. Then, for the first time, she
looked at his face. His eyes were open.

"Tony, Tony!" she exclaimed, "are you making fun
of me? Have you been awake all the time?"

She bent over his face laughingly, and pressed a
kiss upon his cheek.

How stiff it felt! My God! what was the matter?
Could he have fainted? She leapt from the bed, and
running to her husband's side, pulled down the bedclothes again and placed her hand upon his heart. The
body was cold—cold and still all over! His eyes were
glazed and dull. His mouth was slightly open. In one
awful moment she knew the truth. Tony was—*dead!*

She stood for some moments—some hours—some
months—she could not. have reckoned the time, silent
and motionless, trying to realise what had occurred.
Then—as it came upon her, like a resistless flood which
she could not stem, nor escape, Harriet gave one fearful
shriek which brought the servants hurrying upstairs to
know what could be the matter.

"I have killed my husband—I have killed him—it was I myself who did it!" was all that she would say. Of course they did not believe her. They accepted the unmeaning words as part of their mistress's frenzy at her sudden and unexpected loss. They saw what had happened, and they ran breathlessly for a doctor, who confirmed their worst fears—the Signor was dead! The old palazzo became like a disturbed ant-hill. The servants ran hither and thither, unknowing how to act, whilst the mistress sat by the bedside with staring, tearless eyes, holding the hand of her dead husband. But there were a dozen things to be done—half a hundred orders to be issued. Death in Florence is quickly followed by burial. The law does not permit a mourner to lament his Dead for more than four-and-twenty hours.

But the signora would give no orders for the funeral nor answer any questions put to her! She had no friends in Florence—for ought they knew, she had no money—what were they to do? At last one of them thought of the neighbouring Convent of the Annunciation and ran to implore one of the good sisters to come to their mistress in her extremity.

Shortly afterwards, Sister Angelica entered the bedroom where Harriet sat murmuring at intervals, "It is *I* who have killed him," and attempted to administer comfort to the young mourner. But her words and prayers had no effect upon Harriet. Her brain could hold but one idea—she had killed Tony! Doctor Phillips was right—it was she who had killed Margaret Pullen's baby and Bobby Bates, and to look further back, little Caroline, and now—now, her Tony! the light of her life, the passion of her being, the essence of all her joy—her hope for this world and the next. She had killed him—*she,* who worshipped him, whose pride was bound up in him, who was to have helped him and comforted him and waited on him all his life—she had killed him!

Her dry lips refused to say the words distinctly, but they kept revolving in her brain until they dazed and wearied her. The little sister stood by her and held her hand, as the professional assistants entered the death chamber and arranged and straightened the body for the grave, finally placing it in a coffin and carrying it away to a mortuary where it would have to remain until buried on the morrow, but Harriet made no resistance to the ceremony and no sign. She did not even say "Good-bye" as Tony was carried from her sight for ever! Sister Angelica talked to her of the glorious Heaven where they must hope that her dear husband would be translated, of the peace and happiness he would enjoy, of the reunion which awaited them when her term of life was also past.

She pressed her to make the Convent her refuge until the first agony of her loss was overcome—reminded her of the peace and rest she would encounter within the cloisters, and how the whole fraternity would unite in praying for the soul of her beloved that he might speedily obtain the remission of his sins and an entrance into the Beatific Presence.

Harriet listened dully and at last in order to get rid of her well-intentioned but rather wearisome consoler, she promised to do all that she wished. Let the sister return to the Convent for the present, and on the morrow if she would come for her at the same time, she might take her back with her. She wanted rest and peace—

she would be thankful for them, poor Harriet said—only to-night, this one night more, she wished to be alone. So the good little sister went away rejoicing that she had succeeded in her errand of mercy, and looking forward to bearing the poor young widow to the Convent on the morrow, there to learn the true secret of earthly happiness.

When she had gone and the old palazzo was quiet and empty, the bewildered girl rose to her feet and tried to steady her shaking limbs sufficiently, to write what seemed to be a letter but was in reality a will.

"I leave all that I possess," so it ran, "to Margaret Pullen, the wife of Colonel Arthur Pullen, the best woman Tony said that he had ever met, and I beg her to accept it in return for the kindness she showed to me when I went to Heyst, a stranger. Signed, HARRIET PENNELL."

She put the paper into an envelope, and as soon as the morning had dawned, she asked her servant Lorenzo to show her the way to the nearest notary in whose presence she signed the document and directed him to whom it should be sent in case of her own death.

And after another visit to a *pharmacien*, she returned to the Palazzo and took up her watch again in the now deserted bedchamber.

Her servants brought her refreshments and pressed her to eat, without effect. All she desired, she told them, was to be left alone, until the sister came for her in the afternoon.

Sister Angelica arrived true to her appointment, and went at once to the bedchamber. To her surprise she found Harriet lying on the bed, just where the corpse of Anthony Pennell had lain, and apparently asleep.

"Pauvre enfant!" thought the kind-hearted nun, "grief has exhausted her! I should not have attended to her request, but have watched with her through the night! *Eh, donc! ma pauvre,*" she continued, gently touching the girl on the shoulder, *"levez-vous! Je suis la."*

But there was no awakening on this earth for Harriet Pennell. She had taken an overdose of chloral and joined her husband.

When Margaret Pullen received the will which Harriet had left behind her, she found these words with it, scribbled in a very trembling hand upon a scrap of paper.

"Do not think more unkindly of me than you can help. My parents have made me unfit to live. Let me go to a world where the curse of heredity which they laid upon me may be mercifully wiped out."

THE END.

Made in the USA
Coppell, TX
30 July 2020

31990696R00187